Second Endings #2

BRIGHT
Phantoms

Lulu M. Sylvian

GRIFFYN INK

Editing: Full Bloom Editorial

Cover: Laura Medeiros

I should probably thank Edgar Rice Burroughs a whole lot for this one.

Remember: always wear sunscreen.

Thanks to Victoria Raschke for naming Mammoth Hunters!

PROLOGUE

Now **Hollywood Report:** Liam James— best known for his role in the cable series, *Tails from the Urban Jungle*, was unofficially declared dead Thursday after a single-car accident flipped his vehicle across several lanes of freeway in Los Angeles county.

Emergency medical professionals credit a quick-thinking witness who performed CPR on James until their arrival for his survival. Emergency medical responders resuscitated James— who had no pulse and was not breathing on his own when they arrived. James was rushed to Cedars–Sinai where he is currently in ICU. Further details of his injuries are not known at this time.

The accident occurred after James drove off set in a modified Corvette used in the filming of the remake of the 1978 movie of the same title. *Corvette Summer* is mostly known for its connection to the original star, Mark Hamill's reported near-death in a car accident after filming was complete.

Eyewitnesses to James' accident said the car flipped for no apparent reason. It is estimated that his vehicle was traveling at speeds approaching 80mph.

Like its 1978 counter-part, the refurbished 1972 Corvette Stingray was painted cherry red with orange glitter flames and had a right-hand drive. Investigators discovered a malfunction in the motorcycle chain connecting the steering shaft to the left mounted steering box which left James without control of the car.

Ascendant Studio officials immediately expressed grief at learning the news of James' accident and were quick to point out that the vehicle was rebuilt to match a certain look for filming, and was not sound for freeway speeds.

1

L unch was ruined by several things— the first being the scowl on my sister Ruth's face. What had I done this time?

"That color doesn't suit you, Dani," she bit out.

Odds were fairly balanced she was complaining about the yellow sweater I wore over my black and white outfit or the new hair color. It had to be the red hair. Typically, I went for platinum blonde, but a few weeks ago, I decided to switch it up and my stylist and I went for a blend of 7/4 and 77/44. In other words, I was Lucille Ball orange and infringing on my sister's hair color territory.

I forgot to mention it to her. I'd been this color for almost a month, and so far it was exhausting. I don't know how she did it. Ruthie had been a redhead since she was sixteen.

"You must be sisters. They say red hair runs in the family," our chipper waiter commented. "What drinks can I bring for you?"

Before I managed to get out that I wanted a strawberry

daiquiri, Ruth ordered waters with lemon for both of us, and announced, "We are sisters, and no thank you, we don't drink alcohol."

Total bullshit. She drank. Did she forget that wine was alcohol? No, she was being pissy and controlling. Nothing new.

"I know. Red is such a hard color to maintain." I gave her that point, I didn't want to fight over lunch. "I'm having it stripped out starting next month. I'll have an ombré fade for a while. Apparently, this color stains the hair quite a bit, so my ends that are already fried, won't let go of it easily."

"Then why did you do it?" She still sneered, not giving up, not recognizing that I had already conceded to her.

"I wanted something fun and different. Nothing as extreme as black, but I wanted something dramatic for the premiere last month."

I loved movie premieres. For a few minutes, I got to pretend I was a starlet. I'd walk the red carpet, and sometimes I'd even have my picture taken. Of course, my boss, Charlie Davenport, king of *King of the Scene*, would say I'm a star when it comes to set design and construction. What can I say? I loved making things look like they aren't. And since King of the Scene was a top special effects set company, we got to go to some great opening nights and premier parties.

"Oh, which schmaltzy flick did you work on this time? *It Came From the Black Lagoon*?" She let out one of those fake snobby as shit laughs.

I don't know where my sister got her high and mighty attitude, but there it was competing with the penthouse of the Burj Khalifa for loftiness. She didn't have to work, somewhat of a rarity in Los Angeles these days. Her current husband was boring as fuck, but he made the big bucks, and surprisingly enough he wasn't in the industry. I was, and

Ruthie hated it. She was not concerned with my feelings and frequently let me know how stupid I was for getting involved with the Hollywood machine.

She had a personal grudge against the movie industry. His name was Daddy. Well, I called him Daddy, she called him Frank Kensington. Never just Frank, always both names like it was a cuss word. She followed along with what Mom did. Frank-fucking-asshole-Kensington. It made custody weekends interesting until she stopped going when she turned fourteen.

Neither of them got that using "Kensington" like it was bad would set me up for some therapy issues when I was older. I mean, how else is an eight-year-old supposed to take it when her last name becomes the equivalent of running around calling someone a "motherfucking cunt?" Yes, in Mom's eyes Kensington was as bad, if not worse than the C-word.

Ruth thought I was rebelling against her and Mom by working in the industry. Dad worked in the industry, and when I was seven he traded Mom in for a younger model, who just happened to be an actress he met on set.

Daddy was a cameraman. Still was.

Being in set design, I got to build some of the weirdest stuff for some of the best science fiction movies, and that included the rash of recent monster, excuse me, kaiju, movies that were popular again. The premier had indeed been for a monster movie.

I laughed, "You're thinking of that Oscar-winning movie with the fish-man." I shook my head and muttered, "*It Came from the Black Lagoon.*"

Our chipper waiter delivered the waters and announced he would be right back to take our order.

I took a sip.

"No, this one was based on that multi-player video game. It's more fantasy than monster. But it does have some great big burly Orcs in it."

Ruth raised her eyebrows at me. It didn't matter if I gave her the title or not. She wouldn't know what I was talking about.

"You should grow up and stop playing around. You could still be an architect."

I was reminded why, even though we lived in the same greater metropolitan area, we didn't see each other more than a few times a year. I loved my sister, I just wish she would accept my choices.

Our waiter came back and I ordered the grilled salmon. I really wanted the steak, but Ruthie was in her holier-than-thou Ruth mode; I didn't need or want more judgment from her over my food choices. She ordered a large salad with strawberries and feta.

I took a sip of water to wash the foul taste out of my mouth that appeared suddenly. Everything went wrong all at once. I lost any strength in my hand and my water glass slipped, spilling all over the table. I couldn't breathe. My chest wouldn't move. I couldn't suck anything in, or even blow anything out. I could barely manage tiny shallow breaths.

The look of horror on Ruth's face added to my already terrorized state. Her lips were moving, but she made no sound.

My vision blurred, and gray crept in around the edges. The more I panicked the less air moved into my lungs.

I passed out.

When I came to, an off duty EMT had a warm hand on my neck checking my pulse. Someone handed him a paper bag and he had me breathe into it. By the time the emergency crew arrived, Ruth was berating me again, only instead of not approving of the shade of yellow my sweater was, or my choice of hair dye, she was letting me know how inconvenient and inconsiderate making a scene in the middle of the restaurant was to her.

It didn't matter to her that my oxygen levels were crazy low, or that I was bawling as if my world had ended. Yet again, I had embarrassed her.

In my head, I called out for Flint. He didn't answer. That seemed to make everything worse, and I sucked in more air and cried some more. Ruth declined the ambulance ride to the hospital for me. I didn't mind; I didn't need that bill. But she promised the EMTs she would take me.

Our waiter was a dear and he packaged up our lunches in to-go containers and gave us some forks.

Ruth didn't talk on the drive over to the Emergency Room. Maybe she was scared more than pissed off. Pissed off Ruth never shuts up.

She dropped me off at the ER doors and went to park. I sat on a bench. I wished Flint would show up. He was typically so good about being there when I needed him. And I really needed him now. I needed him to slip into my head and let me feel his arms around me, even though I couldn't touch him. And if I caught a glimpse of him, it was never more than a flicker of light and shadow.

I was too wobbly to walk. My whole body felt like it was in the process of recovering from being full of bees. I didn't know how else to describe it, there was a residual buzzing over my skin, that felt numb as if it had been hurt and stung, and was now easing back. Just there hadn't been the initial stinging sensation.

Ruth guided me in, and the triage nurse got me situated in a wheelchair. She took my vitals, and checked my oxygen levels, still low, and said they would get me back in a few minutes.

Ruth and I sat in a corner eating our lunches. I wasn't very hungry, but I felt like I needed strength. Food was fuel. Fuel was strength.

Ruth stayed uncharacteristically quiet the entire time. I really had expected her to continue going off on me. Maybe the EMT said something to scare her. They finally got me into the back.

I hate ERs, there are too many spiritual residues. At least I didn't see the flicker of any full ghost this visit. I saw ghosts, and I'm highly empathetic, and that can be exhausting at times. Especially when I'm sick or hurt. My barriers were so far down as to be non-existent this afternoon. They felt raw too, that was an unusual sensation. The residues didn't bother me any more than random shivers down my spine. Had Flint been around I would have not sensed the other wisps of spirits, his would have taken all of my attention.

The ER nurse placed sticky sensors against my chest, and I cringed knowing the adhesive would either stick to me forever or peel the skin away when they were removed.

Ruth was back to her old self, blaming me for the world's most dramatic panic attack, by the time they released me. Nothing was wrong that they could find. But something was wrong, Flint was gone. I couldn't sense him, couldn't pull him to me.

"I love you, don't scare me like that again," Ruth said as she pulled away from the curb.

At least she drove me home. I more than half-way expected her to put me in an Uber and tell me to get over myself. I'm sure Mom had something to do with Ruthie making sure I got home safely. Mom had been sweet on the phone, she had even asked if she needed to get on a plane and come see me. I told her no she could stay home, but that I might come down for a long weekend. I needed the peace of some Santa Fe time.

I thought some-how my boss had found out about my afternoon in the ER when he called.

"Hey Charlie," I said. I sounded so tired to my own ears.

"Are you under contract right now?" he asked.

"Yeah, with you. What's up?" If Charlie forgot I was already working for him then something hot had just come in. I hoped.

"How long have I got you for?"

"This is week four of six. Are you going to tell me what's going on?"

"What happens after that?" His answering questions with questions was going to make me batty. Something I didn't need after the day I just had.

"I make phone calls unless you decide to hire me on full time." I loved working for Charlie, I would love it more if I was permanent.

"Make sure you're here on Monday by ten AM. You're gonna love this. Oh, and I'm extending your contract out by at least three months." He hung up.

The man was a tease. My heart rate zoomed, still not quite regulated after this afternoon's freak-out. I was too exhausted for the adrenalin rush to do much more than crash hard and fast. I was good for nothing else, except to cause damage to a pint of ice cream.

I curled up on my couch and watched TV— still worried about what happened with Flint, where was he? Flipping through channels I learned that actor Liam James had offi-

cially died, but had been resuscitated after a nasty car accident that had Hollywood reporters digging up the details on
a car accident from the nineteen-seventies that left a major
film actor with a broken nose, a concussion, and a slew of
rumors that followed him around for forty-odd years. They
called it the Corvette Summer Curse.

2

I paused as I climbed up the rigging. For the one-millionth time since this shoot started, I couldn't believe I was here on the set of a Sebastian Hale film. I had to pinch myself. Of course part of me kept asking: why had I insisted on coming? I didn't do outside.

I wiped my hand down the thigh of my cargos before wrapping it around the pole above to haul myself up. The climb wasn't far but it was the opposite of gravity, and today that seemed harder than usual.

I preferred working on a sound stage where there were lifts or stairs, or other bits of rigging designed for scenery monkeys like myself to crawl around on. Let's be real, set designers build-in easy access. We didn't like unnecessary work. Outside in nature was different. Well, this nature was different. We had to build around the landscape, and we couldn't bulldoze any rocks that were in our way. I had been lucky enough to accompany the boss on the scouting trip so that I could help to determine how our sets would integrate into the natural landscape. I should have built-in more stairs.

By the time filming was wrapped at this location and everything cleared out, there would be no evidence of our constructed sets. No one would know we had been there at all.

I had just swung my leg over the rail to the high platform when I heard my name.

I peered down over the edge. It wasn't far. I wasn't the climbing type though, so it seemed farther away than it really was.

"Yeah, that's me," I called down to the runner who shielded his eyes with a clipboard.

"They need you down in makeup."

"What?" That made no sense. I wasn't a make-up artist, and I wasn't an actor. "I don't do makeup, you want Mary." She was the head of special effects makeup and I knew she was on set this week.

"Nope, they sent me after Danica Kensington. Said you knew about sunscreen." His conversation made less than no sense. "Can you come on down? Glenn requested you specifically."

Oh shit, wonder-kid Glenn Russell was asking for me? Okay, he wasn't a kid anymore, he was older than me, but he came on the scene with a big splash fresh out of UCLA film school, and that reputation clung like glitter— there wasn't any easy way to get rid of it.

Well, never let it be said that I left the director of a movie waiting on me for long. I swung my leg back over the side rail and climbed my way, even more slowly than the haul up, down.

"What the hell does Glenn want me for? How the hell does Glenn even know who I am?" I shot off questions a mile a minute as I followed him down and around the path into the ravine where the makeup trailer was parked.

Glenn Russell was at the point of his career where he could write his own paycheck. He hit Hollywood hard with a lightning strike on his first film. Number one box office ticket sales first two weekends, and that was during the Christmas release season. His next film pulled the same magical numbers, but for a total of four weeks and with a June opening. He was movie magic himself when it came to action-adventure. Having him on this project was just another insurance that the studio would have a hit on their hands.

To be honest, the studio was stacking the cards at this point. A *Sebastian Hale Adventure* was a guaranteed hit no matter what. They always earned enough at the box office to ensure there would be more movies made. Then they added to the mix the hottest director of the decade, and let's face it, casting Liam James as Seb Hale was not a dumb move at all. That man was...

I stopped walking. I may have stopped breathing. I didn't get star struck on principle, plus it makes my job really hard to do, but damn. There was no way anyone would have guessed he flat-lined in a car wreck eighteen months earlier.

Liam James stood in front of me, half-naked, wearing only his Sebastian Hale requisite loin cloth. Okay, for this particular adventure it was a linen Egyptian kilt. That was part of the story's shtick, no matter where in time Seb Hale ended up, he somehow managed to lose all his modern trappings of civilized clothes. Except for his shoes, and frequently for comedic relief, his sock garters.

I was saved that particular ridiculous look today, he wore proper English riding boots up to his knees. Those were some fine looking knees.

His arms were crossed, and damn if that pose did not make his shoulders look a mile wide and his hips distracting. Kilts shouldn't hang, clinging just below the hip bone like that. It was almost indecent. Not that I was complaining. Liam James was an incredibly good looking man. He had built his career as a blond. After his car accident, he let the natural dark coloring grow out. I now gazed upon the new Sebastian Hale for the first time, and he stole my breath.

Yeah, I'm one of those geeks. I read all thirty *Time Traveling Adventures of Sebastian Hale* books by the time I was a senior in high school. I grew up watching the movies, after all, they had been making a new batch every few years ever since the stories were first published in the early nineteen hundreds.

And after Flint left me, I binge-watched every single episode of the Sebastian Hale movies he had starred in. Every night I fell asleep on the couch watching a half-naked black-and-white Flint be the hero over and over again in the five movie serials from the late nineteen-thirties. *Sebastian Hale and the Temple of Ahmentari* was one of my favorites, it combined all the prowess and attraction of Seb Hale and had a heavy dose of ancient Egypt. What wasn't there to love? I got a good dose of inspiration for these sets from those films.

In *Sebastian Hale and the Princess of the Taj* time travel plopped Seb Hale in the middle of pre-empire India. It got all of the histories wrong. It got all of the religions wrong, but there was Flint Reese kissing that actress from Tasmania, the one who ended up actually being Indian, but no one found out until after her death. At least once in her life, she got to be an Indian princess.

Sebastian Hale Before Time featured wooly mammoths and dinosaurs at the same time, plus the sexiest cave girl until Raquel Welch wore a fur bikini in the nineteen-sixties. Same plot, same cheesy lines repeated over and over again.

And I ate them up, hour after hour of them in glorious black-and-white.

Flint's slicked-back hair said more about the era of the filming than anything costuming did to convey the character. I missed that hair. It worked as an Edwardian style, but it was so very thirties, long to his jaw with the back short. When he didn't slick it back, the dark hair hung in straight lines across his face. I loved threading my fingers through those silky strands.

By the time I finished all fifteen episodes of *Sebastian Hale and the Horse of Troy* I didn't think I could cry anymore but I managed to sob my way through the twelve episodes of *Sebastian Hale on the Silk Road*.

The movies weren't sad. They were schmaltzy, feel-good adventure flicks. They were familiar and comfortable like a warm blanket at a time I was sad because, after years of being so certain that I had my very own personal muse in Flint, I had to wonder if maybe I hadn't made it all up in my head.

With Liam, it looked like they got Seb right: larger than average, an inverted triangle of a torso with lean rippling muscles, and wild disarray of formally controlled Edwardian male hair fashion; short on the side and back, with longer hair on top that hung down into his eyes. A basic wedge cut, but with the longer hair uncontrolled. Flint Reese had been my favorite Seb Hale. God, Flint had been gorgeous, and I was biased for other reasons. But I think his position as favorite flew right out the window as soon as I saw Liam James.

Mr. Hale, I had to remember on set to call him by his character's name— that was one of Glenn's particular rules. Glenn made the big bucks happen, so we followed orders—

was looking over Glenn's shoulder as the two of them intently focused on a monitor in front of them.

"Hey Glenn, I got Danica for you," the runner announced. I didn't get his name until later.

Glenn grunted and Mr. Hale lifted his head and gave me a quick glance.

"Davenport tells me you are the palest person he has ever met," Glenn said without even looking up.

"I don't know about that, but I am pretty pale." I was more than pretty pale. I made pasty white look like a tan. Another one of the plethora of reasons I did not insist on doing outdoor location set work. I had idiopathic hypo-photosensitivity. It basically meant I had some kind of extreme sun allergy and could get sunburned just thinking about it. Yeah, working on set in the Utah desert wasn't the brightest idea I ever had, but this was a Sebastian Hale film, damn it.

"What do you know about sunscreen?" Glenn asked.

I had no clue what information he was looking for. "All kinds of things. What do you need?"

"Come here." He waved me over, and with a hand on my back positioned me so that I could also look at the monitor. The screen was protected with a black plastic hood to keep the glare of the ambient light from interfering with visibility. Best guess is, we were looking at dailies from yesterday.

Seb Hale was speaking intently with the dusky Egyptian beauty. They were close enough they could kiss, but they wouldn't. They wouldn't kiss until the very end. Sebastian Hale done right was rife with sexual tension. And the heroine was always a dusky local beauty.

Well, fuck a duck, if the local beauty this time wasn't played by Cecilia Saaid. At least they cast an Egyptian in the role. How had I missed she was playing Nefertari? I may have groaned out loud.

"You see it too?" Glenn asked enthusiastically.

I shook my head. I confessed, "I'm sorry, I'm not sure what you want me to be looking at. The shots are so tight on the actors I can't make out anything going wrong with the set."

"Not the set, look at Sebastian's shoulders."

I had been trying not to. They were distracting. And the real thing was perilously close behind me.

Glenn pointed, and traced his finger just above the surface of the monitor, not touching it. "Look, pink."

"Well, yeah, that happens with naked skin and sun." Liam drawled.

Something in my body went sizzle. I don't think I had ever heard Liam James's natural speaking voice before. And if I had, I hadn't been paying attention. It was low and swirled with the sexiest hint of a British accent. It wasn't the accent he used as Sebastian Hale, which was a proper upper crust Londonian aristocratic sound. His natural voice had hints of almost Scottish. I didn't know the various regional accents in England, but this was definitely Scottish adjacent, and very familiar.

Something in Liam's voice reminded me of Flint. He had been from northern England and immigrated with his mother when he was a kid. I didn't want to think about him anymore. I was done being sad over Flint. He left me. At first, I thought something may have changed in my brain to affect my vision of *the other*, after all, I had passed out pretty spectacularly at that restaurant. Maybe Flint was around and I could no longer hear him or feel him. But he hadn't come to me in my dreams either for eighteen months. I didn't think the problem was with me. I still saw other ghosts.

What could have made Flint so suddenly move on? He completely ghosted on me. I had to laugh, if I didn't I would cry. Ghosted by a fucking ghost.

"Well, it doesn't happen with Sebastian Hale. He is more dignified than that," Glenn replied.

He was right. Pesky natural elements never impeded Sebastian Hale. Locals learned his language, not the other way around. Sun did not burn him. Hell, rain barely made him wet. Animals did his bidding, time made adjustments for him, and he always got the girl. A different girl in every century as it were.

How many little bastard Seb Hale babies would have been left throughout history if he really had been able to time travel, and wasn't just a ragingly popular pulp fiction character? I bet there would be more of his progeny than the world population of Genghis Khan's offspring. I know I'd volunteer as a not-quite virginal sacrifice.

"Can you make it so he doesn't get more sun?"

It took me a minute to figure out Glenn was asking me a question.

"Um, why ask me? Why not see what your make-up artist has?"

"She let him get color."

"Did she use anything on you?" I turned to ask the man in question.

"She sprayed something over me before filming." God his voice was yummy, even when talking about sunscreen.

I raised my eyebrows expecting him to say more. He didn't.

"That's it? Just a spray? How many applications?"

He shook his head. "Once in the morning."

"How many days have you been out here?" Glenn asked.

I turned my attention back to him, and he was giving me a serious once over, and once again look.

"You don't look like you've been outside much."

I huffed a laugh. "I got here the week prior to filming with the rest of the set crew." We had done most of our pre-construction back at the warehouse in LA, so all we needed to do once here was refine some of the fittings and put it all together like a big puzzle. It saved us hundreds of man-hours from having to be on location, which cost a serious chunk of change.

"But you're so pale." Thanks for the observation Seb.

"I'm mostly covered, and I am well slathered in sunscreen. Sebastian Hale has to be exposed. There is bound to be some color to his skin." I pointed out.

"Can you make it stop?" Glenn asked.

"I can show you how to apply sunscreen that will mini-mize the sun's effects, but he's all exposed. He is going to get some color."

"Great, tell Lake what you need." Glenn clapped and rubbed his hands together. "You're now in charge of keeping our hero proper British Lord pale."

I swallowed the lump in my throat.

I needed to tell my boss, Charlie, that I had been usurped by the director to ensure the hero didn't get a healthy tan.

"Give me a shopping list, and by the time you let Daven-port know what's going on, and get back here, I should be back with sunscreen." Lake, holding onto his clipboard gave me a weak smile.

I nodded in return and left to find Charlie and let him know why I wasn't pulling my weight on set.

3

Marcia, the makeup artist, and Mr. Hale met me back at the makeup trailer. One look at her and I understood why they had sought the assistance of someone else. Marcia was gorgeous but the word sunburn did not exist in her vocabulary.

She held out a can of SPF 4. "I used this yesterday. It always works for me."

Of course, it did. She was a dark-skinned beauty. I'm sure she used sunscreen daily on that gorgeous skin of hers. After all, skin cancer was in everyone's vocabulary, but sunburn not so much.

"Has Lake gotten back with the stuff yet?" I looked around to see if the runner had beaten me back and was hiding.

"He left all of this." Marcia picked up a plastic bag full of bottles.

I looked in at the assortment of pink and blue. Perfect, he had gotten creams and sprays. I pulled out a blue and gold spray can, set the bag down, and pulled out a second can. I handed one to Marcia and said, "This needs to get applied every hour."

I unwrapped the second can and sprayed some onto my fingers. "You can just spray his neck, shoulders, and arms, but"— I held up my fingers showing her the lotion— "this is how you need to apply it to his forehead ears, cheeks, nose, chin. All the high points that the sun is hitting."

I bit my lip and then thought about it. "They're using reflectors, right? Right," I answered myself.

"You'll need to spray the front of his neck, chin, and chest."

"I'm not doing that," Marcia announced.

"Then who is? Sebastian Hale does not sunburn," Liam's voice rumbled like distant thunder.

I looked over at Liam for the first time since Marcia and I started talking. A second ago he had been nose down in his phone. Typical talent, ignoring the people there to make his efforts look, well, effortless. I didn't think he had been listening. Truthfully, I was trying not to gaze over at him. I didn't do celebrity crushes, well not with the live ones anyway. And, I had never been distracted by an actor on set before. There was just something about him that pulled me in like a magnet.

I took a deep breath, told myself it had everything to do with Sebastian Hale and not the fact that he smelled like clean earth and sandalwood.

"What do you mean you aren't doing it? He's right, Sebastian Hale doesn't burn or tan or... anything. He's Sebastian Hale."

She rolled her eyes. "Oh great, another mighty white savior saves the day storyline, cause the brown natives can't take care of themselves." Her tone overflowed with raging sarcasm.

I cringed. She was not wrong. The premise of *The Time Travels of Sebastian Hale* were all very much turn of the twentieth-century colonizers and imperialists save the day.

Liam scoffed. Mr. Hale scoffed. Had to remember to call him Mr. Hale on set.

Marcia and I turned to him.

"Have you read this script? Nefertari is the real hero. I'm just there to do her bidding. It's flipped the Sebastian Hale mythos on its ear. William Powers Stapleton should be spinning in his grave. She saves me from the slavers, she comes up with the plan. Seb Hale gets to be noble and mighty, and he is a completely feminist social justice warrior."

I felt my eyebrows crinkle together. This was Liam James speaking to minions, and not barking? The man had a bit of a surly reputation. So far he wasn't upholding it very well. I wasn't complaining.

"I thought this was based on *Seb Hale and the Temple of Ahmentari*?" I asked.

"Based on. Loosely. Egypt, temples, Nefertari, I think that's where the similarities end. Look who is doing this?" He looked right at me and I swear those teddy bear brown eyes melted all the connective tissue in my body. "Aren't you the woman who Glenn brought in specifically to make sure I don't get any color?"

The expression I made was not a smile. I showed off my teeth in a grimace, I guess that's what that had been all about. I thought it was for a consultation, maybe it was a job interview. I wondered how I would be credited in the film. Would my name show up under Charlie's and the crew's with King of the Scene, or would I be Mr. James's sunburn consultant?

I sighed, "I guess it's me then. Okay, let's get to it."

Marcia made a sort of snorty laugh and told me good luck before disappearing back into the trailer.

"Okay." I handed out a pink bottle of lotion to Liam. "You need to slather this on."

He looked at me, didn't say a word, popped an earbud in, and dove nose first back into his phone. There was *the* Liam James ... with the reputation.

I tapped him lightly on the front of his shoulder. I was perilously close to his pectoral muscles. I swallowed sand. This probably would not have bothered Marcia in the least. But I didn't work directly with the celebrities, ever. And certainly not with one like Liam James who was flipping every hormonal switch I had. I needed to shake that BS off. The attraction was purely a Seb Hale fangirl moment. It had nothing to do with how his voice had a physical aspect to it, or how his eyes made me think of Flint.

I squeezed my eyes tight at the sudden and surprise sting of tears. Curse Flint. Curse him straight to hell and back in a small hand basket with only cookie crumbs.

Liam lifted his attention to me.

"Hi? You need to put sunscreen on." I held the bottle out to him again.

"No, you need to put sunscreen on me."

My head made a sweeping nod on its own as I realized what needed to happen here. "Okay, I can do that, but, um, look, I'm not a makeup artist so I'm going to need you to help me out here."

"Fine. What?"

I started to say something and then stopped, not sure how to approach this. I tried again. "Okay, I need permission to touch your body, I guess, and I need you to apply the sunscreen here"— I motioned my hand in a circle in front of his chest and abs. There was no way I could touch him there, that was entirely too intimate.

He snatched the bottle and put a small dollop in his palm and began smearing it into his skin. This was hard to watch. I had a reason to stare at all the rippling muscles of his torso, but he was doing it all wrong.

"That's not going to do you any good." I grabbed his hand and squelched a blob of lotion onto it. "Now rub that evenly on, but don't rub it in. It has to sit, give your skin a chance to absorb it."

He began rubbing it over his chest. The white cream clung to a few chest hairs that the waxing clearly hadn't caught. It was hypnotizing. I blinked away images of being in a shower and watching him do that with a bar of soap. *Dani, bitch, get it together.*

"Make sure it's evenly spread out and you'll need to go just below your waistband. I'm going to start on your legs."

"My legs and the skin under the waistband are covered."

I'm surprised he didn't hit me with a "well actually," before he informed me of where his clothes were. His attitude was making it very easy not to be attracted to him. I needed to focus on that and not his body.

I knelt next to him and rubbed lotion between my hands so it wasn't cold when I touched him. "Clothing moves. You'd be amazed by how much. Now, don't jump I'm gonna touch you."

I wrapped my hand slowly around his leg just below his knee. He stiffened and hissed a little. I didn't mean to tickle him, but it was his knee. I now knew that Liam James had ticklish knees. I didn't need to know that!

I didn't need to register how muscular and firm his thighs were, and I stopped because I really didn't need to be applying sunscreen that far up his leg. I shifted to his other leg. Again, ticklish knees.

I had him coated in white cream and told him to just hang out while I ran over and knocked on the make-up trailer's door.

Marcia stuck her head out.

"I need to do his face, has he already had makeup done?"

I figure he had since he was already in costume, but sometimes, they did costume first, depending on who needed how much work, and how many chairs the trailer had, and... well, lots of factors.

"No, not yet. They needed to deal with the sunburn issues first."

"Do you do a full face?" I knew next to nothing about regular movie make-up, how much coverage was he going with. How much protection did he really need? The more make-up he had on the less sunscreen because make-up provided some coverage.

She shook her head. "We keep him pretty minimalist."

I nodded. "Okay, I'll get his face covered."

I left Marcia and returned to Liam. It wasn't that far from the trailer to the tent we were working under.

I dragged a chair over so that I could reach his face. He was substantially taller than me, I needed him to sit. As I leaned in close to apply the specific facial sunscreen Lake had purchased at my direction, I knew this was going to be a challenge. Something pulled me into this man in a way I had never experienced before. I wanted to caress the planes of his face like a lover. Stroke along the side of his cheek and down his jaw. With his eyes closed and even breathing, I felt that magnetic tug again.

I rubbed a little too vigorously trying to jerk myself out

of it. Not only was it a bad idea to even think about, but it was also not allowed. Getting involved with the talent was a contractual no-no with Charlie. Absolutely no involvement with talent while on set for the duration of a shoot.

"I thought we were supposed to leave it sit before rubbing it in." His eyes opened and it took everything I had to back up a step. The brown pulled me down into their depths.

I cleared my throat. "That's for the rest of your skin. Your face can get applied once since you'll have on make-up."

He gave a little *harrumph* noise in reply.

Back on his feet, I instructed him to start rubbing the sunscreen in. I worked on his back, shoulders, and legs.

"We're done here?" He clapped his hands in a way that announced he was done.

"Not quite. I need you to stand like a T."

I proceeded to spray him down with another layer of protection.

"Now you can go to make-up."

I followed him over to the trailer with the bag of bottles. Lake had purchased doubles of everything. It wasn't going to be enough.

I stuck my head in the door and caught Marcia's eye. "Can we leave these in here?"

She pointed to an out of the way corner on the floor next to some cabinets.

"Thanks." I bounced out the door with two cans of spray and went in search of Lake. I had some questions, like was I really supposed to now be slathering up Liam James before filming every morning, and who was going to be in charge of his hourly applications?

～

I wiped my hands down my thighs, again. I still felt slick with sunscreen, and I didn't want slick hands as I hauled myself back up the scaffolding. Once at the top I wiped my hands again. My skin was beautifully hydrated, but my fingers felt slippery.

"What happened to you?" Nolan asked as I made my way across the platform to where he secured some cabling.

"Apparently I'm the only person on set who wears sunscreen."

"Bullshit." He coughed like some middle schoolboy in the back row of English class.

"I know, right? But Charlie threw me under the bus. Now I have to trowel up Sebastian Hale every morning." There was no way I would let him know that my job now included man handling Liam James in a very personal way. Sorry, not sorry, I looked forward to skimming my hands over his shoulders. It was so sleazy in my brain. And that's where those thoughts were going to stay. I would be completely professional, and I would not do anything inappropriate.

"Does this mean I'm down a set of hands?" he asked.

"It might. Once they start shooting, I have to get back down there and monitor and reapply the sunscreen."

"And that, Dani, is why I sent you down there." The boss man swung up onto our platform. Charlie wouldn't have sent me down there if he didn't think I could handle it, or wasn't the right person for the job.

Charlie was like the dad I never had. I mean I have a father, he just wasn't around much. Charlie, on the other hand, over mentored everyone. Those who couldn't handle it finished a contract and were gone. The rest of us worked for him like we were in some kind of cult. We got a boss we liked, good jobs, encouragement, and a den mother in his wife Linda.

I didn't have to worry about Charlie getting upset with me. He knew how important being here was for me, and not just because he had tricked me into designing the sets when I was drowning in a deep depression over missing Flint— okay he didn't know about the Flint part— but because he knew I was a huge Sebastian Hale geek.

"Who else would realize that sunscreen needs to be constantly reapplied if the makeup people didn't?"

I sighed, he was right. "Point taken."

Charlie turned to Nolan, "I need your eyes on Nefertari's bedroom."

"Isn't Viv on that?"

"We've run into a snag, and I want your input before it turns into a SNAFU. Dani can finish this up." Charlie was right, I was just lashing down columns. Viv was working on some rigging that suspended Nefertari's bed, and another system that would fly in the gods. Carlos Constanza as Horus was a big freaking deal. And we needed to keep the chick who played Isis safe, even if she wasn't a big name, yet.

I might not feel bad if something happened to the bed with Cecilia in it. Not that anything bad would actually happen if the bed fell or dropped the eighteen inches it was suspended. But I liked Carlos and didn't want to see him get hurt.

I sat on my ass to take a breather. My feet swung over the edge of the scaffolding. The view over the production sets from up here was pretty cool. The people below moved about like ants. They weren't that small, it was more along the lines of a scaled model village. I wasn't very high up, but high enough for a change of perspective.

I saw the top of Liam's dark head. I followed his path as

he strolled through the canyon from catering to the main set. I should head down that way soon. He paused. Tension bunched in his shoulders. Headed toward him I saw the tall crown of Nefertari bouncing along the path. I leaned in. This was going to be interesting.

Cecilia had a reputation of hooking up with every leading man she ever worked with. Every one of them. I believed the rumors. While most of Hollywood was working hard to do away with the casting couch, Cecilia wasn't ashamed to be single-handedly bringing it back. Well, in her case that would be two hands and a mouth.

The only time I bothered caring about Cecilia's sexual habits were when they had a direct impact on me. Fine, she could bang Liam all she wanted, I had no claim on him. I actually didn't want to like him much, he was eye candy. However, if she pitched one of her infamous fits that delayed shooting, she was messing with my job.

She changed her pace and really wasn't walking anymore, she slithered. I almost wondered if her eyes emitted a targeting beam and if Liam had a red laser dot in the middle of his forehead. Talk about body language—her's radiated sex, his was a frozen block of terror.

Oh, this was good. Liam didn't like Cecilia, assuming I read his posture correctly. Yep. There it was. She reached out for him and ran her hands across his collar bones in a way I wouldn't dare touch him. He captured her wrists in one hand and pulled them from his chest. I was too far away to hear anything clearly. She was probably talking in a low seductive voice.

With a sudden gesture, her hands were released and Liam made a loud growling bark. I stood up so I could visually trail him from above. He stormed off in the direction he had come from. I glance back at Cecilia. Her arms were crossed and she stomped her foot.

I smiled. I was inclined to actually like the man now. Good looking, check. Playing Seb Hale, check. Not a fan of Cecilia Saaid, double-check.

Liam stopped as he was approached by another actress. Isis, what was her name? Emi Paul. She didn't walk; she flowed. She moved like that when up in the aerial silk rigging for Isis. Liam opened his arms and she moved in for a hug. Oh, well, that would explain why he wasn't interested in Cecilia if he already hooked up with Isis.

She backed out of the embrace, laughed, swatted at him as if he teased her. One second he moved as if he were relaxed, the next he clutched at his head and fell to his knees. Isis had her arms around him and helped him down to the ground. I had heard about these attacks. After the accident, the rumor was Liam had debilitating headaches, they came on suddenly and left without any after-effects. This had to be what was happening. I hadn't realized he had them on set.

I held my breath as I watched the action below me. There wasn't much to it. Isis seemed to be comforting Liam. And then she helped him back up to his feet. He gave her another hug, and instead of continuing in the direction away from Cecilia and the Nefertari encounter, he followed Isis in that direction. I watched until they turned a corner and were out of sight.

4

"Cut! Cut cut cut cut cut!" Glenn yelled. And then he muttered, "Cut a fucking bitch."

He was one hell of a cranky director this morning.

I sat behind a few rows of camp and director style chairs lined up for support crew. That was me, support crew. I grabbed one of my blue and gold cans of spray-on sunscreen and wandered up toward the scene being filmed. If Glenn decided to not get started right away, I needed to sneak in and spray Seb Hale down. So far my over the top application of sunscreen was keeping the lead almost as pale as he could possibly be. And that was saying something since his skin tones leaned toward the swarthy olive completion of a Greek god.

"Why are there clouds? Who told me it would be clear today?"

Great, Glenn was going to fight the weather?

I looked up into the sky. It was crystal clear and, oh, wait, there it was a single little puffball of a cloud.

"I should have green-screened this," he continued to complain.

I quietly walked over to where Liam stood and showed him the can. He looked at me with brown eyes and nodded. I thought we might be awkward after this morning...

I had just finished applying the first layer of lotion when all the muscles in Liam's body tensed. Immediately he grabbed his head and curled into himself, letting out a low moan of pain.

I dropped the bottle in my hands and tried to hold him up as he fell into me. He was big, and all that muscle was heavy.

"Mr. Hale? Sebastian?" He didn't respond, and he stopped making noises. But he shivered as if the pain were too much to process.

This had to be one of those episodes, what I saw happen when I watched him and Emi Paul in the canyon. I began to lose my footing.

"Liam, I can't hold you." Set names be damned, he couldn't hear me anyway.

He looked up at me. His entire face twisted in a visage of pain, brows sweaty, eyes bloodshot and blue.

"Nica?" he asked. Someone asked.

I stopped breathing. That was my name. That wasn't his voice. Those weren't his eyes.

"Flint?" I don't know if I made a sound or not. My knees gave way at that point, and I landed on my ass. Liam followed me down and curled into the fetal position across my lap. There was nothing I could do, and I wasn't capable of doing anything anyway. I lay across him to the best of my ability and held on until it was over...

Liam acted as if nothing had happened earlier, so I would too. I might as well do my job while Glenn was on a tear. I lifted the spray can and pressed the nozzle.

"Why are you still doing that?"

I jumped at Glenn's loud tirade now directed at me.

"He hasn't gotten any sun for days now."

I looked at the man like he had lost it completely. I held up the can. "Right, it's working because I put sunscreen on him throughout the shoot."

Never considered that sunscreen consultant would ever be a job I held. Glenn just stared at me, holding my gaze. It looked like I wasn't going to have the job much longer. So far, it had been an odd week, starting with him pulling me away from my job on set to manage Sebastian Hale's pale skin.

Every morning, I met Liam and applied thick creamy lotion to his ridiculous shoulders and ticklish knees. And every morning, I had to insist he do his own chest and abs. I let my hands glide over his skin and up and over the ridges of muscle in his arms and back, probably enjoying the touch a bit too much. He stood there oblivious to my presence, focused on his phone, thumbs flying over text messages.

He wasn't exactly impolite, he was just used to having people wait on his snobby, but hot, ass hand and foot. If he wasn't a job, I wouldn't even attempt to speak to him. But I did have to tell him how to stand and move so I could rub him down. And why not try to get as much enjoyment out of a job as possible? It's not like anything would ever happen between us. Even after this morning, I seriously doubted Liam James would be able to pick me out of a lineup of tall black men, and I am most definitely not tall or a man. And I'm about as far from black as you can get without being albino.

Glenn nodded and I was allowed to go back to my little chair in the back and wait until the next time I needed to spray down the star.

I watched the edges of the filming, where people were

doing their behind the scenes job, so many people just to make the two actors in the scene look fabulous. So many people to create a few hours of escapist entertainment for the world. It really was movie magic, and I adored every second of it. How could I not?

We were all here to create one of the most beloved action-adventure heroes of the past century. Sebastian Hale could not come to life without the contributions of everyone here, including me.

It made me giddy. I loved my job, even if it meant that this week I had to slather up Liam James while keeping my clothes on. At least I didn't have to work with Cecilia. There was no denying she was gorgeous in all that Egyptian finery. Hell, she was gorgeous in jeans and a T-shirt. But she was only pretty as a picture. She opened her mouth and venom spewed forth, well, at least in my direction.

Sebastian pulled Nefertari to his chest. Damn, but they could pose. I couldn't really hear what the actors were saying from where I sat. I didn't need to. They were overemphasizing their actions as if everyone was here to shoot an old fashioned black-and-white silent movie. It looked kind of hammy right now, but on screen, it would be glorious. And it would look like still frames ripped out of the comic books.

Glenn was good at his job, and he was an industry wizard. But some of the credit needed to go to Liam and Cecilia.

They shot, and reshot the scene several times. Starting and stopping over and over again. Glenn didn't pitch another fit. I never did figure out what had been bothering him. More clouds wafted in on the breeze.

I wasn't expecting him to call it a wrap for today so soon.

But when I looked up I realized those were no longer happy fluff ball clouds.

"Hey, Danica!"

I looked up into the scaffolding to find the source of my name. I saw boss man Charlie waving at me. I shoved the bottle of sunscreen into one of the many pockets of my shorts and headed over to him.

"What's up?" I asked. It felt weird not being on his team for this job. Especially since the only reason I was out here was to be on the crew for the sets.

"Looks like a storm is rolling in. Can I get you to help out, or are you too good for us now?" Charlie laughed.

I whipped the spray can out of my pocket and held it up threateningly. "Watch it, I have sunscreen and know how to use it." I slid the can back, and hauled myself up the scaffolding.

"I need you to make sure the portico is lashed down." Charlie gave me instructions, and continued with what he was doing, folding up yards and yards of silk drapery.

We had to secure Nefertari's luxury patio furnishings and the rigging that would fly the gods in and out at her beckoning. The incoming storm gave us plenty of warning, which was good because we had a lot of work to do. Glenn was right, it might have been easier to green screen all of this. But he would never get that authentic shot in the desert feel.

Glenn was a curious director that way, if he could do it authentically he would when other directors would green screen and motion capture as much of everything as possible.

The wind kicked up. I snatched my hat before the wind could steal it away and rolled it up, shoving it into my back pocket. At some point, I determined that there were enough clouds that I could afford to take my over shirt off. I tied it around my hips and enjoyed the rare feeling of air on my bare shoulders.

My work uniform was the same every day— tank top, cargo pants or shorts, a UV shirt, a wide-brimmed hat, utility belt, red lipstick. I felt naked without my lipstick. The only thing I put on before I put on lipstick every morning was sunscreen.

Soon the air was full of sand, and the entire crew had tied handkerchiefs around their faces or had pulled up their T-shirts to cover their mouths and noses. The sand stuck to my skin, and it actually hurt when I tried to wipe it from the back of my neck. That was some seriously scratchy sand.

Fortunately, we just finished when the rain started falling. Ancient Egypt was now lashed down with webbed belting, bungee cords, rope, and covered in bright blue tarps. I'm pretty sure those ancient architects would have laughed at us, then again they were working in limestone, and we worked in foam and plaster.

I felt absolutely beat rolling into Base Camp. I was gritty and dirty and didn't want to touch anything. The rain wasn't helping. It was spitty and making things damp, and not washing away any of this afternoon's grime.

"Hey Viv," I called in through the door. I really did not want to track all of this sand and dirt into the RV. I knew she was in because the door was open, with just the screen closed.

"Yeah?" My RV-mate called back.

"Can you hand me my shower caddy?" I also asked for my towel and robe.

"I need to take a shower too. Glenn decided to hold a big barbecue tonight." She smiled as she handed me the plastic basket I kept everything together in.

"What?" Why tonight? Those things usually took place as a wrap-up party, not an 'oh, hey, it rained' party.

"Glenn decided tonight was a good night to have the entire cast and crew have the big feast he always does at the end of a shoot. So dinner is on him."

"Why isn't he waiting until the last day of the shoot? That makes no sense."

Viv shrugged, she didn't have any answers either.

It wasn't until I had been under the falling water for a minute I realized I had made an incredibly stupid mistake.

I had sunscreen all right. Apparently, I did not know how to use it.

I followed Viv and a few other crew members into the oversized ballroom at the luxury Sunset Sands Resort. According to Nolan, who rode in with us, the dinner was scheduled for tonight because when they wrapped this location there wasn't going to be any time for cast and crew to have an informal gathering. It had to be informal since most of us didn't even know this was going to happen, and all we had were our work clothes with us. I did put on a clean black and white polka-dotted shirt, worn with a sassy knot at the waist, tied my hair up in a red bandana and rolled the cuffs of my cargo pants up exposing my white socks and a flash of the sunburn on the back of my legs. The one cute outfit I had packed was too scratchy against my legs to be comfortable.

Glenn rented out the entire ground floor and outdoor party space of the exclusive resort to host this shindig. Outside wasn't so bad now that the storm had passed. But I planned on finding a dark little corner, hopefully somewhere cool, and grit my teeth.

My stupidity rankled harder than usual because I had a fucking can of spray-on sunscreen in my pocket the entire time.

Charlie greeted us with a big smile. I swerved to miss his hand, and...

"Ah, no!" I cried as his hand landed on my shoulder.

"What's the matter?" He stepped back and looked at me with concern.

I gingerly pulled the collar of my shirt away from my neck and leaned, exposing the bright red skin of my shoulders.

"Oh, Danica," he exclaimed.

I felt the disappointment roll off him.

"I know, stupid. I thought I had enough sunscreen on, and I figured the cloud cover from the storm would be enough. It wasn't."

Charlie eased the rest of my shirt back to get a look. "How bad?"

"Shoulders and backs of my calves."

"Your nose looks ok, only a little pink on your cheeks. Hat?"

I nodded. "Hat and better sunscreen on my face. I got lax being able to hang out under a tent this past week."

"Oh wow, that looks bad. Should I trust you to keep me from turning red like that?"

I cringed at the sound of that voice. I hadn't heard Liam come up while Charlie examined my burn. Charlie repeated what I had just explained, how my own stupidity resulted in a sunburn.

"Do as I say, not as I do?" I shrugged.

Liam smiled and laughed. It looked good on him. I was

more than a little surprised when he continued to chat with Charlie about how much he appreciated the set designs as we waded through the catering buffet. "They really bring a sense of urgency and realism into the production."

"What, you don't like jumping over green rocks in a green room with sensor dots all over your body?" I joked.

"Don't get me wrong, I can act my way through any situation. But, it's a whole lot nicer to have place and time to interact with."

This was the most he had said to me all week. He actually was a nice guy, but he was the star, and I was crew. Charlie, on the other hand, was King of the Scene, and as such was a mucky-muck, upper echelon, crew without being a peon. He was allowed to rub elbows with the elite.

"Enjoy your dinner. I'll see you later," I said with my plate full of ribs and salad.

"Danica, please, join us."

"Thank you, Mr. Hale, but I can't."

His jaw dropped a little and then his face set. He gave me a sharp nod.

"My name is Liam, Mr. Hale is a character on set. And please join us."

I tilted my head toward the table with the other leads, slightly separated from the rest of everything. Nefertari interrupted her conversation with Horus to give us a glare. Cecilia was one of the reasons that the table was separated. Liam also had a reputation of not being overly friendly toward crews on set. There was no way I was going to play stupid and try to go sit there while she was around.

"Social ranking is alive and well on set. But there is nothing stopping you from joining us and the crew," I said.

"I thought talent couldn't..." he began.

I shook my head, "Flip it. Crew can't."

Liam looked at Charlie. He gave a confirming nod. "I don't count."

"Yeah, Charlie is crew the same way Glenn is crew." I snorted. It wasn't a pretty sound, and I was keenly aware of that.

"Come on." I turned and headed toward the mass of tables.

I found a half-empty table and took a seat. Liam sat opposite of me and introduced himself to everyone as if no one knew who he was. We all knew who he was, he was the reason we were here.

"So, how's the new gig, Dani?" Nolan asked.

I turned to my coworker and smiled around a mouth full of food.

"She's doing great, I haven't gotten a lick of sun all week." Liam gave me a glowing reference.

"Yeah, but I'm failing at protecting myself."

"Huh?" Nolan asked.

"I was stupid and thought the clouds with the storm were heavy enough to not let as much sun through as they did."

"Those UV rays are getting stronger every year, I swear," Viv said from another table, joining our conversation.

"Seriously. I got my legs and shoulders pretty bad."

"Let's see." Nolan reached up and pulled my shirt back. "Damn woman, you're neon."

I winced. Light hurt.

"Can't you put anything on it?" Liam asked.

"I haven't had a chance or a car to try to get to town. And unfortunately, the shop in the lobby only has a treatment that requires a tub. I don't have a tub."

"I do," he replied.

I leveled a glare at him. His tub didn't do me a whole lot of good.

"You can use it if you like."

My eyes had to have jumped out of my head. "Really?" I wondered how I would be able to get myself over to Beverly Hills, that's what we all called the luxury trailer village where the talent and directors and other elites like Charlie lived during filming. The rest of us lived at Base Camp. However, their trailers were swank, while ours were musty and old RVs. Base Camp was also set up several miles away from Beverly Hills. I wasn't sure if that was because of the classist bullshit on set, or topographically there just wasn't room for everyone to be in one location, or a combination somewhere between.

The conversation took a hard left turn and I forgot about taking a bath in a luxury trailer as the guys all discovered that Liam played Dungeons and Dragons. They all rambled on about quests, and Liam confessed it had been a long time since he played. "I haven't found a regular group. And it's not something you can bring up like you can fantasy football."

"Tell me about it. Role-playing geeks are pushed farther back in the closet every year."

"Hell, fantasy football is just D and D with quarterbacks. You are more than welcome to join our group."

I left them to their male bonding over magical quests.

I got up and took my paper plate to the garbage. I grabbed an icy can of cola and headed outside.

If it wasn't D and D, it was some other online role-playing game. It cracked me up that actors and other film-makers liked to play pretend when their jobs were bringing pretend to life for other people to watch. I guess it wouldn't be any different if I liked to paint as a hobby while I designed and built sets for a living.

I sighed. It was nice outside. The air had cooled off, and there were no lights. It wasn't exactly hot inside, but the light on my skin reminded me that I was burned. I couldn't see any way for me to get over to Liam's trailer and then back to mine. I guess that bath wasn't going to happen.

"Nica?" Liam's voice rolled over me like thunder.

I felt the rumble deep in my belly. I wanted to lean back against the presence I felt there. I wanted his hand to reach up and caress my neck. My breath caught, and for a second, I felt frozen in time. *Flint*. Oh, how I missed him. Time spun back up and I breathed him in and suppressed a groan. I wanted so much from him, but I knew Flint could not give me what I needed.

I stopped moving. The fine hairs on my neck stood up and a chill shivered down my spine. Suddenly my burning skin turned freezing cold and pebbled with goosebumps.

Flint had called me Nica. He had been the only one, everyone else called me Dani or used my full name. Why did Liam remind me of Flint so much? There was more to it than this whole Seb Hale thing. Maybe the darker hair? The same deep soothing tones to his voice? His eyes? I couldn't ask Liam, he would have me committed. I couldn't ask Flint, he had left me, and I hadn't let anyone else into that empty space his absence created.

"It's nice out here," I said, not knowing what else I could say. I couldn't turn around and face him. I was terrified I would start babbling about Flint as if Liam would know who or what I was talking about.

"It is. Different from the hot day on set, that's for certain." Liam fell into pace next to me as I slowly strolled around.

I had to blink hard a few times when I looked up at him. I saw a flicker of light as if an image was projected onto Liam's face. I swear his eyes changed colors. I saw Flint there. I swallowed hard.

"I want to thank you for the offer of your tub, but I don't think it will work out."

"Why not?" he asked.

"Logistics. I don't see how I can get over to your trailer and then back to mine. I don't have a car, and it's not like I can call a cab out here." I grinned weakly up at him.

"I'm not staying in a trailer. Didn't you hear?"

I shook my head.

"There was some kind of carbon monoxide leak from the air conditioner. So they're putting me up here for a couple of nights. I have a huge tub, and you can go use it now, while your friends are still enjoying their evening." He hitched a thumb over his shoulder indicating the crew in the ballroom.

I spun to face him. "Really?"

My eyes darted around landing my focus on nothing, on everything, as I thought about what I needed to do to make this happen.

I needed to tell Viv and make sure she would wait, I needed—

"Come on." I followed Liam as he took long brisk steps away from the party. "You can call the concierge from my room and order your skin treatment stuff. I'll find your friends, Viv and Nolan, right? I'll let them know what's going on."

His room was grander than I could have imagined. It wasn't a hotel room, bed in the middle and a bathroom attached. It was a full suite and bigger than my studio apartment at home.

I wandered around the cavernous space in awe, my jaw dragging along the floor. I squealed when I found the bathroom and the indoor pool Liam referred to as a tub. I felt the urge to run to him and tell him there was room for two.

When I returned to the main room Liam finished a phone call and hung up. "The concierge is bringing up an oatmeal bath. That's what you wanted right?"

I nodded.

"She also suggested some vinegar, and is having the kitchen send some up."

"Oh, nice. Clearly, she understands." I sighed.

"Vinegar? Won't that sting?" he asked.

I laughed; most people gave me that same perplexed look. "You'd think it would, but surprisingly enough, it does just the opposite."

We stared awkwardly at each other for a few seconds. Liam broke the silence. He turned to leave. Opening the door, he said, "I'll head back now and let everyone know. You take your time."

My knees went weak at the smile he flashed before closing the door behind him.

5

I may have fallen asleep in the tub. I thought I heard whispered voices and doors closing. Even if I hadn't heard anything, the water was now cold and I needed to get out of the tub. Wrapped in a large fluffy white towel, I padded out into the bedroom. The bed looked so soft and comfortable and inviting. I'd only close my eyes for a few minutes.

Flint was back, but he wasn't Flint, he was Liam. But he was definitely Flint. I kept trying to ask him what had happened, but he made soothing shushing sounds and wrapped me in his arms. I lay my head on his shoulder and thought this was all right. I missed him so much, it was so nice to be back in his arms.

And in that perfectly acceptable but weird as hell dream way, Flint was no longer dressed in the form-fitting band shirt and jeans Liam had been wearing at the party. He wore the linen kilt and riding boots of Sebastian Hale. I stood naked in the middle of Nefertari's patio, frozen in place while Seb Hale looked for a place to hide me.

"What the fuck are you doing in here?" Nefertari's sharp voice pulled me from my dream.

I pushed up from the bed and blearily stared at an out of focus woman.

"You? Where is Liam? Never mind, Glenn is going to hear about this."

When the door slammed closed I realized the screaming banshee had been Cecilia. When I fell back asleep, I didn't dream about Liam or Flint.

∼

The next morning, I was too embarrassed to show my face on set. I really did not want to be there. I hadn't returned to Base Camp, and as far as I knew, not only had Liam told everyone I was up in his suite taking a bath, but Cecilia had found me there at some point in time during the night.

My stomach folded in with knots. I guess there was some truth to the rumor about something going on between her and Liam. Then again there was always some rumor, and some truth to her hooking up with her lead counterpart in a lot of movies.

This morning felt a hint worse than a walk of shame, I was showing up at work in the same clothes everyone saw me in last night after I spent the night in the lead actor's room. I knew nothing had happened, but no one else would. And Charlie enforced a strict no fraternization rule. My job was in jeopardy if I even had one after this.

I tried to hide as I walked down the canyon that led to the set. I wasn't the only one slinking through the canyon trail. A few shadows skittered past, probably the spiritual residue of desert rats.

The entrance canyon split, I needed to follow the gully to the left to take it to make-up, the open space in front of me eventually led to the set. Nolan passed me going from the ravine on my right, where King of the Scene had storage containers, headed toward the set.

"Hey, Dani, how's that sunburn? Feeling any better? Man, did you piss Nefertari off." I couldn't believe my luck running into Nolan first.

I grabbed his arm and pulled him to the side against the wall of rock. "Nothing happened last night," I growled between clenched teeth. Nolan would have my back and squelch any whispers that might make their way to Charlie's ears.

"Bullshit," he laughed. "Everything happened last night and you missed it."

"What?" I was so confused.

"The queen of de-Nile last night got drunk off her ass and moved in hard on our new bard. We wanted to eliminate her, but no one rolled high enough."

I backed up and squinted at Nolan. "You had dice on you? You guys played last night? Who's your bard?"

"Joe always has dice on him. Liam is a blast. We did a mini-run just to pass time while you were taking a bath. Anyway, Cecilia tried to convince Liam she was his for the taking, and he told her she was drunk and found a female crew member to make sure she got back to her room okay. I guess when she found out he was in the hotel, she pitched a fit until she was put up there also. So was the bed any good?"

"What?"

"Was the bed comfortable? Liam said you were out like a light when he went to check on you."

"And you didn't wake me up to take me home? Now everyone is going to think I slept with him."

Nolan just shook his head. I felt like he wasn't understanding how stressful this was for me. Sure hooking up on set happened, but that reputation could get in the way of being hired for the next job with Charlie. I did not want this kind of reputation. I liked working for Charlie, he paid well, and on time.

"No one is going to think you slept with him. But frankly, if you do, we won't give you any grief. The guy is a real gentleman. After he came back to let us know you were asleep, he told us to leave you be, and he went and got himself another room for the night. We were all there." Nolan grabbed my upper arms to hold me steady. "Including Charlie, it's all good."

It was a good thing he held on, I think I might have collapsed with relief. "But Cecilia? She saw me in his room."

"Yeah, and she's made herself look like the drunk idiot she is. She's been telling everyone how she convinced some poor security guard, who has probably lost his job over this, that it was her room. But when she went to seduce Sebastian Hale properly, you were passed out on his bed, and he was in the shower."

"She didn't use my name did she?" I started smiling. I couldn't feel sorry for her. I just couldn't.

"No, she used some delightfully descriptive epithets including sunburned girl, so everyone knew she meant you."

I cringed. There it was, named and shamed.

"No worries, Dani. Liam already made sure everyone knew he wasn't there and you needed the rest. I've got to get. We have to dry everything off after last night."

I let Nolan go and he disappeared down the gully and

around the rocks. Great, so everyone knew that a whole lot of nothing happened, and now because of that, Cecilia would have an extra grudge against me.

I shook my head. Cecilia wouldn't have a grudge against me. That would mean I was important enough for her to remember my name. She made it clear years ago I wasn't that important to her. If she called me sunburn girl, then I was safely off her radar.

"Good morning, Nica." The way Liam said my name this morning made my toes want to curl. The purr in his gravelly voice sounded like something had happened last night. "How are you feeling this morning? Did your bath do the trick?"

"Good morning, Mr. Hale. It sounds like I need to not only thank you for the use of your tub and bed but for putting the kibosh on a rumor someone is trying to start."

He huffed out a half-laugh. "I've been putting the brakes on that woman for weeks. Sorry you got mixed up in it. And my name is Liam."

He took a step toward me and nodded at my shirt. "May I?"

I pulled back the collar so he could take a look at this morning's rosy glow of my burned skin.

He hissed. "It's not as bright. How long before it turns into a tan?"

Every cell of my body was keenly aware he did not replace my collar; he stood close, focusing on my back. His breath swept gently across my sensitive skin.

A bark of a laugh escaped my lips. "You're cute. I don't tan. It will stay pink until it fades away. And it will hurt the entire time."

I twisted to get a look at him. He was so close my breasts

brushed against his chest. His hand let go of my shirt and grazed down my arm.

"Liam." The sound was barely a whisper.

"Better not let anyone else hear you call him that," Marcia said louder than necessary.

Liam and I jumped away from each other. It was suddenly very chilly in the canyon. I ran my hands over my arms.

The other woman held out a bag for me. "Your tools, can't rub him down with sunscreen without the sunscreen." The tone in her voice made me wonder which she heard first, Nefertari's report of my presence in Liam's hotel room or Liam's claim to have gotten another room for the night.

He nodded at her as she turned to leave. "Marcia."

She winked at him. "Mr. Hale."

I did not miss her saucy walk, with all the hip motion back to the makeup trailer.

I tried to put the whole incident behind me while I coated him. He made it difficult. While I stood in front of him applying lotion to his face, he grabbed on to my hips and pulled me close. I could have complained but I liked it. I liked being that close to him, gazing into his face with his eyes closed. I liked how he held onto me.

"You're taking your time this morning," he commented as I stroked my fingers across his cheekbones.

"Am I?" I was and I knew it. I tried not to admire his features, but this morning I wanted to remember everything about his face. The way his lips curved into a slight grin, emphasizing his cheekbones, the way his dark lashes fanned across those cheeks, I wanted to freeze this moment forever. Something in me needed to commit this to memory for future recollection.

I trailed my fingers down his neck. Liam hummed low in

appreciation. I don't know what exactly had changed, but I knew I could touch him this way and he wouldn't object. When I had worked the lotion down to the base of his throat he grabbed my wrist, keeping my hands splayed across his collar bones.

"Keep going." He dragged down on my arms pulling my hands down onto his chest.

He opened his eyes, and they were the blue of Flint's eyes. We both froze. Held in each other's gaze.

"I can't," I whimpered. "You can't either. Not after last night, not after you made such a show of being noble and getting a different room. Thank you for that."

"Nica." His voice was a familiar caress that matched the way his warm hands held my hips and ran over my backside. Flint.

I stepped out of his grasp and handed him the bottle of sunscreen. "Not while we're on the same set."

"And once filming is done?" He rubbed the lotion across his pecs and over his abs. I longed to touch him, but that was dangerous territory.

"Filming isn't scheduled to be over for another eight weeks, but I'm done with this production when this set wraps at the end of the week." I folded my arms around myself.

"You aren't going to London?" he asked. His eyes never left mine. He reached out and caressed the side of my face. I couldn't stop myself, I leaned into his hand.

"I signed on for this bit only. I'm not even on the books for the green screen work." I shrugged. I should have been all in for this production, it was Sebastian Hale after all. London was not an option, they had an entirely local team that would deal with Sebastian Hale before he decides he has to fire up the time-traveling machine, and again after he returned from ancient Egypt.

This time, he would not be bringing the beautiful beauty of the past back with him. Nefertari would be left Queen of the Nile Delta, pining for her lost proper gentleman. And then it was back to the states for the core group of actors and filmmakers to finish anything forgotten on a green screen sound stage.

The six weeks in London was too long to wait for their return without work, and not long enough for me to accept and finish a contract from another production. And since Charlie didn't have enough work for me, I had accepted a contract on a sci-fi pilot for network television. I took what I could and I counted myself lucky to have been a part of the production.

"Next week I'll be transitioning the big pieces we have here for use on a sound stage. The week after that, I'm on a TV show," I explained.

"Then what happens when we wrap here?" he asked, his voice thick and seductive.

"Actors go on to London, and I spend the day breaking down and packing up. I take the RV back to the lot and make sure everything is ready to go for when it's needed again." I dropped my arms.

"That's not what I meant." He reached forward and caught my hand.

He tugged me back into his sphere of personal space. His eyes had transitioned into a hazel color, half blue, half brown. The breath caught in my throat.

I found my spine and my words. "I would very much like to see you."

"You're seeing me now," he teased.

"Fine. I would like to kiss you Liam James, and I'd like

for you to kiss me back." I gave a shy smile and looked at him through my lashes.

I wasn't exactly shy, but a little flirting never hurt.

Without letting go of my hand he stood up. "I very much look forward to the day we finish filming. I think you missed my knees."

Every nerve in my body thrummed, and I knew exactly why. Glenn's final shot was this morning. Yesterday's work had gone better than expected, and they had been able to make up for the lost time. That meant this morning would be the last time I rubbed Liam down with sunscreen, and tomorrow, I would be rubbing him down with me— if he was agreeable to the idea.

I was pretty sure he would be. Yesterday had required a very cold shower after work.

I floated down the canyon to the make-up trailer. My bag of sunscreen bottles unceremoniously kicked to the curb. Marcia must have placed it out on the step earlier. Fine, I could take the hint, she didn't want to be bothered.

I grabbed the bag and waited anxiously for Liam to show up. Nerves bounced through my skin like a super bouncy ball in a small room knocking over lamps and causing general havoc. My feet bounced, and my knees jumped. I could barely drink my coffee this morning; my stomach buzzed.

The nervous energy compounded itself and by the time Liam arrived, I was ready to throw up. I have never been so anxious to see anyone that I could remember. Okay, maybe Santa when I was little, but never as an adult, and not like this.

He didn't arrive alone, and I did throw up. My nerves had topped out and seeing Cecilia hanging off his arm this morning was more than I could handle. They didn't see anything, and by the time they were under the tented application area, I appeared to be calm as a sunflower in full daylight. The poor mint I sucked on would testify otherwise, if mints could speak.

"Mr. Hale, Glenn, good morning, Nefertari," I greeted each of them and was ignored as if I didn't exist. So, I pretended they weren't there and set about getting ready for Seb Hale's arrival and sunscreen session. I passed behind Liam and the hand not occupied by Nefertari reached out and grabbed mine, squeezing twice. Okay, so he knew I was there and he wanted me to know he was aware. At least, that's how I interpreted his actions, why else would he, mid-conversation with the director and costar, grab me?

Once I had everything set up to my best, assuming I would be judged on having a professional-looking workstation, I sat and lazily bounced my legs. The rattling nerves from earlier completely replaced by boredom and annoyance.

I had no intention of eavesdropping, but that was impossible considering they were in my space having a conversation. I tried not to grin too hard when Cecilia began pouting about how Liam changed his flight and she couldn't get the airline to change hers as well. Glenn insisted that shouldn't be a concern of hers, after all, he needed her in London a few days for some press opportunities.

While Nefertari would stay in ancient Egypt, Seb Hale would, of course, run across an alluring woman in Edwardian England who reminded him of the lost love he left behind, so of course, Cecilia had a few scenes in Edwardian England. Technically, Liam needed to be in London longer than Cecilia, but from the sounds of it, she would get there three days ahead of him. My stomach flipped. Did that mean what I hoped it meant?

Liam peeled the appeased Cecilia off his arm and draped her on Glenn. He stood with his arms crossed watching them leave. Damn, they walked slowly. I didn't say anything either. As soon as the two interlopers turned out of the canyon, Liam spun. I was out of the chair and our lips met.

I had never kissed him before, and yet it felt familiar and like I hadn't kissed him in forever and I had missed it. His lips slid across mine in a familiar caress. His hands fisted in my hair and I grasped the big muscles in his arms. We pulled each other into our gravities and held tight. Kissing him was ambrosia and perfection. His lips teased and caressed mine. His tongue slid and tangoed with mine in a sexual give and take. He held my face and changed his technique to a repetition of shorter, harder presses of mouth against mouth. Finally, he pulled back and stopped kissing me.

I swallowed hard. That's not exactly what I had thought was going to happen. I wasn't complaining, not one bit. He continued to hold me to him. His body was strong and warm. I felt his thick desire press into my belly. That costume wasn't going to hide anything. He would need to lose the erection pretty soon.

"You heard?" His voice was raspy.

I nodded. "You aren't going to London right away."

"I need to touch you, Nica. I need you touching me." He buried his face into my neck. His lips tickled against my skin.

"Liam, we shouldn't, not here, not now."

"When, where?" he growled as he trailed small kisses along my jaw.

Here! Now! My body screamed. "Tomorrow. You will officially be done and we can be together without the fuss of having to deal with everyone."

"You mean Nefertari?" He stood back, releasing me.

I didn't stop touching him, resting my hand in the middle of his expansive chest. "Yes, I mean Nefertari—Cecilia, Glenn, my boss, and any other list of people whose business they would make it out to be. Liam, I don't know what's happening between us, but I want it between us and not involve every other person on set."

He wrapped his fingers around mine and held my hand to his skin. "I understand. My part is done this afternoon. Instead of leaving in the morning, I'll meet you back here?"

I nodded. "And then you can either follow me back to Base Camp or wait around and ride back with the gang."

"You're okay with your coworkers knowing about us, but not my coworkers?" There was a sharp edge in his voice.

I smiled and leaned into him. "My coworkers think you're a good guy and would love another chance to quest with you. Your coworkers would roast me on a spit and make sure I never worked in film again. Just a bit of a difference."

"Cecilia hates everyone, don't take it personally."

Oh, I was definitely taking it personally.

"Come on, let's get you slathered up for one last day of no tan." I reluctantly pulled my hand away from his skin.

He grabbed my hips and pulled me against him. "You know one good thing about no tan?"

"Hmm?"

"No tan lines."

I squirmed away from him with a giggle.

It was a good thing this was the last time I was rubbing him down with sunscreen, it was impossible not to touch him inappropriately. I tickled his knees intentionally and ran my hands up his thighs substantially higher than the sun protection needed applying. He hissed in a breath between teeth.

"You know you can go up even higher," he teased. His breathing was as heavy as mine.

"It wouldn't be professional," I managed to say.

"I don't want you to be professional. I want you touching me." His words came out like a breathy growl.

When it came time to do his chest and abs I handed him the bottle. It was still too intimate for me. Too awkward, especially now that I would have problems stopping. He grabbed my hand and filled the palm with lotion. And then he placed my hand on his chest. He made a noise deep in his throat. I scraped my teeth along my lower lip. This job was not supposed to be sexy. All I needed was to keep the man from getting a sunburn. I closed my eyes and reveled in the feel of him under my fingers.

It was too much, and I tried to squirm away. "Liam, I shouldn't."

He didn't let go of my wrist. I leaned my face into his arm.

"Touch me, Nica." The sound barely a whisper.

I thought I would cry when he said my name. I had to open my mouth to get enough air in my lungs, and my lips caught on the skin of his arm. He ran my fingers below his waistband as I had originally instructed him to. I think I let out a mewling sound as he guided my hand back across his soft skin and strong muscles. I felt him push lower down past the waistband of the kilt. I know I let out a whimper of surrender when my fingers grazed the scratchy hairs above his sex. I gasped when my hand spread around the base of his hot, thick manhood.

"Please," I whispered against his skin.

He released his hold of me, and I slowly trailed my hand back up his abdomen.

"Tomorrow is a very long ways away," he spoke softly into my hair.

I couldn't agree with him more.

6

The canyon was empty. The makeup and caterers had thoroughly removed themselves the day before.

Glenn had called a wrap on the location's shoot by noon. No more spraying down the hero to prevent him from tanning or burning. And I was back to working with the KoS crew and taking down the set. This time I remembered to use the bottle of spray sunscreen on myself. I also kept my over shirt on, no matter how sweaty I got.

We had worked as late as we could and being mid-summer, that was fairly late. We weren't allowed certain types of lighting on sight, so once the sun had set, we could basically see enough to get ourselves safely back to the parking lot. I didn't see Liam for the rest of the day, so I was anxious for this morning.

Not as anxious as I had been yesterday, and that made no sense. Today, I didn't care if anyone saw me fraternizing with the talent. There was no talent on location, so Charlie could not complain if Liam showed up on his own.

Nothing familiar but the red rock walls looming over

me. It seemed surreal that twenty-four hours ago this had felt more like a room and less like nature. Now, I expected a coyote and a roadrunner to come dashing through with a beep-beep.

I found a rock ledge to perch on while I waited. Would Liam really show up? Was the heavy petting of yesterday a reality or a crazy desert induced dream?

Touching him was so familiar. There was a connection there with him and Flint. I knew there was, there had to be. He tasted right, he smelled the same. And the eyes. Brown they were Liam's; blue, Flint's. Why did they change? I know people thought Liam looked like Peter Keith, but that was only with blond hair and a horrible mullet. He didn't exactly look like Flint Reese but there was a heavy similarity there. I was making shit up in my head, I had to be. I had been in love with Flint. Maybe I was in love with Liam and I was mixing the two of them up together in my head.

"Nica?"

I wanted to moan in pleasure at the sound of my name rolling around that man's mouth.

Nica. Maybe it was the stupid nickname that was having me confuse Liam with Flint.

I lifted my eyes to meet his gaze. Hazel. What did that mean? Damn. Liam James out of costume, with his clothes on, was breathtaking. Who knew a tight tee and butt hugging jeans could be sexier than a low slung kilt and riding boots. And I appreciated a man in a kilt big time.

I jumped from the ledge and made my way to stand in front of him. No sunscreen, no limits. I could touch him and not feel guilty. I could call him Liam and not worry about someone with a stick up their ass calling me on proper set etiquette.

I reached forward and twisted a finger into a belt loop. I focused on my finger, and not his face. "I have about six hours of tear down to finish. Viv is driving herself back to LA tonight, and I'll drive the RV back to the studio in the morning."

"I have a book. My driver can wait and take us back to your camp this evening. Can I catch a ride back to LA with you?"

I looked up into his face then. "I was hoping that's what you'd want."

He smiled, his eyes sparkled blue, and I melted. His lips were super soft and coaxed sounds from me I didn't expect to make just from kissing. I wanted to pull him into me and consume him.

He sounded as hot and bothered as I felt when we finally broke apart. "Hurry up and get finished. I'll be in the parking lot."

There had only been four hours' worth of work to finish. We packed the last of the storage containers and locked everything up. Nolan would supervise the trucks loading the containers. I was done. I was one of the last ones from King of the Scene crew to leave. Viv had left about an hour earlier. Charlie was already back in LA getting everything ready for the set to come rolling in in the afternoon.

I headed out to the parking lot, really just a flat spot in the desert where park rangers said we could put vehicles.

A long black car sat in the middle of the lot, doors and windows open. I could see the driver leaning back in his seat. He looked asleep.

"Hey handsome," I said leaning into the back.

Liam smiled and pulled me in. The plush seats felt soft and comfortable as Liam pressed me back into them. He lay against me, body to body. "Hey yourself. Ready to say goodbye to this place and get some privacy?"

"Hell yes."

Liam knocked on the roof. "Henry, my good man, get us out of here."

I could hear the smile in the driver's voice when he said, "Yes sir," and closed the open doors. I told him where he could find Base Camp and ignored everything but Liam's lips the twenty minutes it took to drive there.

Henry carried Liam's luggage into the RV and left us with a nod. Liam followed him out and I'm sure arrangements were made to pick him up in LA. Liam jumped into the RV with enthusiasm. He stood in the middle and looked around. He looked huge, and his presence made the space look small. It wasn't nearly as large as his luxury trailer, but it had a bedroom in the back, and pull out bed above the driving cabin.

"This is bigger than I thought when you first described it. I thought you were going to be in one of those dinky pop-up trailers." He sat in the side chair with a flop.

"It gets tight when there are two people moving around in here."

"Two? You mean you had to share?" He raised his voice slightly since I was in the bedroom gathering towels and my shower basket.

"Yeah, we don't have the privilege of not sharing. Look, I need to take a shower. You don't mind waiting a few more minutes?" I stood in front of him a stinky sweaty mess.

He smiled up at me. "Nica, I've waited all day, and I suspect somewhat longer than that to be with you. I think I can handle another thirty minutes."

I only made him wait for another fifteen. I hadn't bothered getting dressed and wore my robe back to the RV. Liam was already shirtless when I got back. We were both adults. We both knew what we wanted, we didn't waste any more time with needless flirting.

I took the time to put my shower basket away, and that was it. Liam was in my arms. The tie to my robe fell open and we were skin to skin. He felt heavenly. After days of rubbing lotion into his skin, I was not surprised at how soft it felt against mine. He was warm and smooth, and I loved how he crushed me to him. I'd spent weeks admiring his thickly muscled arms, now I could admire how they felt around me. Cradling, protecting, claiming. We fell onto the bed and his weight pressed me into the mattress.

His lips scorched my skin as he trailed kisses across my jaw and down my neck. I did not stifle the little sounds of want and joy as he bit at my collarbone, before lowering his head further down my chest.

His tongue traced a circle around one of my nipples and I cried out. He sucked the nub into his mouth and I held his head to my breast, reveling in the sensation of him.

There was a knock on the door and he paused. He went back to his ministrations when there wasn't another sound. God, his tongue licked and pulled at me. His hand cupped and kneaded my other breast. I was worthless as he made love to me. I was nothing but melted nerves and goo for brains. I bunched blankets into my hands, not knowing what I could hold on to, afraid to pull on Liam's hair. A particular aggressive pull on my nipple cause me to call out.

The RV door burst open. "Dani, are you all right?"

Liam sat up.

Nolan froze by the door took one look at us and swiveled to look away. "Oh God, sorry. Didn't realize you had company. Sorry."

I rolled over, pulling my robe closed. Liam stood to block

Nolan's view. "Glad you're keeping an eye on her. But, we're all good."

Nolan stepped down to leave. "Lock the door this time. Oh, and hey, we're having a last night pot luck. If you two decide you want to be sociable. You know the drill, Dani, clean out your fridge, bring what you've got."

Liam patted Nolan on the back. "Yeah, we'll see ya later."

I watched him figure out and throw the locks on the door.

He stalked back to me on the bed. "Now where was I?"

I bit my lip and threw open my robe. I guess it was a good thing I hadn't remembered how to use my hands earlier, or Liam's jeans would have been at least partially off.

This time my hands got busy and as Liam sucked and licked and bit my breasts, I fumbled and finally unfastened the top button on his jeans, eventually freeing his erection. Hot damn the man wore jeans commando, or maybe that had been for my benefit. I didn't care, I had him in my hands. Hot and heavy, soft and solid, suede-covered granite.

He kicked free of his jeans and lay pressed against me. His fingers trailed tickles and caresses up and down my torso. I lay back and looked at his face as I watched his gaze following his hand over my torso, down to my sex. He ran a teasing finger across the seam of my flesh and back up to circle my belly button. I had some belly padding, but nothing I was overly self-conscious about.

I laced my fingers through his hair and pulled his mouth to mine. His hand continued to trace over my skin. The next time his finger found my sex, I closed my legs together, holding his hand in place. He got the hint and his fingers found their way between my folds.

I sucked on his tongue and tilted my hips, encouraging him to keep doing whatever it was he did with those fingers.

"You want to replace those fingers with something else?" My voice came out low and full of desire. I wanted his fingers to continue, but I also wanted other parts of him there as well. I let him decide which parts I got to sample next.

He rolled up on his elbows, surrounding my head with his arms. I wrapped a leg over him and slid my other leg over his as he repositioned himself. I moaned with satisfaction as he slid into me. He filled me and I still wanted more of him. I thrust up against him and he began a slow and steady rhythm. We rolled and thrust against each other. There was no awkward finding the right pace to match with a new partner. We fell into the precise movements each other needed. It felt like the perfect first time. It felt like we had been doing this with each other for years. He knew exactly how to make me come. And he did. Repeatedly.

Damn him and his slow buildup of pressure. He didn't bang away, pounding me into the mattress. He was deliberate and consistent.

"Faster." I urged him on.

"I know you, darling, and this way, you'll come harder."

He was so right. Even while I lost control of my muscles and quivered and clenched around him, he continued his steady pace. He made me come three times, each one was more intense than the previous. On my last set of convulsions, Liam finally let loose. I cried out in ecstasy as he roared his release. That hadn't been a sprint to see who made it to the finish first, but a marathon of sexual prowess. I lay limp while Liam looked like the cat that got the cream and wanted to take a victory lap.

I reached up to him and caressed his face. He sucked a finger into his mouth, playfully biting it as he shifted to my side.

Liam looked down at me; his face was so serene; his eyes so blue. I was already in love with him. I had no idea how I got there. One minute, my job was to spray his body down with sunscreen, then next, I just wanted to wrap up in the sound of his voice.

"You are the most beautiful woman I have ever seen, and then I walked in and found you passed out on my bed."

I groaned. "I'm sorry about that."

"No, never. I think that's when everything clicked for me. You with your pink and white skin. You looked like some kind of angel. And my God, you have the sexiest ass."

"You looked? Oh no, it wasn't." I closed my eyes, at least I hadn't realized it at the time. But I should have suspected something, I had woken up with a sheet over me.

"It was on display. Your towel had fallen off. And you were completely naked like some Pre-Raphaelite painting."

Together, I think we looked less Pre-Raphaelite and more like a Peter Paul Rubens; rock hard man of heroic proportions, and pasty white marshmallow fluff of a woman.

I closed my eyes and groaned. I really shouldn't complain, after all, I had managed to seduce him by sheer force of stupidity and hips.

"Why do I feel like I've known you for a thousand years?" The earnestness in his expression tightened my chest.

I had an answer, but I don't know if he could accept it. It was easy— because we had.

"So what's the deal with this pot luck?" Liam asked with his head in the mini-fridge of the RV.

I sat on the bed and pulled on a fresh blouse and some retro pedal pushers. I had been saving this one non-work outfit for the big crew party, but of course, I had a sunburn and two days ago my skin hurt too much for these pants. They were a little tight and the lace detail was scratchy on sensitive skin. Normally, I wouldn't have noticed the lace edging, even this evening they felt a little scratchy, but I wanted to look cute. It wasn't exactly a date, however, we were going out together to be social. I didn't want to show up in my standard workwear.

I don't know why I was fussing, the rest of the remaining crew would still be in their cargos and sweat-stained T-shirts. Liam had pulled his old familiar jeans on. I could tell he had them for a long time by how soft the denim was, and the way they fit his body.

Damn that body. All lean and ripped and strong. Big muscles in all the right places. And I had most of them memorized by touch. I loved touching him. And caressing him was so different from my fingertips applying thick sunscreen. That had been almost clinical, detached.

"Last night on set we toss together what we have leftover, and make a party of it. Usually, there are hamburgers or hot dogs, and always a lot of salads. What have you found in the fridge?"

"So far, you have dressing, an onion, half a bell pepper, some crumbled feta, and a jar of olives."

He pulled everything out and placed it on the small counter behind him. "It would be criminal to share that lettuce with a rabbit."

He popped the top to a plastic container, his face wrinkled in distaste. "This is dead, whatever it was." He dove back into the fridge. "Eggs, half dozen. We can make small omelets."

I sat on the end of the bed, staying out of his way. "Are there any noodles in one of those over-head cabinets?"

He turned around and began pulling a few cans and two boxes of mac and cheese from the cupboard.

"This is it. Black beans and mac and cheese."

He examined the choice ingredients, hands on his hips. "Let's make a big thing of mac and cheese for tonight, and save the rest for breakfast."

"Sounds like a plan." I fixed my makeup and he figured out the small stove and began boiling noodles.

He cooked. Okay, mac and cheese out of a box barely counted, but some people didn't even know how to do that.

A robotic tweeting sound came from the floor next to the bed. I looked over and found Liam's phone ringing. Caller identification said "Da." I handed him the phone. "Hey, I think it's your dad."

"What's up?"

Liam stopped stirring and pulled the pan off the hot burner. He sat with a fluid motion and relaxed back into the couch. He stretched one arm out along the back of the couch and held the phone to his ear with the other. One long leg crossed over the other. He looked like a magazine ad for an expensive watch— extremely gorgeous shirtless muscled god in old jeans, an old worn couch, shaggy unkempt, sex rumpled hair, and a watch that cost more than my car.

He twitched his fingers at me, and I left my perch on the bed and slid in next to him on the couch.

"What do you mean? Mum hasn't called me at all."

I leaned against his smooth chest. I wanted to but didn't think it would be a good idea to play with the chest hairs that I saw starting to grow back. Sebastian Hale may have been an enlightened man from Edwardian England, but I'm pretty sure the character wouldn't have shaved his chest. That was done for the benefit of Hollywood.

"Damn it. No, of course. Everything is fine. Yeah."

I couldn't hear what his father was saying, but Liam wasn't happy. Not upset, just not pleased.

"No, I had to let her go, she's the one who sold those pictures of me. I know. I know."

His hand dropped to play with the ruffle on my blouse.

I really wanted to know what he was talking about. If it was about the pictures from his recovery, I remembered those. Not that I paid attention to the gossip magazines, but these even made the regular news. They were pictures of him post-accident. He had fallen asleep on a couch. No shirt on. He didn't look good. He was still banged up, bruised, loss of muscle tone, and scars. His hair was shaggy, and half bleached out, with long dark roots. I had to look close, and be very intimate with his skin to know where those marks had been. He had recovered, and his muscles came back with work, and the bruising and red marks of healing wounds had completely faded.

"Put Mum on."

There had been a mini-scandal with someone who worked for him, taking and selling those pictures. That wasn't cool. I don't remember if he sued them or they had sued him. I had heard about it and went on with my life.

"Hullo Mum, no I haven't been ignoring you. I think it's another assistant problem."

Besides back then, it was over a year ago, I was still reeling from the absence of Flint in my life.

"Yes, she is very beautiful. She is also nucking futz. I'm going to program your number back in immediately. Bye, I love you too."

Okay, a man who still told his mom he loved her, now

that was a good guy. I already knew Liam was good. I had a suspicion about him, that if it was true, he was one of the best guys around.

He ended the call and began hitting things on his phone. "I have a new assistant and..." he paused. "Fuck."

"What's wrong?"

He stood up and held his phone out to me shaking it. "My mum, my sister, gone. All my contacts. They're just men."

He pulled the phone back where he could look at it. He started laughing in a menacing tone. "That stupid treacherous bitch."

"Which one?"

"Cecilia. She's the one who recommended my current assistant to me. I have had the absolute worst luck with assistants since the accident."

"Oh, like the woman who sold those images of you?" I sat up a little.

"Exactly. Had to sue her. Then I had an assistant who forgot to make sure my bills were getting paid. This one Cecilia recommended. I have been suspicious of a few things, like how Cecilia knew what restaurants to show up at and join me for dinner. And now," he focused on his phone. "It looks like she went through and blocked all female contacts. Moron, all the names are still here."

He looked up at me and laughed. "This had to have taken hours. Anyone with a feminine first name. My personal trainer Tracey is in here. Tracey is a guy."

He shook his head and then stopped, tossed his phone onto the couch and hauled me up to stand next to him. "I'll deal with that later. You are stunning, and I only have a few days before I have to fly off to London. I'll fix the stupid phone on the flight, give me something to do. What time is

this get together? Do I have time to make love to you again?"
He lowered his face to mine.

I shoved him back before he could mess up my lipstick.
He rerouted his lips and kissed my neck. I seriously thought
about skipping out on the guys tonight and dragging Liam
the few feet back into the bedroom.

7

The firelight was mesmerizing, but it really was too warm to sit around a fire. I stood and pulled on Liam's arm.

"Fellas, it's been real, it's been nice." I wanted to get Liam back to bed. Besides, we had to drive back to LA tomorrow, and it was a long drive in an old RV.

"But you can't say it's been real nice," Nolan finished for me. I swear we had been at this for too long, and my exit speech was too old and trite.

Liam nodded at everyone as he stood.

It wasn't a big group tonight. Viv had left to drive home earlier this afternoon, so had at least half of the crew Charlie had out here. Besides, Nolan was his foreman, and he would be the last one to leave.

"Can we interest you in a quick quest?" Joe asked fishing dice out of a pocket.

Liam chuckled. "Not tonight. I need all my stamina points."

I shook my head, boys and their D and D jokes. "You had better roll a twenty for endurance too," I teased. I needed to be one step ahead of the rest of them on the innuendo.

We all said goodnight, and Liam guided me back to the RV with his hand in the small of my back. I loved that little touch. It said, "Mine."

"It must be nice to work with the same group over and over again," Liam said.

"It is," I replied. "You've worked the same director before. Don't you get the same camera crew and other actors?"

He shook his head. "That doesn't happen all that often. And those few directors who always work with the same core group of actors or the same film crew, yeah, I haven't fallen into a steady groove like that. I think I liked working on the series."

I slid a glance over at him. His successful four year run as Johnny Urban in the cable series *Tails from the Urban Jungle* had been before the accident. "You think?"

He tapped his temple. "Memory issues, dying will do that to you apparently."

"Was it weird? Dying?"

He chuckled and wrapped his arms around me. "I think you are the first person to ask if it was weird. Everyone usually wants to know if there was a light."

I rested my hands against his chest and gazed at him. "Well? Was there?"

"Someday, when I don't think it will scare you off, I will tell you all about it. But, I can tell you one thing, I never want to get into a sports car again. Let's stop talking about bad memories and make some good ones."

I couldn't agree more.

Liam had been right, he knew me, knew my body. His lovemaking had me flying high. I had only one lover who had come close to this level of expertise, and he was the reason Liam was so good.

Liam came hard and loud. I laughed with delight. It was euphoric how I could reduce this strong man to need and urge, and human sweat noodle.

"I don't think I could move if I wanted to," he said with an exhale of breath.

I know I couldn't. I curled up against him, warm and sated. I hummed in agreement, eyes closing in post-coital bliss exhaustion. His fingers began drawing lazy shapes on my shoulder. My eyes opened wide before I settled again. Did Liam know? Maybe he didn't. Maybe he thought his hand was moving absently, but he was writing, spelling L-O-V-E, over and over again.

Just like Flint. Exactly like Flint, except Flint knew what he was doing. Flint had said he loved me. Liam knew how to make love to me so perfectly because he had for years. I knew somehow, someway, Flint and Liam had merged.

My subconscious picked up the hints, and it felt right. My brain hadn't yet been able to connect the dots. How, when, where? None of that mattered. My heart knew, from him calling me Nica to writing words of love on my shoulder, he was Flint.

The drive back to LA took hours longer than it should have. And that was all our own damned fault. That and the fact the RV had a bed, and there were plenty of rest stops along the way. We didn't rest much, spending almost as much time connected at the hips as we did actually driving.

It was late, well past dinner and the sun was already setting when I finally pulled into the lot of the RV rental place. It was a commercial lot where they rented everything from RVs to panel trucks to companies in the industry. I swapped the counter person RV keys for my car keys, and we transferred our stuff into the back of my bright red Mini with checkerboard roof, and cherries painted on the back. Liam's bags almost didn't fit.

"You going to be okay in this?" I asked about my small car.

"Just don't play race car driver and I should be fine." He slid into the passenger seat. "I honestly don't have freak outs or anything, I'm just being careful these days. No classic cars, no specialized tricked out cars, nothing that doesn't have airbags and seat belts."

"This puppy has all standard safety features," I announced as I revved the engine. It did not give off an aggressive throaty growl. I hoped to impress Liam with the meekness of the vehicle.

We spent another hour in traffic and then I was pulling into my driveway.

"This is a nice house," Liam said as he unfolded out of the Mini.

"It is, but I don't live in the house." I tilted my head indicating the garage.

He pointed and raised his brows. "You live in the garage?"

I nodded. "It's a converted flat. It's nice. Maybe not as nice as the house, but they have never raised the rent on me in eight years. And I don't have to worry about anyone watching out for my stuff if I go on location for any length of time."

"So, you travel for work a lot?" he asked as he carried an arm full of bags behind me.

I unlocked the door and led him into my studio. "Just dump everything on the couch."

I liked my place, inside it looked like a New York loft, long and narrow. The recovered vintage wainscoting wall panels in oak created that old building feel. Above that, the walls were painted a deep teal. Vintage Sebastian Hale and Tarzan movie posters and small pieces of original artworks covered the walls that bookcases didn't hide. The door opened directly onto my living area, two long bar counters and a short wall created the narrow kitchen, and behind the kitchen on a raised floor was my bedroom. There was a curtain I could pull to visually separate the bedroom. I had a nice space in an upscale neighborhood that otherwise I never would have been able to afford to live in.

"I travel enough," I answered.

Liam kind of froze and looked pale. I mean paler than normal, after all, I had spent the better part of three weeks making sure he didn't look like he was working outside in the sun most of the day.

I put the bags I carried onto the kitchen counter and stepped over to him.

"You okay?"

A fine sheen of sweat glistened across his brow, and beads of it appeared above his lips. His skin felt clammy under my fingers.

"Sit down before you fall down." I guided him to one of my mix-matched chairs. Interior decorators specializing in shabby chic had nothing on my style of curbside finds.

He looked a little dazed. I rushed over to the kitchen and grabbed the pitcher of water from the fridge. I always had water in my fridge.

"Here." I poured some into a cup and held it out to him.

I watched him carefully as he took a drink. His gaze moved around the apartment, slowly taking it all in.

"I've been here before." His voice was barely above a whisper.

Another puzzle piece. I bit my lips together to stop me

from grinning like an idiot. Yes, he had been here before, but not. It was very complicated and I knew I would have to explain it to him at some point, just not today, not this week.

He pointed to the short wall that defined the space of the living room and prevented the kitchen from being as wide as the entire garage. "That's a closet, not a bathroom. The bathroom is deceptively large and behind the back wall."

He was right. That wasn't something most people could figure out when they first walked in, because the door to the bathroom wasn't visible from the living room. Most people, not that I had a lot over here, thought the short wall was a small bathroom and not a storage closet pantry.

"The walls should be purple."

I swiped at the tears that welled in the corners of my eyes. Goosebumps formed all over my body. Yes, the walls had been purple. I changed the color last year in my boredom after Flint stopped showing up. Flint never saw this new color. Flint knew this place with purple walls.

I nodded, quick little movements. "Yeah. Purple."

"Nica?" His blue eyes held questions as he turned them toward me.

I stepped into his personal space, positioning myself between his knees. Running my fingers through his hair, I eased him against me so his cheek rested on my belly.

He crushed his head against me and groaned. I held him close, expecting him to collapse again, but he only held on tight.

Okay, this felt like he didn't know. He was freaking out, so maybe I wouldn't spring the whole, 'yeah honey, I think you somehow sucked up the ghost of my fantasy lover' thing on him for a while.

Liam pressed his face into my belly and took several

long, deep breaths. I sensed more than felt the slight shiver in his body.

His arms wrapped around my hips, holding me in place as he came to terms with whatever realization or freak out that was taking place inside his head.

Slowly, I felt his energy change. His attention shifted, and so did how he held me. His face no longer pressed into me; he ran his cheek up and down, around like a cat. His hands didn't fist into my shirt, they smoothed the fabric over my hips. And then they pushed the fabric away from my hips so that I felt his warm palms directly on my skin as he pushed my shirt up and tugged at my pants. The movement of his face continued to push my clothing out of his way and his lips were on my mid-section with sucking bites and fluttery soft kisses.

I tightened my fingers in his hair, holding him to me. My need to provide comfort rocketed straight into a need to cradle him in my body.

He stood, lifting my shirt with him so that he continued to pull it up and off as he towered over me. His head lowered to mine, and those soft kisses of his now demanded returned lust from my lips. His teeth scraped against my lower lip before he plunged his tongue into my mouth to lay claim to the desire that was now his.

He tore away from my mouth and rotated me so that I faced the chair. He forced me forward so that I knelt facing away from him. I pushed back with my hips, letting him know what my expectations were. A zip and a tug and my pants and panties were around my knees, acting as an effective binding. Liam pressed the hard ridge of his erection behind jeans against my ass.

I whimpered, unable to get to him with the sensitive flesh I wanted him pressed against. I backed off the chair and Liam took my pants all the way off. With his thigh, he lifted me back onto the chair. A hand on the back of my neck held me in place. I slid my hips back and forth over his crotch. He removed the hand from my neck. I heard fumbling sounds and then his hands were on my hips pulling me back against him as he thrust home.

"Yes!" Oh, he felt so good shoving into me. We had only done this four times already today. I should be too sore to walk, but every time he touched me, I was wet and ready and needed him like I hadn't had sex in months. Maybe it was because I hadn't had any in over a year, and before that, it hadn't exactly been earthly physical.

His fingers bit into my hips and he slammed fast and hard, his need so much greedier than before. I moaned and made little whimpers of sheer pleasure as my body jerked in reaction to his. With each thrust, his balls caressed my clit with a small kiss of impact. At first, I found the touch to be nothing more than a tease of sensation, but it built with each stroke, each lick of flesh on flesh. I came around him with a sudden spasm of delight. He couldn't crash into me fast enough, I couldn't push back hard enough and I found it difficult to even try to move in response.

"Fuck me," he roared as he spilled into me with a rush of wet heat.

"I am, trust me, I am." I wanted to keep on doing what we were doing for a very long time, even though we had both reached the pinnacle of abilities for the act.

He pressed in tight and continued to rock my hips back against him. "I think you need to talk dirty to me some more."

He redoubled his grip on my hips and pressed harder. "Who can think to talk? You are sucking everything out of me through my cock." He shuddered.

It caused a shivering shudder in me and I fell forward onto my arms, detaching us in the process. I panted, trying to catch my breath from the sudden and unexpected shagging.

"That was intense." Liam leaned over, wrapped an arm around my middle and pulled me onto my feet. With wobbly legs, we stumbled up the two steps to the bedroom. He divested himself of the rest of his clothes and helped me to lose my bra. Pulling back the covers he guided and then followed me into bed. He lay back and I draped over his chest.

"Are we making up for lost time or stocking up for time apart?"

"What's that supposed to mean?" I asked.

"I mean, darling Nica, your body is very demanding and I can't seem to not touch you, not want to be inside of you."

He guided my hand down to his crotch. I expected something soft and pliable, a toy to wiggle around. Instead, he was already growing hard again.

"This isn't normal. I don't have the return rate of a porn star or the ability to blow your head off with firehose reactions. And feel this"— he thrust into the hand that cupped him— "it's ready to go again. You are an aphrodisiac."

I gave him a little laugh. "You have been on me like some carnival ride. I am tired. I need a nap before we go another round."

"Fine." He pouted sticking out his lower lip. "Take a nap, be that way."

I played with his lower lip. "You sleep too, and when we wake up, we can fuck like bunnies. At this rate, I'm gonna need an ice pack on my lady bits, and you aren't going to have any skin left."

He flipped me so that I looked up at him, his longer hair

falling in his face so that his eyes peered out like a predator looking through tall grass. I sucked in my breath. Nerves in my stomach flipped and my pulse quickened. Those eyes were split, half and half, blue and brown. The colors danced together without blending. Two men looked out at me from under that hair.

"Must take care of your lady bits." He gave me an evil grin and then slid down my body.

His tongue was cool and I levitated off the mattress as he sucked me in. I didn't think there was any way he was going to get another orgasm out of me today, let alone so close to the last one, but I was wrong. So gloriously wrong.

I was nineteen when I lost my virginity to a ghost. And a few years older when I lost it to a living man. I spent the next ten years comparing any real lover I had to some near mythological construct. I didn't know about anyone else dead since Flint was the only spirit who seduced me in my dreams. No one, and I meant no one alive, could compare to Flint. I tried for years to find someone who could. It took that long before I realized I would never physically know anyone like him.

Until now.

Liam felt like Flint. He moved like Flint, touched me like Flint. Had eyes like Flint.

Sitting up, I gazed down on his sleeping form, his hair draped across his face. He didn't look like Flint. There were similarities in coloring and haircuts— that had more to do with the fact they both took on the role of Seb Hale than anything else— and they both had similar eyes, but that was it. It wasn't a physical reminder, it was emotional.

How could I be so certain? Wasn't this more wishful thinking? Ruthie had told me I was being weird the one and only time I tried to tell her about Flint when he first showed up in my life. I always had invisible friends guide me, help me make big decisions, but they never stuck around for very long. Flint manifested and stuck. I knew about his secret wife and child. I knew the truth about how he was discovered for Hollywood. And I knew these things because he told me. I had to look them up to make sure I wasn't going crazy. Every little detail I found out gave me goosebumps and a stomach ache when I learned they were true. I wasn't crazy.

I was a Sebastian Hale fan, and of course, I knew things about the various actors who played him. Rumor had it that Tom Mix almost played him, but producers decided that went against his cowboy image. Even Valentino was considered for the part. The role went to a then-unknown named Hamilton Klein. I've only ever seen stills from the production since the master film was destroyed in a fire before it was copied for release. It was another fifteen years before Hamilton Klein became a superstar of early sound films.

I can name most of the film actors off the top of my head. Hamilton Klein, Emilio Charles, Flint Reese, Toby Heath, Tom Bakersmith (not Thomas Baker-Smith, different actor), Umberto Moore, even that hot underwear model Ash Simms, and now Liam all played the part. And those were the most famous ones. I have the radio shows on CD. I might be a little obsessed. But I was obsessed with a proper Edwardian English gentleman who could travel through time using his father's mausoleum to find love and adventure, not some action actor who was considered a hot commodity in the nineteen-thirties and forties. So wouldn't it make more sense if I were to invent some imaginary friend that it be Sebastian or someone like him and not one of the actors?

That was the argument I told myself. Eventually, I stopped trying to find any explanation I could that did not end with the ghost of Flint Reese haunting me in a very sexy way. And he was sexy, but also very kind. Had he been flesh and bone he would have been "Best Boyfriend Ever." And the fact that he was damn near perfect was the argument I used to remind myself that maybe I was making everything up.

That never explained why he suddenly stopped showing up in my life, in my dreams. And now, here was Liam in my life and my very cells told me he was Flint. Or why I swear I caught glimpses of Flint in his face, or why his eyes changed color. So why hadn't he come and found me before this? What had happened to Liam that Flint was in his body? It wasn't reincarnation, because Flint had only vanished a little over a year ago.

I padded off to the bathroom. My brain was addled after a day of barely being able to keep my hands off the man. Maybe this was merely middle of the night existential contemplation.

I didn't crawl right back into bed when I returned. I stood there and kept looking at him.

My brain was very much not addled. I was as clear-headed as I ever could be. "I know who you are, I just don't know how you got in there," I whispered.

Liam cracked an eye open and looked up at me. "We died."

Breath caught in my throat. A shiver zinged down my spine and all over my body as my skin pebbled with goosebumps.

His eyes closed and he rolled onto his side, making a

snoring snort of a sound before settling back into a deep sleep.

That's what I needed to do, go to sleep. I slipped in next to Liam and pulled an arm over me like a blanket. He wiggled in closer and made more sleeping rumbly sounds. His even breathing and comfortable warmth lulled me back to sleep before I could think of anything else that would keep me up late contemplating.

8

I didn't even bother getting dressed. I would take a shower after his car picked him up. Besides if there was even half a chance I could have him one last time before he walked out that door, I would. Clothes would only get in the way. I didn't want him to leave. I really didn't. If I could have kept him in bed another month it would not have been long enough.

I sat on the bed wrapped in a robe and watched him finish packing.

"So, it's back to life?" I asked. I didn't really want his answer. I hadn't exactly been living in the real world the past few days in and out of bed, and generally being all happy and in love.

Oh God, I was in love with him, wasn't I? I had transferred all my feelings for Flint onto Liam, and I still had doubts.

I mean, I knew he was Flint, I knew it. Why didn't he?

Why would he say things like Flint, but not come right out and say, "Hey babe I'm back." Okay, Flint wouldn't say that, but he would let me know somehow, and I think by more than just calling me Nica.

Liam stopped and looked up at me. His lips twitched into a little half grin and he put down his packing.

He walked around the bed and sat on my side, sliding a hand up my leg.

I caught my breath and smiled as my pulse picked up. His hand reached under the robe and he stroked and fondled my delicate flesh. I closed my eyes and breathed heavily through my mouth.

"More like life comes to a crashing halt." His voice rasped in my ear.

I turned my face to him, and our lips were instantly consuming each other. We barely had time before his driver arrived, but I lay back pulling him down on me, letting his weight crush me to the mattress.

"Nica." My name was a sigh on his breath.

He wasn't complaining. Before too long his jeans were around his knees and we were thrusting against each other, hip to hip. Liam took his time with a slow and steady pace. I didn't understand how he could do that. I was completely frantic, scrabbling to hold him close, pulling him in deeper. Wanting every inch of my skin branded by him.

I didn't want to cry, but after coming down off the orgasmic euphoria, I continued to crash. My emotions plummeted past sad and straight into the pits of despair over dealing with losing him.

He swept a thumb under my teary eye.

"Hey now, it's only going to be for six weeks. And I do have a phone, you can call me."

I wrapped my fingers around his wrist. "What if your assistant blocks numbers in your phone again?"

His eyes held me in their gaze, it was soothing and calm and felt like a caress.

Liam stood up and adjusted himself back into his clothes. I pushed back against the wall, pulling the robe closed.

"I texted my manager to fire her, and I have asked for a male assistant while I'm in London. Hopefully, no more crazy women trying to be helpful."

"Oh yeah, women are crazy?"

He returned to his packing.

"You know that's not what I meant. I meant those specific women were. Blocking my mother's number is a little crazy if you ask me."

"I know, I was just giving you a hard time "

"I thought that's what I just gave you?" He looked up at me through a fall of hair hanging in front of his eyes.

I went weak in places that were still quivering from the last hard time.

"Yes, you did." I purred. "Six weeks, huh? And then what?"

"By then, Glenn will know if we're missing anything, and then it's off to New Zealand for a mini-series."

"You're doing a new series? What's it called?"

Series were good work, but that would keep him away for a while. I sighed. I couldn't tell him what I wanted to tell him, couldn't lay claim to him. A few days of hot sex was not a relationship.

"It's called The Odyssey."

"Wait, what do you mean it's called... are you remaking the Odyssey?" I loved that story, I didn't realize that was going into production again. Every few years, it was remade. And every few years, I watched it. I'm a sucker for a good old fashioned adventure. And well, nothing is older than the Odyssey.

"I was a shoo-in, being part Greek and all."

I crinkled my brows at him trying to see his Greek heritage. He was hot. He was a Greek god, marble statue hot.

"I didn't realize you were Greek. Never actually thought about that," I said.

"Yeah, my da is half Greek." He nodded.

Our conversation turned dull and mundane. Neither of us facing the inevitable— that he was leaving as soon as he received a text message announcing the arrival of his driver.

Liam's lips were so soft against mine. He didn't press in, didn't plunder my mouth with his tongue, didn't coax more from me. And I didn't either, even though I wanted to. I wanted to suck him back in through my mouth and never let him go. I wanted hot clashing mouths and flicks of tongues against teeth. I wanted to take his air and give him my moans of pure unadulterated joy.

My fists grabbed onto the front of his shirt, a faded often worn Johnny Urban shirt. If I had wrapped my arms around him one more time this morning he would have been deep inside of me. At least that's what I wanted, and since it was what I couldn't have, I didn't go after it, again.

I let Liam go. I let him leave my body weeping with need and emptiness and loneliness. It was just me here, empty arms. Broken emotions, empty shell.

He picked up his smaller suitcase and tossed it into the trunk next to the larger case the driver already put in. The driver closed the trunk and Liam climbed into the back of the car. He looked back at me. His expression could have been a mirror of my own. Sad with a brave veil.

I wrapped my arms around my middle and gave him a weak smile. He needed to go off and be the proper gentleman Sebastian Hale and make thousands swoon, while I had to go create an alien landscape for a pilot being shot after a short two weeks of set creation. We had lives and we needed to live them.

Did it matter I didn't think I'd be able to live mine to the fullest without him in it?

Did he feel the same?

The car pulled out of my driveway. Liam's hand pressed against the window for a brief moment in a final goodbye.

Damn. I swiped at the tears that had stayed in check until the car pulled out. I had found Flint, and I had lost him a second time.

I found Flint. I let out a choking laugh. He was in Liam some way, yet how? And why didn't he say anything? I was going to sound like a complete idiot if I mentioned it. Or maybe not. Maybe he knew and I just needed to trust.

I watched Mrs. Pearllop from across the street walk down her drive and up the sidewalk for a bit. She waved before she faded. I wondered how long she would roam the neighborhood looking for her cat before she realized she was dead. Had been dead for over a year now. Before she realized the cat had been gone even longer?

I wondered how many of our neighbors thought I was an utter nut job standing outside in my robe, crying, and waving at nothing they could see.

I went back inside. I should shower, do some laundry, go to the grocery store, do all those things that didn't happen while Liam and I tangled in the sheets for the past few days.

I hated my apartment. It was too small, too confining, and entirely too empty.

I took a deep breath and centered myself. Now would be prime meditation time. Time to recenter and focus my energy inward. Time for some self-care.

I picked up my phone and texted Liam. "*I miss you already.*"

Damn, I was clingy. I honestly did not expect him to reply.

"*I wondered who would cave first. Your text came in as I was typing.*" He responded. "*Is it a character flaw that I find that I enjoy breathing more when you are around?*"

My heart thudded in my throat. It wasn't fair. We had only been able to be together for a few days. A few intense, glorious days, and I was already deeply in love with him.

My go-to gloomy depression-related film-watching typically leaned toward Seb Hale adventures. Any of them, even the short-run series from the nineteen-nineties that's only saving grace was just how incredibly pretty Ash Simms was. But I didn't think Seb Hale could save me right now.

"*Will you hate me if I confess to watching Tails from the Urban Jungle because I miss you?*" I typed as I scanned my DVD collection to see if I even owned the show. Liam had really become a name in the acting world when he had taken on the role of the burly blonde shape-shifting hero Johnny Urban.

"*I don't think I could ever hate you.*"

Oh God, I was a goner. I held the phone against my heart.

I flopped down on my couch and stared at my phone. I wanted to tell him so badly, but if I spooked him now, he would run, and keep going. Besides, telling someone you're in love really isn't something you should do the first time over a text message.

"That's good. I don't think I could ever hate you either." That was as close to me telling him how I felt as I think I could manage at the moment.

"Good, because I stole a pair of your panties to keep me company in London."

My stomach felt hollow and dropped out of my body. I didn't have anything of his to hold onto. Not true. I smiled wickedly. I had lots of dirty, nasty, sexy DNA evidence of him all over my sheets. But that really wasn't something I wanted to snuggle with, because as sexy fun as it was to destroy my sheets, they really were nasty and needed to be washed. Body fluids were fun at the moment, but they are not the kind of thing you wanted as a keepsake. They turned all crusty and gross.

"Don't have too much fun with those." I didn't care if he used them for his own personal spank bank. Actually, I would find that totally hot if he used my undies to help get himself off. For some reason, that right there was the ultimate compliment.

I mean it was up there with watching certain movies while enjoying a little personal massager time. Hello vibrator, hello visual enhancement. I was going to need to invest in the entire *Tails from the Urban Jungle* series. All four seasons and Liam was a bit more than half-naked in almost every episode. I know there were lots of naked butt shots and some seriously hot sexy time scenes.

Okay, so Liam was blonde in that show, and he no longer had the blonde hair. But that's okay. Johnny Urban had a huge tiger tattoo and could shift into a were-tiger. Liam had neither the big chest tattoo nor the supernatural skills.

"*I don't think I could have nearly as much as I would if you were in them. Or taking them off.*"

Liam had other skills that could make me scream. I needed a cold shower. In a bit.

"*You know you left here with me not wearing any panties.*"

"*Don't tempt me.*"

I laughed. Maybe he didn't know me well enough to realize that was a challenge. Then again maybe he knew exactly what he was setting up.

"*Are you going to text me when you get to London?*" I asked.

"*Of course. I also speak over the phone in case you want to hear my voice.*"

Yes, I wanted to hear his voice, but I wanted to hear it while I could also feel his breath on my skin.

"*Some phone calls might be dangerous if someone overhears.*"

"*Oh yeah?*"

"*You should never put me on speakerphone, even if we are talking about groceries.*"

"*What's on your grocery list that would make a call so scandalous?*"

"*Cucumbers.*" I typed.

"*That's not so bad.*" I could picture him laughing at me.

"*Cucumbers and lube?*"

"*I will be sure that no one is around when I have you on speakerphone.*"

"*You'll play?*" I asked.

"*Most definitely. But this probably isn't the best time. I don't want to go through security with a hard-on. TSA might get the wrong idea.*"

Damn, I missed him.

"*I'll be good.*"

"*You are the best.*"

Double damn.

"*Text me when you get in safe and sound. I should go pretend that you leaving hasn't destroyed my day. New job starts tomorrow and I have a lot of laundry.*"

My phone rang.

"Nica." I closed my eyes against Liam's voice.

"Hi." I couldn't stop the smile that split my face.

"What, you aren't going to flirt with me over the phone?"

I didn't want to flirt. I wanted to get straight to talking dirty, but he was in a car where the driver would be able to hear him.

"You already said that might not be a good idea before you go through security. I'll get flirty and talk dirty when you make it to your hotel room."

"You are such a tease," he chastised me.

"Giving you something to look forward to," I purred.

"And I do look forward to it."

Eventually, we did end the phone call. He made it to the airport and I took a shower. Life without him wasn't nearly as interesting.

Turns out that wasn't true.

It was almost exactly a year later before I saw him again.

9

"Liam, you know Danica?"

The nerves in my belly flipped. I had been wondering how to approach him all afternoon. I saw him several times during this afternoon's events leading up to the actual premiere screening, and at the launch party for *Ahmentari*. Dressing up for today's premier had required a new dress, none of my standard premiere party dresses fit at the moment.

Marc Stainn from Ascendant Studios guided Liam toward me, a hand on his upper arm. It was a perfunctory move by Marc to look like he gave a rat's ass about the production crew. About half a second after I managed to have that judgmental thought my eyes locked with Liam's.

God, they sucked me into their brown depths. He looked the embodiment of a contemporary Sebastian Hale. The cut of the chocolate brown waistcoat and trousers tucked into riding boots screamed proper English gentleman. The open neck collar showing off his Adam's apple oozed maximum sex appeal. His stylist knew what they had been doing when selecting the dark brown tones and plaid sports coat, and the cool clear blue of his silk shirt. How had they known that blue was a perfect match for Flint's eyes? The tight muscle in his jaw relaxed, and his lips parted. I saw the pink tip of his tongue dart out to lick his lower lip.

I gave him a weak smile.

"Of course I know Nica." His lips curved into a smile as he said the nickname only he used. Liam resumed his composure in a blink. Maybe I imagined that reaction. Maybe that reaction was because I gained some weight, but his gaze burned like fire as he looked down and back up. I didn't miss how long he lingered on my chest, clearly appreciating the gifts of the boobie fairy. They ached in response, a reminder of their lack of use. He stepped in close, and his hand grazed along my hip. It wasn't a quick platonic touch. To me, it felt as if he wanted to let his hand linger. He left it a little too long, moved it a little too slowly.

His fingers curled against my lower back. His breath caressed my ear.

In a low gravelly voice, he said, "You are beautiful."

I didn't miss the whispered "as always." When he stepped back, leaving me alone again.

My nerves danced and screamed. My body wanted him back within arm's reach again. The pounding in my chest and my shortness of breath were clear indicators he affected me on a physical level. I hadn't let myself think about him this way in so long, but clearly, logic and analysis had nothing to do with how I felt about the man.

Marc clapped him on the back, laughed at something he said. Patted me on the shoulder and left us alone. Off to play social butterfly big-time producer man.

I wasn't sure where to start. I had so much I needed to tell Liam.

Liam cleared his throat, "How have you been?"

I didn't want to simply say good. I hadn't been good. I had been everything from abandoned to depressed, to so freaking high it made euphoria look like the doldrums. I opened my mouth to say something and closed it again. I tried again, but before I could make a sound Charlie Davenport's big meaty arm was around my shoulders and squeezing.

"How's that gorgeous baby of yours doing? Who is watching her? You know Linda said she will babysit for you at any time."

"Hi, Charlie." I laughed. He had just taken care of the hard part for me.

"She's with my sister tonight. I thought Linda would be coming with you."

"She hates these things and she adores that baby. Is she walking yet?"

Charlie knew better, but that was just how he teased.

"She can't even sit up. How long has it been since you had a kid? They don't pop out walking and talking."

"Are you sure? I think mine did. Do you have any new pictures for me?"

I pulled my phone out from my clutch. I should have sent these over earlier, but this week's schedule had been all out of whack with the premier. So I had forgotten my weekly update to all of the surrogate grandparents.

I handed Charlie my phone.

It always amazed me when he saw Myrna. His huge demeanor would somehow soften, and he cooed. The ruler of King of the Scene turned into a babbling ball of goo around her. He had actually been on the receiving end of her very first smile. He even cooed at my phone.

He held it out toward Liam. "Is this not the most beautiful baby you have ever seen?"

Liam looked from the phone to me. "May I?" he asked as he reached to take the phone.

I nodded.

Charlie moved to lean across Liam so they could both look through the baby pictures.

"See I told you, most beautiful baby ever. Just look at those big eyes."

One second Charlie was smiling at my phone, the next his head was pivoting around as if he heard his name. He waved at someone, straighten back into the big man he was, and gave me a quick side squeeze. "Call Linda, okay."

"Will do, Charlie." And again Liam and I were alone. And for a second time that evening, he was slack-jawed.

I saw an extra glisten of moisture in his eyes when he looked back up at me.

"She's mine." It wasn't so much a question than confirming it for himself.

I nodded.

There was no way he could miss those eyes. He looked into his own in a mirror every day. I was glad he recognized them in the little round bald face of his daughter. Hers were blue like Flint's, but the shape was pure Liam.

"Why didn't you say something? Can I meet her?" His gaze was back on my phone, and I noticed he was holding it as if it were as precious as the baby girl herself.

"Of course you can meet her." My throat was dry, it was hard to speak. But he was enthralled by the images on my phone.

"When?" His voice was quiet. Maybe he was having a hard time with this too.

I sighed and squared my shoulders. "How about tomorrow? We aren't doing anything."

He didn't look up at me, kept his eyes on Myrna's

pictures. "I fly out for the European release tomorrow." He lifted his head, and his eyes locked with mine. His eyes burned intensely. "My flight isn't until after lunch, can I see her before that?"

I nodded. "Sure. You remember where I live?" He wasn't going to remember.

"You still in that converted garage in Sierra Madre?" He remembered.

"Yeah, but if you're flying out of LAX..."

"Right. I'll be over after breakfast. About nine. Is that okay?"

I nodded. The timing was good. Myrna went down for her first nap around ten anyway. This way she would be good and tired.

Liam looked up at me. "I don't know what to say. She's so beautiful."

Horus, Carlos Constanza, slammed into Liam's side. They both staggered under the impact. He snatched the phone out of Liam's hand. "Cute kid. Yours?" He thrust the phone out to me without really focusing.

"You have got to come see this. Cecilia is doing body shots off the bartender's abs." He jerked Liam away with him. Liam turned to look back at me as he was swept away.

"I'll see you tomorrow. Maybe." I didn't say it very loud, just enough so Liam could possibly read my lips.

Briefly, I wondered what else was going on at the party that Cecilia felt the need to behave like she was at a frat party, calling all the attention to herself. She may pretend to not know who I was anymore. But I remember how she was in middle school and high school, she never did anything that wasn't a calculated move. Including having been my friend.

The first time I met Cecilia...

Halfway through science class, the principal opened the door, interrupting Mrs. Brandt. I was drawing leaves and diagramming how light converted into energy.

A small girl with long messy dark hair stood between the two teachers. She looked scared, or maybe that was just the way the thick lenses of her glasses bent the light around her face. She wore long to the knee pink shorts and hugged a fat binder blocking the design on the front of her T-shirt.

I smiled as she passed my seat and slid into the desk behind me.

I spun around in an instant. I knew a like-minded soul when I saw one. We had the same long messy hair and heavy bangs covering our foreheads. We also both still dressed like we were in the fifth grade. The shirt she had been hiding featured none other than Disney's alien Stitch.

"I'm Dani," I whispered.

She gulped and shot furtive glances between me and Mrs. Brandt. "Cici."

"Danica, you can greet your new classmate after you finish your quiz."

"Sorry, Mrs. B." I swiveled back to my work.

I decided it was my duty to make sure Cici knew how to get from one class to the next. At lunch, I found out we didn't have the same electives. That didn't stop me. I waited outside the choir room for when she got out of class and made sure she followed me to math, which we did have together.

Cici had something most of the other seventh graders didn't, or maybe I should say she didn't have what they did. Puberty. As far as I could tell she was the only other girl in my grade who didn't wear a bra, because there was nothing to contain. She didn't wear one of those silly training bras either. We didn't have anything to train. I saw in her a compatriot who wouldn't shame me for not having developed yet.

Cici and I immediately became best friends, not only did we dress the same, have the same stupid hair, we both thought cartoons made the best movies. We were young seventh graders, still little girls at heart tossed together in a sea of raging hormones. Her parents were also divorced.

We hit puberty at about the same time too, at the end of eighth grade. She changed. I didn't.

Cici grew an insane amount in height that summer and gave up her childish nickname. Her unibrow got waxed, regularly, as did her legs. Her awkward bangs were blended into a head full of fashionably styled, shiny dark waves. Her braces came off leaving her with perfect teeth, and her fat glasses were replaced with contacts. Cecilia Saaid evolved like a Pokémon into something fabulous.

My hair got braided, I got a bra and my period. Eventually, I had to get new clothes because the whole changing bodies thing, but I still wore knee-length shorts and Disney T-shirts. Cecilia got designer clothes. We managed to stay best friends because our hearts and our brains were the same.

Ever since Myrna was born I started having dreams where I could actually go back in time and fix things in my life. Not big things, and not world-altering things. Like I couldn't go back and tell the Spanish Armada to hold up for a day or two before sailing toward England and avoid the storm that wiped them out. These were little dreams that were telling me to take that job, or not to take out the last year of student loans. Things like that. Things like, don't go to Cecilia's dad's with her that weekend, and never confess that I though Jaleb Morrow was cute.

"Uh, I don't want to go." Cecilia flopped back on my bed and tossed a stuffed unicorn into the air.

"Yeah, I never have any fun at my dad's either. My stepmom is such a pain in the ass." I flopped next to her.

Of course, Amanda was a pain in the ass, she was trying to help raise two girls who were trained to hate her. Two girls who had very little parental involvement once we hit double digits from our custodial mother.

Cecilia sat up and hit me in the head with the toy. "You should come with me. That way you don't have to go to your dad's and I won't have to be alone."

I gasped, it was brilliant. "And then next time you come with me to my dad's."

"Oh yeah, this will be great!"

We manipulated and connived, and Friday night I climbed into the back of her dad's smelly old car with her. His apartment wasn't the best. I was surprised considering how nice her mom's house was. Like my mom, she wasn't remarried. But unlike my parents, Cecilia's dad wasn't doing nearly as well. He wasn't married, and he was much older than her mom, or my parents.

Everything was dingy because he smoked. I discovered that smoke reveals a lot of things I would have rather not have seen as it floated around the shapes of spirits.

Cecilia had her own room and we whispered late into the night.

"Your dad was in the Middle East wasn't he?" I asked. "Like, he fought there, right?"

"Yeah, how could you tell?" she whispered back.

I gulped. How did I tell her he was surrounded by

ghosts? It creeped me out. No wonder everything was uncomfortable around him.

"Mom says he keeps his demons with him," she told me.

I believed her. I could see them. In the dark, I found it easier to confess certain things.

"If I told you something you won't laugh at me right?"

"Of course not. Why?" She lifted up onto her elbow and looked over at me, we were crammed into her single bed.

I stared up at the ceiling. "I can see things, like ghosts."

"Cool." That was not the reaction I had expected from her. "Like what, where?"

I bit my lips together and thought that maybe telling her about her dad wasn't a good idea. So instead I told her about the old janitor at school. He still pushed a mop cart around the halls when classes were in.

"Oh, that's so cool." She flopped back down on the bed, and I thought right then we would be best friends for always, and she was going to be my maid of honor when I married that pop star with the eyebrows.

10

A fter a year of not seeing Liam, I wasn't sure what to think. He wanted to meet Myrna.

Was I ready?

Okay, stupid question, yes I was. But was I ready for the emotions of having him back in my life? I already felt like Flint had left me once, and last summer had felt like a second time. Could I handle it a third time? Should I allow for it at all?

Too many feelings seeing Liam again, but he needed to meet his daughter. And I needed to finally have some closure of some kind.

I dressed Myrna in one of the ridiculous only-good-for-professional-portrait dresses one of her many self-assigned grandparents gave her. I could not even begin to count how lucky I was so many people wanted to help take care of us.

I thanked my bizarre penchant for stationery stores, and the small collection of beautiful cards I had purchased over the years, for "reasons." I had written so many thank you cards since I was about six months pregnant with her. I knew "reasons" and hunches were always to be listened to.

I hoped Liam made good on his promise and his timing. Myrna had already been up for a bit this morning, so we had maybe an hour to an hour and a half before she needed to feed and sleep again.

I spread her play blanket out and put her vibrating sling back rocker in the middle of it so she could see me as I straightened up. Her toys went in the toy chest, an actual chest Nolan and his wife refurbished and gave to us as a gift. It was the perfect combination of fairy and pirate. I folded a few throw blankets over the back of the couch. The baby show DVDs were pushed into a neat pile and placed on the TV stand. I tossed a fringed shawl over the TV while it played music from some streaming channel. I didn't need or want to see the random graphics the music station displayed. If I really needed to know the band or watch the advertisements across the bottom of the screen I could move the shawl and peak.

The rest of my stuff, shoes, sweaters, clothes that needed to go to the laundry all went back into the bedroom with the curtain closed. I ignored the flutters of anticipation in my abdomen.

The kitchen was as clean as I needed it to be. Liam would have to deal with a few dirty dishes waiting to be washed. I only had a few. I took the garbage out earlier before girlie-pie woke up. One of the women in a single moms group suggested using paper plates during the week. Life was complicated enough, in the beginning, being single with a baby, there was no reason for dishes to add to the issues, not when paper plates were cheap enough. She couldn't have been more right. Of course at the time I scoffed, after all, how irresponsible was it to bring new life to this planet and continue to contribute to the landfills with needless waste? I got over that quickly after I could not find time or energy to wash dishes for a little over a week, and it reduced me to tears. I had to take care of me, so I could take care of the baby.

I knelt in front of Myrna and fluffed her dress. "You're going to meet Daddy." I cooed.

"I think he's going to be cool about it, sweetie. But if he's not, I will always be here for you."

She smiled her big gummy grin and kicked. I know she didn't understand the words, but I did. I wanted Liam to be cool with this. I was pretty sure he had fallen for her last night, but who knows what thoughts rocketed through his head in the wee hours of the morning.

The door rattled with a knock.

Breath caught in my throat. This was it. I stood up and smoothed my hands down the thighs of my pants. I tried to smile but a tick in my cheek wouldn't let those muscles work. Butterflies I hadn't felt since I'd first met him wreaked havoc with my insides.

I opened the door and sighed. He looked gorgeous, as usual. A little disheveled. His hair stuck up in a million different directions like he had been running his hands through it. I liked the shorter style on him. My knees wanted to go weak when his gaze caught mine and he grinned.

"Hey, Liam."

He left a pile of luggage next to the door. "I have a different driver picking me up in an hour. Those will be okay there, right?"

I nodded. "Yep. Come on in."

He took one step in and froze.

I could tell he saw her, and she him, because she squealed with delight. That kid loved everyone she met.

"It's okay," I said quietly like I spoke to a startled animal. And then, he was on the floor in front of her, staring at her like she was magic itself.

"Liam this is Myrna."

I sat down next to her and began unbuckling her from her chair.

"May I?" he asked, reaching to pick her up before I could.

"Of course."

He cradled her into his embrace. Keeping everything slow and quiet. He balanced her on his lap and looked up at me. "Her name's Myrna?"

"Myrna Love."

Liam's eyes flashed for a second.

"Myrna Love Kensington. She was born on Valentine's Day, but Valentine didn't suit her, so I went with Love. I thought it fit better."

"She's so tiny. Valentine's Day?" His sigh indicated he had been holding his breath. Had he maybe for a second there thought she wasn't his?

"Why not James?" he asked.

"I didn't know if you... I wasn't going to saddle you with this. With her."

He huffed and smiled and shifted his gaze to her. "I'm going to claim her if that's all right with you. I have no intention of not being in her life if you let me."

"You want her?" My stomach did uncomfortable flips and tosses. I didn't realize just how nervous all of this was making me. I was scared, and happy, and wanted to cry, and throw up all at once.

"Nica, I... yes, absolutely. Look at her, she is so perfect. She looks like you." He lifted her so she was face to face with him. "Hi little Myrna, I'm your da."

She grabbed his nose and he laughed. I saw tears. Good, I wasn't the only one being overly emotional right now.

"Tell me about your days together. What's her little life like? She's not much for conversation at the moment is she?" He put her back on his leg and bounced it. He knew how to hold her.

"We do this, we have tummy time so she can build all the muscles a growing girl needs. We take walks around the block. We eat and breastfeed a lot."

"Are you working?"

I shook my head. "Not yet. I'll have to go back soon though. Everyone has been so awesome, I can't even begin to tell you. Charlie made me permanent so I could have insurance and take maternity leave."

"I saw how he was about her last night. How many people know?" His big brown eyes left his daughter for a second and locked with mine before returning to gaze at her.

"About Myrna?"

"About me being the father. I mean, Nica, do the math, it's kind of obvious when you got pregnant."

"Oh, I know. Officially, no one knows you're her father except for my sister. And officially, she hates you by the way. Unofficially, only the guys from work who were on set with us figured it out. As you said, do the math. But because I haven't made any claims to who her father is, your name is not on the birth certificate, they are officially not knowing."

"But Charlie knows."

I didn't look at him. I focused on playing with Myrna's toes. "I'm pretty certain that's why he did what he did with the baby pictures last night."

"Why didn't you say anything?" His voice lowered to a whisper.

I was crying now. "What was I supposed to do at the party last night? Hi Liam, by the way, I had your baby? I was going to tell you, I figured I needed to lead up to it."

He huffed again. "I'm glad Charlie barged in and steam-rolled me like that. I deserved to be slapped with it. Why didn't you tell me earlier?"

"I tried, but you had basically disappeared. You never called me back. I left you a thousand messages and texts while you were in England. And then that whole thing with you and Yasmin Montenegro having a custody battle hit. I figured I would tell you eventually. But I wouldn't ever want you to think I had expectations. I didn't keep her because I thought I would get money from you. I kept her because—"

"Love," he cut me off. His eyes met mine, and they did that swirl of color with the blue. I swallowed hard, having forgotten about that little notice of Flint in his eyes.

"Exactly." We had been in love for those few days. It hadn't been all hormones and hot bodies. At least, I had been in love with him, and Myrna was my love child.

Liam closed his eyes and pulled Myrna in tight. She didn't squirm much, no fussing. She pulled at his ear and hair.

"Nica." His tone was low and soothing. It was warm and comfortable like a blanket. And if I had any interest in sex it would have tugged at things low in my body. But that part of my body was all still in post-baby repair mode.

He sniffed, lifting his head and scanning around.

I knew that look. I rolled to my feet and reached out for the girl. "I'll take care of that."

Liam held her close as he stood. "No, I'll do it. Show me where."

"Seriously? You'll change her diaper?" I half expected him to happily be daddy until life got messy.

"I'm going to need some coaching. I've never changed a nappy before," he confessed as he followed me back into the messy bedroom.

He went straight to the changing table and placed Myrna down. He knew enough to support her head as he eased her back.

"Diapers are under there." I pointed. "You have to keep a hand on her the whole time. She can't roll yet, but the second you aren't looking is when she will decide to pole vault off the table."

He did great. He knew enough to ask why I didn't tell him to keep her covered.

"That's for boys with the built-in fountain attachment. If she pees it just sort of bubbles up, it doesn't spray all over."

He laughed. Myrna giggled and kicked. I smiled, and my heart filled with so much love and joy I started crying again.

Liam reached over and wiped a tear with his thumb.

I sniffed. "Did you just wipe baby pee on me?"

I laughed at his moment of panic and showed him where I kept the hand sanitizer.

"It's okay, I've spent the past three months covered in pee, poop, snot, and spit-up. You can use a baby wipe if it's particularly bad, and after you put her someplace safe, you can wash your hands."

"What's safe?" He looked like he didn't want to ever put her down. Clearly, no place would ever be safe enough.

"Her bassinet," I indicated the co-sleeping basket on the side of the bed. "Buckled into her chair. I wear her a lot, and if all else fails, the floor. Well, the floor at home. Other places not so much. Here." I reached out and took her so he could wash up in the kitchen.

"I need to send pictures to my mum. And I need pictures for me."

He had me sit with her in my lap so he could get a hundred shots with his phone.

"I'm sorry you couldn't find me. And it was stupid that I didn't come hunting you down the second I was back in the states."

"Liam, I..."

Myrna began to fuss, she was hungry and had a very busy morning so far. I picked her up and slid my shirt up, and bra over. She latched on and greedily pulled at my milk. I forgot what I was going to tell him.

Feeling Liam's eyes on us I looked up at him. Damn, he was in love with her. I could see it all over his face, and in Flint's blue eyes. I shivered. I hadn't been making that part up.

"I owe you an explanation for this past year. I can only hope you will consider forgiving me."

I opened my mouth to say something, but he held up a hand stopping me from talking.

"I have been in the states long enough and remembered where you lived. I didn't come looking for you because I'm a coward. What we had was intense. What if we couldn't pick it back up? Coward. The Yasmin Montenegro thing was a huge publicity mess. She did not have my baby. I asked for a paternity test because the timing was off. Babies take basically nine months, not a year. She had a beautiful son, but he is not mine. Once the lawsuit went public, the baby's father stepped in. He's another model from Brazil. That kid is going to be a real heartbreaker when he grows up with parents looking like that."

I nodded. Okay, I could handle that he wasn't a dead beat father to one baby while wanting to claim this one.

"I think any of your children would be beautiful," I said quietly. I was biased, Myrna was perfect.

"She really is, isn't she? I think that has more to do with her mother."

I flashed my gaze up to meet his. His eyes were back to being brown.

"If you let me, I want back in your life, in her life. I want to be her father." He said it with such earnestness and conviction I believed him.

"You already are her father. But if you want in our lives, you have to be here. I won't chase you down, not for attention and not for child support. I would love to have you back in Myrna's life." I wanted him back in my life. I was still in love with him. Or maybe I fell in love with him all over again after seeing him with Myrna.

A quick double beep out front caught our attention.

"Since when do drivers beep? I thought they knocked," I said as Liam got up and opened the door to look out.

"Since it's a cab and not a private driver," he said as he came back in.

He leaned over and stroked Myrna's cheek as she fed. "I have your number now, and I'm not letting my assistant touch my phone. I need to tell you that story when I get back. This is a two-week junket. I'll tell you everything, and I want you to tell me about everything I have missed." He leaned down and kissed me on the cheek. "I've missed you."

I couldn't think of anything to say by the time he left. I sat there with Myrna passed out and sucking randomly in her sleep, tears running down my cheeks.

The rest of the day, I felt a slight buzz over my skin. Maybe I was reeling from that brief peck on the cheek, maybe I was losing it. Liam wanted in our lives. And I wanted him in Myrna's.

Ruth wanted me to forget all about him. She had more than enough venom and hatred directed toward Liam, I didn't need to add my own. Besides, I didn't hate him. I never had. Even when I first found out I was pregnant and hadn't heard from him, I couldn't bring myself to even be mad.

11

A *year earlier...*

My foot moved of its own accord. My knee bounced like a ball pit in an earthquake. There was nothing of interest on the waiting room TV. The various magazines strewn around could not hold my attention for long. Well, not until I found a gossip rag with a juicy article on Liam in it.

I couldn't help it, he took my breath away, and these were some rather unflattering shots. I flipped back to the cover, it was an old issue. Based on the date the photos had to have been from when he was in physical therapy after the accident. I let my fingers trail lightly across his image. I crinkled my face and let out a soft growl when I saw the picture of him and the model he was dating at the time.

Who was I fooling? She was... fill in the blank, fill it in with everything I was not. Okay, just because a girlfriend of his from the past and I didn't look the same didn't mean he didn't like me too. Hadn't liked me too.

I had no clue if he still liked me.

"Danica Kensington," the nurse called my name. I tucked the magazine under my arm and followed her back.

She never looked up, just kept her focus on the tablet in front of her. I got on the scale. I was up. Damn it. She took my blood pressure, also up.

"White coat syndrome?" she asked. If she had been my doctor's usual nurse she would have known that was not the case.

"Yes," I answered. I was stressed, but not for any reason she could currently be thinking about.

She led me into a room and indicated I should hop up on the table. "What are we seeing you for today?"

"I am here to fail a test," I said.

Her eyes finally lifted and focused on me. Her brow furrowed and she tilted her head to the side, like a puppy trying to figure out what it was looking at. "Wha...?"

"I need to take a pregnancy test, and I'm hoping to fail gloriously."

"Oh..." realization dawned on her. "Have you taken any at-home pregnancy tests? Those are really accurate these days."

"I have and they are not. The first one said yes. The second one said no." I began kicking my feet back and forth.

"Alrighty then." She handed me a blue-lidded plastic container. "Give me as much as you can. Fill in your last name before collecting the sample. And when you are finished place it on the marked shelf in the bathroom. The doctor will meet you back in here."

And with a little grin, she left me to go pee in a cup.

Back and waiting for the doctor took longer than sitting in the waiting room, but now I wasn't fidgety. I was nervous and scared. Something danced in my lower abdomen and I hoped it was just nerves.

There was a knock, and my doctor came in.

"How are you today?" she asked as she pulled up the wheeley chair and sat down.

"I could be better. This whole thing has me a bit nervous."

She nodded. "Well, you did not get the results my nurse said you were looking for. You are pregnant. When was the first day of your last period?"

"Well, that's part of the problem. I don't know."

Her brows shot up. I could read the expression as 'how could you not know?'

That unspoken question opened the dam on my tongue and it all came spilling out. "My last proper period was April? And then I sort of had a half period in May. On a day, off a day. So mostly just spotting for a week. And the same thing in June, and then nothing. But I started super light bleeding and cramps even last week. And I haven't had intercourse for... since June. And I'm on the pill, and how am I pregnant?" I held my hand up. "Don't answer that."

She scooted up to me and placed her hand on my knee. "So, it's possible you got pregnant in April and have been spotting the whole time."

I shook my head vigorously. "Nope."

"The pill isn't fail-safe, and—"

"The sex wasn't happening in April. If I am pregnant it was either in January and I know that is a solid no, or June. It's June. Shit. But I'm on the pill," I said it again as if repeating it enough would somehow magically change things.

"Were you on any other medications? Antibiotics can negate the effects of birth control."

I couldn't think of anything. I closed my eyes and let out a groan of defeat. That stupid ingrown toenail thing.

"Antibiotics at the beginning of the month. But I thought it only made the pill not work while I was on the antibiotics and I was finished with that by the time I got together with..." I shut up before I announced who the father was. That wasn't going to happen until I had a chance to speak with him. If he ever called me back.

"If you know the exact date of insemination, that helps in calculating how far along you are. And that will help guide you towards what your choices are. You came in here to fail, and you passed. Did you already have a plan in mind?"

I laughed, not a happy laugh but that resigned to your fate sound. "I planned on not being pregnant."

I pushed my fingers into my hair and squeezed my head together. It was going to explode, and there would be no more Danica, no more cells creating a baby, no more connection to Flint or Liam.

I dropped my arms like they were concrete and I no longer had muscles to support them. Flint. Liam. Oh, God.

I didn't realize I was crying until Dr. Farhadi handed me a tissue.

"It's the hormones, they will sucker punch you every time. You don't need to make a decision today. Not to add to your stress, but you do need to make one soon. I need to either schedule you for a procedure or for prenatal."

I wiped my eyes and nodded. I already knew. "Prenatal."

Her expression said 'are you sure' with flashing neon. That woman had better never play poker.

I nodded. I had something of Flint and Liam, how could I not treasure this gift? "Yeah, prenatal."

"Okay." She stood and then held out her hand to help me off the table. "Meet me at the front desk to schedule your first checkup. I have some vitamins you'll need to take, and I have some information to hold you over until that appointment."

I left the doctor's office with a few bottles of vitamins, a stack of pamphlets, an appointment in three weeks, and a knot in my stomach that was either a future baby or writhing nerves.

I called my mom, and then my sister.

The reactions from my family ranged from a joking, "I'm too young to be a grandmother," to a not so joking, "I'm supposed to have children before you."

On the way home I stopped at the book store and got myself a stack of "So Now You're Pregnant" books, and at the grocery store I bought several pints of ice cream, after all, I was eating for two, and this was all fair game. At least it was until I puked, again.

How had I missed the signs? Right, morning sickness apparently came at any time of the day, not just in the morning. And no it wasn't that I was eating too fast or too much. I felt "full" because things were literally filling up down there.

Armed with a bowl of ice cream and my favorite rom-com, I made myself comfortable on the couch and texted Liam. Again.

I hadn't tried to contact him for three weeks. Nineteen days to be exact, and I needed to stop worrying about what he thought about me. If there was no more us, I still needed him to tell me. What I needed and what I wanted were very different things.

I wanted him. I wanted to tell him to his face about the baby. I wanted to feel his arms around me again. I knew he would be happy. He was Flint, and Flint loved me.

Oh God, I hoped Flint still loved me. It had been so long since I'd had him in my arms.

The phone started ringing. Finally, it was ringing and not rolling straight into— shit.

"The number you have reached is no longer in service."

I closed my eyes and replayed our last conversation.

Liam's voice was full of smiles as he bitched about the new assistant. "He is so incompetent. At first, I thought it was the little cultural and language differences since I'm not an American. And then I realized we were in England. I'm so shagged out, I forgot where I bloody was."

I loved how his native accent came out thicker and with more epithets from home. It was so sexy. "At least he hasn't blocked mum from calling. But he doesn't seem to understand I cannot eat carbs during filming, and he brings me doughnuts and fudge. That he makes."

I laughed, "Hey you ate carbs with me."

"I needed to carb load for you, darling."

The whole conversation was full of innuendo and flirting and nothing, absolutely nothing insinuated at him not being interested. Nothing to hint that he no longer wanted to continue with this relationship, even if it had to be long-distance for longer than we had been physically together.

I hadn't said I loved him at that end of that conversation. I felt it, but I hadn't said it.

Would saying it have changed anything?

I tried to call Liam every week until I admitted defeat in September sometime. By then, I didn't have time to chase after him. I was too busy working full-time for Charlie and buying diapers in advanced. I also had to juggle things gently with Ruthie.

I think part of her anger toward Liam was a redirect so that I didn't think she was mad at me for getting pregnant while I knew she and Hugh were undergoing fertility treatments. I didn't really clue into her feelings until early November.

I sat in my brother-in-law's recliner that evening. I needed one of those. Of course, I had no idea where it would fit in my small living room. Feet up and cradled in middle-class comfort, I felt decadent. I rested a bowl of popcorn on my growing belly and began munching before Ruth was able to pick up the remote and turn the TV on.

Our annual Christmas movie watch season had officially begun. Ruth and I had had a ritual, every year starting in November, once a week, we would get together, put on fuzzy slippers, drink hot chocolate, and eat popcorn while binge-watching at least three Christmas movies in a row. The movies had started early this year, a week before Halloween. There were so many holiday rom-coms the cable channel started showing them earlier and earlier every year. At some point, there would be a holiday romance movie channel all year long. But we steadfastly refused to watch Christmas movies until November first.

Celebrity news flashed by as the TV turned on.

"Wait, go back," I said sitting up a little bit. I thought I saw Liam.

Ruth switched the channel back. She groaned. It was Liam.

"Should you be watching this?" she asked with a sneer.

"I want to know what he's up to," I answered.

"It's not healthy, Dani. You're obsessed with him."

"Shush." I needed to hear the news reporter.

Liam's picture flashed up behind the reporter's shoulder next to a headshot of that model he had dated. Yasmin Montenegro, her name was as gorgeous as she was. "Yas-min," I said it out loud letting it roll off my tongue. Another picture of the two of them together was added to the montage.

"Montenegro ascertains had James stayed with her, paternity would not be in question and insists that James pay natal support, and child support after the birth. He has filed a countersuit for a full paternity test and financial damages—"

Ruth clicked the TV off.

"Hey, I was watching that!"

"No. You need to get over him, Dani, and I think suing him for child support is a good idea. He's leaving a trail of baby mammas all over the world. Is that who you really are? Just another…"

"Don't say it," I growled. I had already had enough of her lecturing me over loose morals and random unprotected sex.

It didn't matter that I thought I was protected. It didn't matter that she had a sexually diverse past. No, all that mattered was she was married, I was single, and I managed to get knocked up by the scum of the earth, an actor.

"You were nothing but someone available for a quick screw with no attachments. He's never called you back. He is never going to call you back. Yet you defend that kid of his as if he really cares. He's just like Daddy." She pointed at my baby bump.

I raised my eyebrows at her. "Daddy? You can't put your issues with our father on me over this. Get over it already."

"I'm not talking about our father." Her face turned red with anger. "Baby Daddy."

"Oh yeah?" I surged to my feet. "I have never once referred to Liam as Baby Daddy, he is the biological father of my child. If I can deal with it why can't you? Mom eventually got over Daddy leaving her. Liam never left me, because there wasn't a relationship to have left. You are the only one who has never come to grips with the fact that relationships sometimes end. Our father isn't a half-bad guy, and neither is Amanda. So how about you stop putting your daddy issues on my offspring?"

I kicked my slippers off and stormed downstairs.

I had my feet shoved into my shoes before Ruth finally followed me to the door. "You need to get your priorities straight little sister. You are in no position emotionally or financially to raise that child. You are still hung up on the guy and he clearly couldn't care less. You need to take steps to ensure that the kid is financially taken care of. You know Hugh and I could adopt it. It would be a private adoption, and you would be in its life, and..."

I took a deep breath and calmed myself before I said something I would regret for the rest of my life. "Stop Ruthie, just stop. I am not putting the baby up for adoption. And you need to accept that I don't hate Liam. I never will. When I get another opportunity, I will reach out to him to let him know. But it won't be for child support. He needs to know he has another child, maybe he will want to meet it."

I shrugged into my jacket. Ruth needed to cool down. I could practically see the steam rising from her ears. She was so mad at me for everything from knowing the name of the woman Daddy left Mom for and talking to her, for having an affair with an actor, for getting pregnant while she struggled.

"I'm gonna go home. I have the big ultrasound appointment on Wednesday, are you still going to come with? I could really use your support."

"I'll think about it." Her tone was gruff, she really was pissed. That was on her. There were too many things to be happy about, and I wanted to feed this baby growing inside of me nothing but love and joy.

I tried not to play the flash of news report over and over again, *countersuing for a full paternity test and financial damages. Financial damages.* That couldn't be right. Could it? Liam would be responsible, he would step up and admit and take care of a child of his. I knew he would. Maybe it was his lawyers being jerks, and not really him.

I didn't know and I needed to not focus on it. I needed to focus on light, love, happiness. I needed to focus on a chocolate-dipped waffle cone full of strawberry and banana ice cream. I blinked up at the neon sign of the ice cream shop. Yeah, my driving brain on autopilot knew what I needed.

I ended up getting a pumpkin and apple spice in white chocolate dipped cone. I may have been all set to watch a Christmas movie, but it was barely November, so I went with some seasonal flavors. I paid slightly better attention to the drive home.

I tried texting him again.

12

"I just wanted to make sure your number worked. Sorry to bother you." I texted Liam.

"It works. No bother. I'm headed out for press. Sorry can't chat. Text you when back. Kiss baby for me."

I sighed as I read the message. So many messages sent without replies. So many nights wondering if I would ever see him again. And now, I knew I would, even if it was just for him to see his daughter.

My phone pinged, and I smiled before I even checked the screen. He had found a second to send another text.

My smile dropped. It was from Ruthie. "Please call. Hugh's brother just died."

"Ruthie?" I said as soon as I heard the line pick up.

"Dani, thank you for calling, can you come over?"

"Yeah, we'll be over in a bit. Do you need me to get anything on the way?"

"No. I don't know. We'll figure it out when you get here."

Everyone sat quietly in the living room, everyone except for Myrna. She found it appropriate to squirm and squeal.

Hugh held her on his knee. His big hands wrapped around her middle, and his knee bounced absentmindedly.

No one spoke. Hugh was always a quiet man, but today, he said even less. Ruthie sniffled. She had requested Myrna's presence, thinking a little reminder of the circle of life would lift everyone's spirits. It didn't look like it was working.

Myrna was a bundle of color and light in the middle of a room full of adults in gray and black clothes, with bleak expressions and moods.

I escaped into the kitchen and began making dinner. It was still early in the day, but I needed something to do. I pulled out Ruth's Crockpot from the lower cabinet and got to work. I wasn't making anything fancy, not that Hugh or Ruth would be able to taste anything. Or maybe they could. Maybe their senses hadn't completely shut down, it just felt like it. Digging in the refrigerator, I came up with a variety of vegetables, and half a jar of curry sauce. The freezer provided chicken breasts, and I found onions and some potatoes in the pantry.

I washed, and chopped, and moved handfuls of food into the crock.

Ruth came in carrying Myrna. "I sent Hugh to take a nap."

"Myrna will be ready for one soon, too," I said.

"She is getting fussy. If you nurse her, I'll put her down."

I washed my hands. There wasn't much left to finish with the meal prep, but feeding the baby came first. I sat down and got myself situated before Ruth passed my Lovebug over. She instantly snuggled in and latched on.

"Is Hugh doing okay? I can't tell. He is so quiet." I looked over at Ruth. Her eyes were rimmed with red.

She nodded. "We knew this was coming. Andrew was so

sick. He just slipped away so fast, though. I mean, last week he wasn't feeling well. And he had done that before, gotten a little low, felt not quite right. It was nothing more than a cold. It's almost like going to the ER gave him permission to be worse than he was."

I tried not to glare at Ruth. Anyone who had to go to the ER for a cold was worse off than they led on. And from what she had told me earlier, Andrew really hadn't let anyone in their family know just how bad off he was.

"Is Hugh responsible for making arrangements?" I asked.

"Andrew took care of all of it. He didn't want a service, figured it would only be Hugh and their father anyway."

"What about Hugh's sister?"

Ruth shook her head. "She wouldn't fly in for this."

"Is everyone assuming or has she even been told yet?" From what I knew from Ruth, Hugh and his father made sweeping assumptions and projected their expectations onto others. Hugh's sister would not be expected to fly in for her older brother's funeral, therefore, why would they bother to let her know when it would be? "You haven't told Alice yet, have you?"

"Andrew only died yesterday," Ruth raised her voice in defense.

"He died yesterday morning, Ruth. If you've had time to tell me, then you've had time to tell her. I mean, I get it if Hugh and his dad are too emotional to be able to make the call, but you should have if they couldn't." I huffed at her. This was ridiculous.

"Andrew didn't want a fuss," she began. "He was an atheist so he doesn't, didn't want a service. He didn't even request to have his ashes cast to the ocean or something like that."

"Someone still needs to tell his sister."

Myrna did her last attempt at a suck with a thrash of her body, trying to stay awake enough to eat before she essentially collapsed under her own exhaustion. I disengaged her and bundled her up.

"Take Myrna and go lay down. She's good for your soul. After everyone has had a nap, make sure Alice has been called. But right now, you need to rest too. Emotional support is draining."

I gently placed Myrna into Ruth's arms and shooed her out of her own kitchen. Why did having a baby all of a sudden make me the default adult?

I sat back down with a thump, adjusted my boobs, and then collapsed with my head on my arms on the table. I was tired. I should be taking a nap with Myrna right now, but my family needed me. Ruth needed me to be strong for her, so she could be strong for Hugh.

Truthfully, I thought Hugh would ride this one out just fine. He was the stoic type, limited emotional vocabulary. Limited public displays of affection. Ruth needed to express her grief, not that I thought she was particularly close to Andrew, but still, to have someone you knew closely die was hard. Harder for some.

I pulled myself together and pushed up and out of the kitchen chair. That was not a comfortable place to fall asleep. If a nap on a chair was in my future, I wanted to be in the recliner. I finished chopping up blocks of frozen chicken and stirred them into the Crockpot with the curry sauce, a can of diced tomatoes, and the veggies— lid on, switched to high. I washed my hands and headed upstairs to the TV room for and in-chair nap.

～

I looked over at Andrew. This was awkward. He was large and reserved in his actions. Myrna smiled up at him.

"Oh, what is she making eyes at?" the receptionist at the crematorium asked.

How did I tell the woman who worked with dead bodies that my daughter was trying to get the big quiet ghost to pay attention to her? That wasn't fair; she probably didn't work with the bodies, just the families. But, wasn't she in essence handing over what was left of Andrew's body to me? Either way, I would have bet money, odds against even, that she did not see him.

He looked like Hugh only older and heavier. Stoic, or in shock. I looked down at the bag she handed me, brown paper with handles, like any shopping bag from any store at the mall. Only inside the shoebox was Andrew's remains, and not a pair of Steve Maddens.

"Okay big guy, let's take you home." I directed my speech to the bag, but it was intended for the spirit.

Ruth had called again. She just could not face having to transport Andrew. Hugh was at work, and he wouldn't be available to pick up his brother during office hours. She was taking Andrew's death harder than I ever expected her to.

I placed the bag in the back of the stroller and wheeled everyone back out to the car. I situated Myrna, and then placed Andrew's physical presence into the trunk. "I don't know where you'll be most comfortable. There isn't a lot of room inside." I loved my Mini, but damn, once packed with Myrna in her car seat, and the stroller in the passenger seat, and Andrew in the trunk, I was going to need to climb out of the car to change my mind. Andrew squeezed into the back next to the car seat. He was non-corporeal, and yet he positioned his body as if he were wedged in.

I always kept up a running dialog with Myrna when I

drove. Not that she was much on conversation; I just wanted her to know I was nearby even though she couldn't see me. Today, I directed my babble to Andrew. He never answered. I don't know if that's because of the type of person he had been, or maybe he didn't know he could answer me.

Most spirits were silent around me. I guess they got used to not being seen, so why would they maintain a conversation?

I got tired of my own voice, and I noticed in the double mirror set up I had so I could see the baby, she had fallen asleep. I turned the radio on low and stopped talking. Andrew flooded my brain. He figured out how to communicate.

Most of everything he made me aware of was deathbed remorse. He didn't speak, he gave me images and emotions. He really didn't know his sister, she was seventeen years younger than him, and by the time he was interested in paying attention to her, she couldn't have cared less about the stranger who was her brother. He didn't marry because he never got over the one that got away.

I slammed on my breaks. "Holy shit! Ruth?" The words were out of my mouth, and a little louder than I had intended.

No wonder she was so upset. And no wonder I had never met Andrew, he hadn't even been to the wedding. "You need to tell me more, dude."

And he did. It was very interesting to get the skinny on my older sister. She had a very bad habit of being a bit too sanctimonious at times. And I knew she was no saint. According to Andrew, she was dating him first before she met Hugh. Hugh was younger, closer to her age. It wasn't until she left Andrew that he realized she would have made him the perfect wife. He should have done more.

I wanted to know more. Had there been a dramatic fight over the girl between brothers? Had Ruth been sleeping with both of them before she decided on Hugh? Had she ever gone back to Andrew after she married Hugh?

I wanted juicy dirt on my sister and Andrew clammed up. No more information, no more visions. He had loved Ruth, and clearly, she had loved him at one point in their lives.

I smirked and laughed to myself all the way to Ruthie's house.

I carried Myrna in first and then headed back out to the car to get what was left of Andrew on earth and carry him inside.

Ruth refused to take the bag when I handed it out to her. I placed it on the table.

"You holding up okay?" I asked.

Andrew had died a week earlier, and she still looked rough. Hugh had gone back to work, and Alice was flying down for a family remembrance dinner with her brother and father.

"I'm fine." Ruth used that tone that said I'm not fine and I expect you to know this about me.

Because I did know my sister, I did know that about her. I guided her to a chair, and put my arms around her shoulders. "Liar."

Andrew occupied, to the best of his ability, one of the other chairs. It was going to be really weird if he decided to hang out in this house and haunt Ruth.

"You once told me you saw ghosts." She sniffed.

Oh damn, Ruth had started crying, and she was going to ask me to conjure up a ghost on demand. It didn't help that he was already there, and she had never believed me before.

"Only if they let me, why?" I had to ask even though I knew where she was going.

She dragged her knuckles across her cheek, wiping at the tears with a gesture of frustration. "You know, can you see him? Is he here?"

Yep, saw that one coming a mile away.

"What's up, Ruthie? What did you need him to know?" The dead always wanted the living to know something, the living had one last thing to tell the dead.

"I wanted to know if you could see him, you know, let him know some things." She sniffed again.

I'm not some ghost relay station. If I were, I'd make bank as a psychic or a medium. Nope, some spirits were just visible or decided they could communicate with me. Ha, some ghosts. Only one really, Flint. Well, Flint was the one who stuck around and wormed his way into my dreams. The rest of them were like Andrew. They sat around and didn't realize they could tell me stuff. They, as if this happens to me all the time. Not including small animals, it happened more than I cared for.

I sighed.

"Why don't you talk to him? He is right there."

Ruth looked around anxiously. I indicated the bag.

"That's him, talk to him."

"Now you're making fun of me," she snapped.

"No, I'm telling you that you can talk to him and get whatever off your chest. If he is out there, or around here, he will hear you."

"You aren't going to help me?" she asked.

I looked at my sister with my most level 'you have got to be shitting me' expression I could muster. She didn't get to pick on me relentlessly when I told her about Flint, only to turn around and claim she believed me all along because she wanted to talk to Andrew.

"Fine," she harrumphed. She shifted in her chair and stared at the box of Andrew's ashes. "Why didn't you tell us things were so bad? Why didn't you tell me?"

As Ruth talked I watched Andrew. He shimmered.

"We could have helped with medical bills. I would have had a chance to say goodbye." Her voice hitched and a small sob escaped her lips. That was it, she wanted to say goodbye. "I'm sorry it didn't work out. It never would have worked out. But I did love you. I do love you." She couldn't talk anymore. She sat with her eyes closed, silently crying.

Andrew shimmered. He stood, placed a hand on her shoulder and then faded. He was gone. That was what he had needed to hear.

"He heard you." I patted her back. "He heard you."

I gave her a few moments of peace before I picked up the still sleeping Myrna and headed home. Maybe I was some ghost whisperer, but that was something I was going to keep to myself.

13

Meeting Flint...

Still reeling from the very personal betrayal by my best friend at the end of the first semester of my junior year, I may have clung unhealthily to anyone who offered up their friendship for the rest of high school. I know I did.

How else would I have become friends with the creepy girl, Hester Prynne? But I did, and yes, I know that wasn't her real name. It was the name she chose. I did say she was creepy.

I wasn't going to tell Hester I saw dead people, she would cling to me even more than she already did. To be fair, I clung back. We were outcasts in high school. And that followed us to UCLA where we were the weird girls freshman year. It sucked. High school was supposed to be where you found your tribe, you broke free of the confines of middle school.

No, high school was where the mean girls of middle school really caught their stride. And woe unto thee if you were one of their targets. Hi, my name is Danica Kensington. I have a very large target painted on my back by my former best friend, Cecilia Saaid.

I felt like that target hadn't faded, even though I had left high school behind. I never confessed to Hester about my special talent. I didn't need her to add to my target, even though I'm sure if I had told her about the ghosts she would have dragged me to a cemetery years earlier. When she announced that for my birthday she wanted to do something "fun," I wasn't expecting a tour of the most famous graves in LA. But a cemetery it was, so armed with a map of the tomb sites we headed in.

Hester shivered. "You can just feel the spirits here, can't you?"

Nope, no Hester I can't. That was a breeze.

There were far more living people than dead ones hanging around. I have since learned not that many dead people haunt their own tombs. But there were ghosts and wisps of spiritual residue.

The redhead standing with her hand resting carefully, lovingly, on Rudolph Valentino's name had that frizzy puff-ball head of curls that screamed perm. Her bangs reached straight up from her forehead in a style that identified her as a nineteen-eighties mall rat. A single-stemmed rose hung from her hand. Fresh rose stems scattered about her feet.

What did she think of the people who came and laid roses at this man's grave? Why had she, and why was she still here in her after-life when it was glaringly obvious Valentino was nowhere around?

It was pretty clear from the beginning the cemetery was a pilgrimage site. Fans came here specifically to lay roses, light candles, or recite poetry to their heroes.

I didn't expect to be so fascinated by the architecture and

monuments. Graveyards were places I hadn't ever considered visiting. I was hooked. The mini temples and obelisks declared a grandeur akin to the Egyptian pharaohs. They wanted to live forever as gods, and here in Hollywood, these memories were. Hester stopped to pay her respects to the Ramones while I continued to wander and study the tombs. I needed to come back here with a sketchbook. I no longer wanted to design and build office buildings; I wanted to design and build monuments.

I tried to ignore the spirits when I saw them. I didn't want their attention. At nineteen I still wasn't certain what it all meant. Could they possess me? Would they terrorize me? A combination of too many horror movies, and having no one to actually ask left me mostly avoiding them.

I tried not to make eye contact, but sometimes it happened, and the hairs all over my body would stand on end. If they got too close or touched me, I might cry a little, or shiver. Reactions were different each time.

Flint gave me goosebumps. I knew he was a specter. He sat legs crossed perched on top of Cecil B. DeMille's tomb. A tourist would never have been so rude. Dapper wide-legged, creased slacks, single buttoned jacket, dark brows and sloped nose hidden in the shadow of a fedora's brim, his style was so far out of date it was pretty obvious he wasn't corporeal. Sometimes I couldn't tell, sometimes specters appeared so solid and so real. Other times they were shadows, or translucent, obvious.

He jumped down from his lookout and strolled next to me. His cigarette, don't ask cause I have no clue how that worked, probably the same way he could change clothes, smelled like electricity and ozone.

I tried to focus on my feet or one of the distant tombs,

not him. *I shouldn't keep smoking these. I understand they, in fact, did kill me.*

"Lung cancer," I muttered.

I shouldn't have answered him. It was a stupid move.

He chuckled and flicked the cigarette away from himself.

"Really? That's littering. You might catch something on fire." I groaned to myself, I had just chastised a ghost over a phantom cigarette, even though it flashed out of existence as soon as it left his fingers.

You're cute.

He flashed me a dazzling grin, the one that made him a movie star. And I blushed.

"I really should go find my friend," I said as I scampered away.

What the hell was I doing, blushing and flirting with a dead man? A really good looking dead man?

That afternoon, Hester convinced me to chop my hair to above my shoulders and bleach it. I let her. I didn't want to be alone in my head. I got sad talking to myself, and I know I would replay meeting that spirit too much without a distraction.

I've always been a blonde, but never a blonde bombshell. Bleaching my hair and listening to Hester wax poetic about the energy of the cemetery was a welcome distraction.

For kicks and giggles when we bought the bleach I picked up a red lipstick at the drug store. My signature look was born that day. So much happened that day.

The first man to appreciate my new look was dead. He leaned against a tree planted along the sidewalk in front of Hester's apartment. I should have been offended, and I should have stopped talking to him. So it made perfect sense that I had to quiz him. And I let him follow me to the bus stop.

"Did you follow me from the cemetery?" I asked, a little louder than I should have, seeing how no one else was around.

He shrugged. *I found your energy again.*

"My energy?"

I had to talk low so that everyone on the bus didn't think I was a complete nut talking to myself.

Apparently, once I recognized him as a spirit and engaged, he could feel my energy like a beacon. There was something there that lured him in. *You get a lot of ghosts following you, don't you?*

I shook my head. "I don't talk to them, they leave me alone."

The guy across the bus aisle from me gave me a side-eye and moved further forward in the bus.

"I know who you are. I've seen your movies. You're Flint Reese." It had taken me a couple of hours to accept who he was. I had recognized that smile, but the suit and the hat were a new look to me. "Sebastian Hale."

He was one of many Seb Hale actors. I followed Seb Hale movies, books, and comics. I was used to seeing him either in Edwardian fashion or shirtless. I confess I did enjoy seeing him without a shirt on.

When I looked over again he was in one of his Seb Hale costumes. Wowza. In black-and-white restored film that was hot. But standing right next to me in full color on a full bus, that was just not fair.

I stared at my feet and refused to talk any more. That's when Flint slipped into my mind and I discovered I didn't need to talk out loud. I didn't complain when he stayed with me on the bus the entire way home. And I didn't freak out when he walked into my dreams that night. I totally let him seduce me.

That's also when I discovered that having a ghost as a best friend and lover wasn't such a bad idea. It didn't matter what I told him, he couldn't announce it to the world. And I didn't need to worry about condoms.

"I'm back, headed over now unless you tell me no."

I wasn't about to tell Liam no. I knew he had already fallen for Myrna, but I still needed him to prove we were important to him. Especially after the year I just had without him.

"How soon?" I replied.

We were going to go to the park for a walk. I wanted to see something other than the same old houses again. I wasn't suffering from postpartum. I enjoyed my misery fully. I was fortunate in that I didn't have a heavy dose of post-natal depression as my hormones and body readjusted back to being not pregnant. But there were days it seemed like it wanted to seep in and take over. Maybe at some point, I'd return to pre-baby normal, but I wasn't going to beat myself up over it. I wasn't going to develop new super mom level hobbies that I never considered before, I wasn't joining a gym. A good walk served me well before Myrna, it would serve me well now that she was here. But I did get slammed with heavy-duty feelings of inadequacy from time to time.

Yesterday, not being able to afford a home with a yard for her slammed into me like a brick wall. For now, we did great with the studio, and we would continue to do well in the studio for several years, but at some point, there was going to need to be a bedroom with a closable door. Or maybe I could give up the big bed and put in two double beds? Either way, I just didn't think the garage would continue to be home five years down the road. And how was I going to deal with moving, and how much would I have saved up in five years? After all, five years ago I thought I was going to save for a condo and only be in the studio another five or six years tops. That wasn't happening, and that had nothing to do with Myrna, and everything to do with real estate markets.

The inadequacy felt like a sucking pull, dragging me toward a pit of black sticky tar. I needed to not be around homes. So the park it was.

"On ground still in plane. An hour or two."

Okay, that gave us time to go now. We wouldn't have to wait around.

"Headed to the park for a walk. Should be home by the time you get there. If not please wait, we won't be long."

"Daddy is coming to see you," I cooed, lifting Myrna from her bouncy chair.

I placed her in her car seat, double-checked the diaper bag, pushed my hat down on my head, and we headed out to the park.

This was nice, it wasn't too hot under my layers of UV over-shirt and wide-brimmed sun hat, and I didn't have to feel the pressure of all those houses looming over me. Myrna smiled and kicked for a bit and then began fussing. I found a bench and we breastfed until she got sleepy. I finished my walk as she slept.

Liam sat on his suitcase in front of my door as I pulled up.

I couldn't help but smile. He was here waiting for us. Maybe if I had gotten through to him last year, he would have been here then, too.

He launched to his feet, and I had to scramble out of the car to hush him. Myrna was still asleep.

"How does that work then? Won't getting her out of the car wake her?" he asked.

"Not at all, she won't even notice."

He opened the passenger door, saw the stroller in the front seat and closed the door a little louder than I was pleased with. I shot him a glare over the top of the Mini.

"Hey, baby sleeping. Remember?"

"Sorry." He looked it too, with a furrowed brow and apologetic grimace.

I waved him over to my side of the car.

"Watch." I flipped my seat forward and demonstrated how Myrna's car seat snapped into an installed base.

I eased out bringing her car seat with me. Liam took the car seat and gazed down on her. He let out a breath as if he had been holding one in until he could see her again. All of his hard edges melted and he turned into a giant softy. Yeah, he was hooked. This kid would never want for anything as long as he was alive. I hoped she waited until we were in a bigger place before she asked for a kitty or a puppy.

Damn, there it was, that slam of inadequacy. I bit my lip and willed tears not to form. Blinking helped.

Liam tore his gaze away from her to focus on me. "Are you all right?"

Oh, his voice felt nice, like a warm fuzzy blanket to my shivering sense of self-worth.

I nodded. I was as fine as I was going to be. I showed him how the bar flipped up and turned into a handle so he could carry her more easily.

"How long are you staying?" I asked as he followed me inside.

Liam scanned around looking for a place to put the carrier down.

"Put her on the bed. She'll be asleep for a while. I'm

gonna hit the bathroom." I motioned at the bed as I hurried off to go pee.

When I came out, Myrna's car seat was on the bed with Liam sitting next to it. He looked confused.

His eyes caught mine. "I don't know how to take her out. What if I wake her?" His voice was soft and hushed.

I smiled and wanted to laugh, but I didn't. I remembered that feeling too well. I lifted the car seat and shifted it into the center of the bed. "You don't have to take her out, she'll be fine."

"Now what?" he asked.

Sleep when she sleeps, the nap rule pulled on me. "I typically nap with her. I'm mostly on her schedule, not the other way around."

"I'm sorry, I'm in the way." He looked guilty. "Is there anything I can do to help out?"

I rested a hand on his arm. There was some buzz of a connection there. It wasn't sexual, but there was something between us still. "You aren't in the way. Would you like to take a nap with us?"

The smile he gave me reminded me there was a reason he was Myrna's father. My knees went weak. If my sexy bits were still working, I'm sure they would have spun up into overdrive. As it was, my heart beat a little faster.

I kicked my shoes off and climbed onto the bed. I carefully unbuckled the baby and lifted her out. Liam whisked the car seat away. It was definitely handy to have a second person around.

I moved the pillows so Myrna had a nice space and placed her on her back.

"Come on. Even if you don't sleep you can stare at her." I curled up on my side and rested my head on my arm.

Liam mirrored my actions. His focus all on the baby between us. I let my eyes drift closed.

When I woke, I was splayed flat on my stomach with a blanket covering my legs. I felt that telltale chill of drool at the side of my mouth.

I thrashed up with an instant shot of adrenalin-filled panic. Myrna.

I caught my breath and tried to ease my speeding pulse. Because the curtain that blocked the bedroom was open I could see into the rest of the studio without any issues. Liam had the baby slung in one arm. The man had big hands and long arms and was able to hold on to the girl one-handed. He bounced and moved around in the small kitchen.

"We thought we would let you sleep. You seemed so tired. Didn't we?" He smiled and nodded at Myrna.

I scrubbed my hand over my face, for once not worried about smearing lipstick. I hadn't really been up for wearing any for a while. Besides, I kissed Myrna's little head a lot. She tended to look blotchy if I left makeup on her.

"How long was I out?" I felt rested, it was a glorious sensation.

Liam approached me with a cup of tea, the little tag hanging over the side.

"Myrnoula and I have been up for about an hour. We've had a clean nappy, and played under that padded arch."

Myrna saw me and began wailing. I put the tea on the bedside table and reached for her.

"She is probably hungry. Sounds like you've been busy."

Liam settled Myrna into my arms and sat next to me while I adjusted and shifted my clothes around so she could latch on.

"We really didn't do much. Is this what it's like?" He stroked her leg.

It was so very domestic sitting here breastfeeding our daughter. I didn't want to be sad right now, right now I should have been very happy, content.

"Nica, what can I do to help?" Damn that man and his voice.

Our eyes locked. His were brown and so full of concern. I yawned so that he wouldn't see any tears forming. Baby hormones raged through my system making me unbalanced.

"Thank you for letting me sleep. I really needed that. I don't even know what I need help with right now."

"Are you saying you've got this and don't need my help?"

I huffed half of a laugh. "Hardly. I feel like I'm making this up as I go. Did you get something to eat while I was asleep?"

He shook his head.

"Could I put you in charge of lunch?"

"Making or buying?" he asked. I noticed his chest puffed up as if he were preparing himself to take charge.

"Either is fine. Myrna will go down for her post-lunch snooze in a few, so we'll need to stick around here. If you order anything, so far I can't seem to do Indian anything, and too much garlic makes her miserable."

In what seemed like a single large step, Liam was back in the kitchen, looking in the fridge.

"Any other dietary needs I need to be aware of?"

"Just yours. You aren't working out for a part right now, are you?"

He shook his head and looked up at me. "Nope, so I can have ice cream and bread."

"I don't think an ice cream sandwich would be very tasty at the moment."

I laughed at the expression that crossed his face.

He shuddered. "Gross, you really eat those?"

"Yeah, but they are made with cookies, not bread." Myrna fussed at me as I shifted around with too much laughing.

"There isn't much in this kitchen. You need to go grocery shopping. I'll order something."

I know I needed to go shopping. I just hadn't really had time between naps and dodging any depression triggers. I needed a mommy to protect me from the world, the way I was going to shield the bundle in my arms. I needed an assistant to run my errands, and make sure I had food in the place.

"I need someone to take care of me while I take care of this one," I muttered.

Myrna slept again, and I stared at my food. Not only had Liam ordered lunch, but he also ordered several meals. The deli provided a variety from salads to sandwiches to soups, and he made sure I now had a selection.

"Let me send over my maid service, that will take a huge load from your shoulders."

"This place is hardly big enough for a cleaner, I can do it," I whined. I didn't want to whine, I wanted to be able to handle it all.

"Then I'll come over and do it. Nica, you are very capable, but you are very tired. In a few months, everything will be easier." While waiting on our lunch delivery Liam cleaned my kitchen and insisted I rest while Myrna took her second nap.

"You'll come over and vacuum, and clean the kitchen, and scrub the toilet?"

"I'll come over to be with Myrna, kick you out for some quality solo time, and sneak the cleaner over while you are gone." He winked and shoved a very large bite of sandwich into his mouth.

"You're as backhanded as your last assistant." I smiled. I scored, his mouth was too full to offer up a witty retort.

He swallowed and the muscles in his throat shifted, bopping the Adam's apple up and down. He had a sexy neck.

"Danica, you have no idea. They just keep getting worse and worse."

"Seriously? How can they be any worse than the assistant who blocked your mom from your call list?"

"How about the one who paid a thug to mug me?"

I put my fork down rather suddenly. "What?"

"So much has happened this past year, it's been insane. I know at some point you must have thought I stopped caring and simply stopped calling you back."

I nodded, that's exactly what I thought. He had been complaining about his assistant at that point too. "So was this the one trying to feed you doughnuts?" I asked.

Liam rolled his eyes so hard he had to have seen brains. "So I had told you about him? Did I tell you the chick who blocked all the numbers did so on Cecilia's orders? I'm tired of being someone's one true love but not knowing it. I think I should be in charge of deciding who I'm in love with."

He held my gaze for a little too long. His eyes shifted, letting the blue in. Neither of us made a sound. I swallowed hard. Now was not the time to ask if there was still something between us; it was not the time to bring up the whole Flint history. Not that I had been planning on it, but definitely not now. Not for a while. If ever.

"Wait back up. Doughnut Boy was in love with you?" I hadn't expected that. Assistants fell in love with their celebrity bosses all the time. It was right up there with nannies on who is next in line for an affair. So why not Doughnut Boy?

"Yes, Harlen. Harlen believed if I pudged up and dropped out of acting, I would realize he had been my lover in a previous life, and we could finally be together. I don't know if he was gay in a previous life but I was not." The look he pierced me with nailed me in place. Maybe that was supposed to be my opening to bring up Flint? Did he know? He had to.

Maybe not. I took another bite of my chicken salad trying not to look guilty, hoping I did not have *you were my lover in a previous incarnation come back to me we belong together* in flashing neon tattooed on my forehead.

"I was a little sad when he left."

"A little?" I was surprised I could actually speak, still caught up on the fact that someone else pulled the past life lover card on Liam when that was my reality.

"I will deny it if you ever tell anyone, but he was really good. I snuck a few of those baked goods he had brought."

"You're telling me you'd go gay for a doughnut?"

Liam chuckled, "They were really good."

It was my turn to roll my eyes and look at my brain. "So he had you mugged?"

"He did. And it went completely wrong." He stood up and picked up my hand, pulling me out of my chair. "Come on, I'll tell you all about it."

Liam guided me to the couch and had me sit. He sat near but not next to me and picked my feet up. Dear God, the man was going to rub my feet and tell me a story. Maybe I should just forget about the whole Flint Reese business and fall in love with Liam for Liam. I could do that, I already had.

I relaxed back and closed my eyes. Liam had one of those "he could read the dictionary to me and I'd be happy" voices. And he could tell a story. I'm not sure which made me go limp more, his capable hands on my feet or the soothing tones of his voice.

He pressed his thumb into that spot where the arch meets the ball of the foot and I stifled a moan. If I didn't edit myself, I would make indecent noises and wake the baby.

"So I want you to picture this, I'm walking along the canal after dinner."

"Canal? I thought you were in London?"

He chuckled, "Yes, canals, London has quite a few. Haven't you been?"

I shook my head.

"It can be lovely, I'll take you and Myrna sometime."

My stomach did a little flip. It certainly sounded like Liam planned on being around for a while. "After dinner, would it be safe in the dark?"

"It was still fairly light out. Some areas are like a park with trees and some are more like a city street with shops and cafes. There I was enjoying the evening, walking around not paying attention like some chump tourist when this asshole gets up real close behind me. He made some comment that made me think I was only getting mugged because he thought I wasn't a local. Okay so I'm not, but he didn't necessarily know that, so I told him to sod off and go bother a real tourist. Words were exchanged until a knife came out. I handed him my wallet, he pulled out some cash and chucked it into a shrub. I thought we were done and then he reached into my pocket and pulled out my phone."

I started to say something about how I was glad he didn't get hurt.

"Before you say anything about why didn't I fight him back, I'm not a trained fighter. I am essentially a dancer. I learn a set of moves to look a certain way. I don't fight."

"I wasn't going to say anything like that, Liam."

"It didn't do any good anyway." He pouted.

"What didn't do any good?"

"I punched the bloke full-on in the nose. So he tossed my phone into the canal. I stood there gasping at my stupid phone, he took off. Eventually, I gathered my wits about me and retrieved my wallet."

His hands on my feet continued rubbing and his voice soothed me into a semi-comatose state.

"I returned to the hotel and decided to let my assistant deal with it in the morning. And that's when it got weird. Now, remember this guy thinks if he can get weight on me, I'll see the error of my ways, give up acting, and settle down with him. I already figured he had a thing for me. I've dealt with that before, so I was already looking for a good opening to let him down nicely. As far as he was concerned, I wasn't dating anyone. I still had to deal with Cecelia and keeping her in check, and he didn't see me with anyone. I guess he never listened in on any of our conversations, so maybe he thought there was a chance."

"Just to be clear, you can't be seduced with doughnuts?"

"For the record, I'm more likely to be lured with a good cream tart." He smiled and his hand ran over my shin.

How easy would it be to just pick up where we left off, and ignore the past year?

Myrna made distressed noises as she woke up alone. There was no ignoring the past year. No picking up where we left off. After all, where we left off was all sex all day, and right now I was more interested in Liam in his ability to have food delivered than the fact he had a hot body and knew how to use it. Actually, I had no interest in that at all.

I kicked my feet out of his grasp and was standing in an instant. I didn't rush to Myrna's side. I wanted to see if she could start developing self-soothing skills. Okay, I was months off from when she should start developing those skills, but I could hope. Her next sounds were definitely distress.

Liam was up and ahead of me into the bedroom.

He lifted her from her bedside sleeper. They both looked at each other with such amazement. I didn't want to ignore this past year, I just wish he had been in it. She continued to fuss until she saw me.

I took her into my arms and she settled. I changed her diaper while Liam continued to tell me how Doughnut Boy organized the whole mugging and got caught because the mugger was his brother, and he was supposed to have stolen the phone, not toss it in the water. They were found out because the brother visited Harlen on set and Liam walked in on the two of them arguing. Turns out non-fighting Liam had managed to break the bloke's nose. Harlen was fired on the spot, and both he and his brother were escorted off set.

Cecilia reinserted herself into the works at this point and had her assistant help Liam get another phone. With a different carrier, on her plan as a child account so she could actually oversee his usage and contacts. Not that he had any contacts. The new plan was unable to make use of any backup Liam had managed with the previous carrier.

He sat with one hand holding Myrna. He ran the other hand through his hair. "I blame the accident." He sighed, not happy. "The doctor's said I didn't have any brain damage, but I don't remember things I should. I feel like cell phones somehow appeared while I was unconscious. Almost as if they did not exist before the accident. I know that doesn't make any sense."

It did and it didn't. Flint had never lived with cell phones. He may have been around with me and was aware of them, but as a spirit, they weren't something he used. I fell back on the Flint excuse again. I needed to stop or get some kind of definitive proof as if the freaky eye thing wasn't enough.

"It doesn't have to make any sense, Liam. That part of your brain decided that phones weren't a memory priority. Cell plans are a pain in the ass."

"They really are. It wasn't until I landed in New Zealand that I finally got things straightened out. Oh, speaking of cell phones." He reached into his pocket and pulled his phone out. He fiddled with it before turning it to me.

I took the phone and looked at a baby picture of Myrna, only it wasn't Myrna. This was a Christmas picture, and Myrna wouldn't have her first Christmas for another six months.

"I showed Myrna's picture to Mum without saying anything and she said, 'Now, this one is yours.' I asked her how she knew because I only see you when I look at Myrna. I don't think she looks like me at all. Mum showed me this. That's my sister Kendall."

I held the phone up next to Myrna so I could see the similarities better. "They could be twins."

He nodded.

"How did your mother handle the Yasmin Montenegro situation?" I wanted to know what kind of a man his own mother thought he was.

He shook his head. "That hit so hard and fast. I didn't even get a chance to discuss it with her before it hit the gossip outlets. Something I told Mum, that I can say now that Myrna is in my life is true, I would never knowingly abandon my child. And I will do anything and everything to provide, care for, and protect my child. Nica, you can count on me from here on out."

I could have fallen forever into the deep pools of warmth that were his brown eyes. Myrna's eyes reminded me of his, only hers were dark blue. They were Flint's eyes.

"I believe you, Liam, I really do."

I really did.

14

"Are you sure you trust him?" Ruthie asked for the bazillionth time this morning.

"Yes, I do."

"He is late."

I stopped getting the bottles of breast milk set up and looked at her. "You did drive to get here right? So you are aware of traffic?"

Liam arranged to show up just before nap time. I could nurse Myrna to sleep, then run off to my appointment. I wouldn't be gone very long, and I had rented a breast pump so I could prepare bottles for my return to work, and I prepped a few bottles just in case I didn't get back in time for her next feeding. This would be the longest I had been separated from Myrna, other than the premiere last month. I was already nervous enough as it was. Ruth wasn't helping matters.

There was a knock on the door and then it swung open. Liam stepped in. "Sorry, they took longer at the dealer than I expected."

"Oh hi," I said as I turned to him.

He went straight to Myrna in her bouncy chair and picked her up. "Are you ready for an afternoon with your da?"

Ruth made a very loud harrumph noise. She did not approve on so many levels. I decided not to count the ways.

"Oh hello." Liam shifted Myrna in his arms and extended his hand. "I'm Liam."

Ruth left him hanging.

I stepped over next to him and fussed with Myrna's outfit. "This is my sister Ruth. She knows who you are."

"Right, she does not approve of me."

"It's rude to speak about me while I'm standing right here," she sneered.

"It's rude of you to ignore Liam when he is introducing himself." I sat on the couch and reached up for Myrna, shifting my shirt to the side.

"Try again?" Liam quirked an eyebrow at her and extended his hand again.

Ruth took it with so much obvious disdain I was surprised she didn't drop his had as if it burned her skin.

I ignored her and looked up at Liam. "There are three bottles in the fridge. I don't know how well Myrna will do with them. She's never been good with a bottle. Warm the milk up, but not in the microwave. That blue contraption is a bottle warmer. It should be pretty self-explanatory. But we should be back before she's ready for her next feeding. My car keys are on the counter in case you need to take her anyplace, like the ER."

"Nica, we'll be fine. Go to your appointment, spend some baby-free time with your sister."

"Dani has needed her hair done for so long. It's been ages. She looks so unkempt with her roots showing like this. It's a good thing you could babysit."

"I think Danica looks great. And I'm not babysitting. I am Myrna's father. I am doing my part to help parent."

"Oh, so you have no problems changing diapers and letting Dani date?"

Liam's jaw dropped, and his face lost color before darkening. His eyes cut from Ruth to me.

"Stop it, Ruth. I am not interested in dating." I turned my focus to Liam. "Ignore her, she's stirring you up. And thank you for being available to spend the day with Myrna."

I deposited the drowsy baby into his arms. "I won't be gone long." I gave Myrna a soft kiss on the head and looked up at Liam. I wanted to give him a kiss too, instead, I rested my hand on the front of his shoulder. "We're good?"

Liam nodded to move me out the door.

A large, shiny new SUV sat in the drive next to my Mini. In comparison, it really made my car look like a shoe. In similar colors, the shape of the cars looked like a baby version and a mama version of a boxy red car.

Liam must have gotten a new car. I didn't think he drove much since the accident.

"That's a bit much, don't you think?"

I closed my eyes and smiled, right now Ruthie was being a bit much. I get it, she wanted to protect me from having my heart broken again by him. But she didn't see him the same way I did. She didn't see how he was with his daughter. Myrna was his whole purpose for being when he was with her. And that not babysitting remark, dude was earning some serious brownie points with me.

I slid into the passenger seat of Ruth's own SUV, only hers wasn't red and therefore not "a bit much." I was pretty sure her SUV was "mucher," it was larger and very top of the line luxury. Hugh made a serious salary, and Ruth certainly spent it.

My hairdresser tisked over how long I let my roots go for. I confessed to loving having someone else wash and fuss with my hair. It felt so good, and for once, someone was taking care of me. I may have fallen asleep enjoying the sheer relaxation of it all. I could do this every week. However, I was a single mother with a newborn, not working, not in a position to maintain my hair every six weeks like I used to be. I needed to consider doing this myself or changing my style.

Eh, maybe not. Last time I went red, and things did not go well. Besides, I loved playing up the whole blonde bombshell look. Right now, I just felt bombed out.

Ruth suggested we get lunch, but my boobs were aching. I needed to get home and nurse. Instead, we got drive-thru and ate hamburgers while she drove home.

"You sure you don't want to come in?" I asked when she dropped me off.

"Not really in the mood to look at your boobs. You're just going to feed the baby then take a nap. We'll hang out later."

"Thanks for driving and getting me out. I'm forgetting what it's like to talk to adults on a daily basis."

"We should all have that problem. See ya." Ruth waved and pulled away from the curb.

I took a few minutes to check out Liam's new car. It was nice, all shiny and red. It screamed "family car," without being a minivan or station wagon. It was nice and looked expensive. The dark windows prevented me from seeing the interior very well, but they made great mirrors. I smoothed on a fresh layer of lipstick. New hair and a little makeup made me feel human again.

I glanced over at my car and winced at the size. I loved my sassy little Mini, it wasn't something I was able to purchase new; it was a low mileage used car. And even though it was too small for our needs at the moment, it wasn't something I could afford to replace.

Listening carefully at the door, I decided that bursting in and announcing my return wasn't the best idea. I didn't hear anything, no noises of anyone moving about, no talking or fussing. Figuring they were asleep, I slowly opened the door and walked in.

Toys were scattered everywhere. Every bottle I had pumped was out on the counter— okay I hadn't pumped that many, but they were all out. Every pacifier I owned was on the floor. So were random items of clothes. It looked like there had been a super ninja smack down of a fight, and passed out in the middle of it all were Liam and Myrna. He lay back on the couch with one arm flung to the side, the other hand holding Myrna on his chest. He was shirtless, and so was she.

Skin to skin. He must have run into a problem soothing her. My blood turned to pure guilt. I didn't mean to leave them alone for a few stressful hours. That's what it looked like happened because this is how the studio always looked on the harder days. At least they managed to have fallen asleep.

Liam was my hero. He hadn't called me once. His brow was furrowed and his jaw pulsed. I think he was clenching and grinding his teeth. Myrna made small unhappy mewing sounds.

I slowly sat down next to them, not wanting to disturb them. I opened my blouse and then reached over to ease Myrna from his hold. My breast pressed into his chest. His skin was warm. I froze. He stirred. Skin on skin, it did soothe, but it meant something completely different for me. At one point, it would have been a wholly erotic sensation. Today it felt presumptuous, making intimate contact when it wasn't appropriate. I would love to feel his skin on mine again and have him hold me. Just hold me, I had no interest in anything else.

I pulled Myrna to me, and in her sleep, she fastened and began to pull hungrily at my milk.

Liam jerked awake. "Myrna."

"I've got her," I said softly.

He eased back against the couch. I could feel the tension rolling off of him as he truly settled.

"Tough time?" I asked.

"You could say that." He ran both hands into his hair and held onto his head. "She slept for a nice chunk of time. She woke up, got a new nappy, had some tummy time. We danced around for a bit, and then everything fell apart. She got fussy but she wouldn't take any of the bottles. I tried warm, I tried warmer, I tried cold. I squirted milk into her mouth and she would lick her little lips, but she would not take the fucking nipple. Sorry."

"It's okay. It's okay. There are days nothing goes right. You got her to sleep again."

He looked down at her and ran a knuckle over her head.

"What do you do when she is so distressed? It hurt. I cried with her. I didn't know what to do. I read in one of the baby books—"

"You got baby books?" The man surprised me at every turn.

"Yeah, I did. I want to be a good father, Nica. I want to do right by her." He let out a big sigh. "I read skin contact with the small ones calms them. They can feel your heartbeat. She eventually cried herself to sleep. I think she was so hungry she didn't know what to do. I'm sorry I didn't do a very good job today." His gaze met mine. "Your hair looks lovely."

He noticed my hair. After all of that, he managed to notice my hair. I wanted to laugh and cry. Myrna's hard days could be brutal.

"I don't know what her fuss was all about. She's taken those bottles before. Ruth said she doesn't like them, but she eventually eats."

"Your sister is still mad at me, isn't she?" he asked.

"I think Ruth will always be mad at you. She holds grudges, so fair warning."

"I didn't know, Nica. I'm—"

"I know, I know." We sat quietly for a moment, watching the baby feed. She was so precious to both of us, maybe she would help heal the chasm in our ability to have a relationship.

"I like your new car," I blurted out, breaking the silence.

"I got it for Myrna. It's her car."

I chuckled, "She's a bit small for driving."

He smiled. It erased the worry from his face. "It's for her. I saw you unfolding out of that Mini. The stroller takes up the entire passenger seat. You've no room for groceries. You can't go anyplace with a second adult right now. So, I got you a bigger car."

"You got me a bigger car? Liam, I can't afford a second car."

"I will take care of everything on the car. It's Myrna's car. So, if I'm going to take her for the day, we can swap cars, or you have the Mini and I take the Flex. It's paid for. It's on my insurance. And I will make sure it's filled up at least once a week. I had the dealer install a second base for her type of car seat. That's what took so long."

"Okay. I need to fill you in on a little secret then. Car naps. Next time she gets unmanageably fussy, try putting her into her car seat and go for a ride. It seems to work really well." I rested my hand on his chest. "Thank you for everything. I'm sorry you had a hard time with her."

"Never apologize for the baby, Nica. She is always perfect, always."

"Even when she's screaming?" Myrna had stopped suckling, so I pulled her off and cuddled her sleeping form. She made a soft contented sound and smacked her lips.

Liam was right, she was perfect.

15

Liam had been over every day, so he had been with me when I got the call from Charlie to return to KoS at least part-time. And I had been with him when he got the call that filming on some prehistoric caveman type action project had their schedule fast-tracked. He needed to be on set next week— in Canada.

Liam closed the lid to the trunk and looked back at me. I wanted him to come back and pull me against him. I wanted a searing kiss to remind my soul that this man loved me until my bones went limp. He trotted back and gave Myrna the tenderest of kisses on the top of her head.

He lifted his face to me and kissed me on the cheek.

"You sure your sister will be okay watching Myrna?"

I nodded. "We've been practicing with the bottle. And I'll only be gone for half day at first."

"The second you even think you want a nanny, you call me. You hear me, Nica?"

"Liam," I sighed. "We'll be fine. We've been working out this plan for a while. Ruthie will watch Myrna while I'm part-time. When I switch to full time in a few months, Ruth will have her part-time and she'll be at daycare part-time. Ruth has already started shopping for a situation, and when she finds a few she likes, then I'll go check them out."

"I don't like it. I can cover your expenses so you don't have to work."

I gazed at him and the concern on his face. I wanted to take him up on his care of us so desperately, but I needed to stand on my own two feet. I couldn't be that completely dependent on him. "You agreed to pay for the daycare, remember?"

He nodded and wrapped me in his arms. I could have stayed there forever, Myrna in my arms, me in his.

"I'll miss you," he whispered.

He held us in a gentle hug and then let us go.

He disappeared into the back seat and the car door closed with a soft thunk.

"Daddy is off to be a hero." I turned and we went back inside. "Well, he's going to pretend to be one."

Myrna gurgled and pressed her face against mine. She still didn't quite have the muscle control to be giving me a proper kiss, but I took it as a kiss. "You do things like that so I just think you are adorable."

Another day and Myrna would not take a bottle. I had only been back to work for three days, and I had managed to work on-site for less than three hours each day before I had to leave. Charlie hadn't said anything yet, but he would have to say something soon. And it wasn't like I could work from home.

I pulled up to Ruth's house. I sat there for who knows how long, staring straight ahead into nothingness. I felt beat, but my baby was in distress. I was going to have to suck it up and figure this out.

Work could wait, Myrna could not.

"She has been a pill all day, Dani," Ruthie announced as she handed Myrna over. As if the infant could have an attitude and be doing it on purpose.

I held my unhappy one close, and I hurt for her. Her eyes were red and she had the hiccups from crying so hard. I sat in the recliner and held her to my breast. Myrna worried my nipple like a predator shaking the life from its prey. The poor girl was starving.

I fed Myrna and got her settled against the back of the couch with pillows blocking her in while she slept. How was this supposed to work if I had to come to Myrna to feed her every day?

"I'm sorry this isn't going smoothly," I apologized to Ruth. She volunteered to watch Myrna when I worked. But if Myrna wasn't going to settle while I was away, I just didn't know how I was going to be able to keep working. I groaned. If I didn't work, how was I going to survive?

Why did everything have to be so difficult today?

"She just needs to adjust and then she'll stop giving me a hard time." Again, there was Ruth's attitude that Myrna was doing this on purpose.

"It's not like she is doing it to annoy you, Ruthie."

"She wants her mother, that's why she's doing it," Ruth said.

I sighed. Myrna wanted to be fed and to be comforted. She didn't want to be left alone in her sling chair. She wanted to be held. I didn't have a clue how much Ruth was changing her routine to fit in the baby, but I suspected she expected Myrna to be ready for mimosas and gossip at brunch.

"I'm going to take her home and spend the day cuddling," I announced.

"If you don't let her work it out of her system, she'll constantly be manipulating you."

"Oh come on, Ruth. She's a baby, she is not manipulating me." I was so frustrated with Ruth. Had been for months. Had been my entire life.

"You came didn't you?"

"Of course I did. You called. Myrna was inconsolable and distressed." I threw my arms up and let them fall to my side.

I grabbed the car seat and brought it over to the baby. Careful not to wake her, I buckled her in.

"Keep the bottles I brought over this morning. They'll still be good tomorrow."

I waved over my shoulder as I carried Myrna out to the car. Liam had been right, the Flex was easier to maneuver in and out of. Fortunately, she slept the entire drive home. However, once home she began fussing again. I picked her up. She felt warm. Not snuggly baby warm but like she had a fever. No wonder she had been upset all morning.

I checked her temperature, a violation of her dignity, and called the nurse at her pediatrician. I needed to keep an eye on her temperature, and make sure she was feeding, and making wet diapers. The nurse also told me how much of a dose of baby Motrin I could give.

I ordered some Chinese delivery, turned on the TV, found a movie I liked and kicked back on the couch. I spent my afternoon holding Myrna, letting her nurse when she needed comfort, and eating Chow Fun and Orange Chicken.

We napped off and on. Her fever never got too hot, and I felt as if I was mastering my baby's first illness.

My phone buzzed. "Daddy is calling to see how you are doing," I told Myrna.

I had texted Liam earlier to let him know the girl was running a small fever.

"How is she?" he asked.

"She's not happy, but she'll be okay. Her fever hasn't gone over 102. She's nursing, she has pass through. Mostly, she sleeps or wants to be held."

"Are you going in to work tomorrow?"

"I can't. I can't give Myrna to Ruth when she's like this. Today, Ruth said that Myrna was being manipulative. She's barely five months old, she's not capable of being manipulative." I sighed. My mama bear came out strong today.

"What did Charlie say?" Liam reminded me that I needed to talk to Charlie directly. This working situation wasn't working. I needed more time or something else.

"He hasn't said anything yet. I haven't talked to him."

"Give him a call. Kiss my girl for me." He sounded concerned.

"I will. Goodnight, Liam."

"Goodnight, Nica." He ended the call.

I immediately called Charlie.

"I'm sorry to bother you at home," I said as soon as he answered.

"How's the baby?" His concern for Myrna filled my heart. No chastisement for ditching work again, straight to asking about my daughter.

"She's running a fever. The nurse said everything is fine, and I'm watching her temperature."

"If you need anything, you let us know. You know Linda thinks the world of that baby."

I smiled. Charlie was a good guy. I hated to be such a

lousy employee. "I'm going to need to take a couple of days, I think. Make sure Myrna is okay."

I could hear him making noises, so I knew he was listening, but as soon as I started talking work, he stopped talking.

"Charlie?"

"Dani, you need to take care of that baby. We'll figure the rest of this out. You've been in for a few hours for a couple of days. So next week, let's try again, maybe for a few more hours?"

"Thank you, Charlie." I blinked back tears. Maybe next week I could propose doing some design work from home. Compartmentalize the job instead of taking a project from start to finish, to working on set.

I still had baby hormones surging through my system, and crying seemed easier than blinking some days.

I bundled Myrna up in my arms and crawled into bed. She nursed off and on all night long. I felt like I slept maybe five minutes. I gave up and decided to get out of bed. Maybe if I got the day started, I would feel better. I sat up and tucked my boob back into my sleep bra. I felt kicked. My forehead felt slightly feverish. Maybe I was getting the same thing.

Panic flooded my system. What if I had given Myrna the mini flu or something? I made my baby sick. What kind of a mother was I? If I found out one of the guys at work and brought in something from home or one of their germy kids. The rage left me as quickly as it reared up. Only it left me completely wiped out.

I staggered to the bathroom. My eyeballs felt warm. I hated that feeling. I popped a few ibuprofen and made my way to the kitchen. I made some tea since Myrna didn't like second-hand coffee converted to breast milk, and heated up some of the Egg FooYung I ordered the day before.

I ate less of my breakfast than expected. Once the food was in my mouth, I wasn't hungry anymore.

I lay down and watched Myrna sleep. Her forehead felt normal. I hoped she was in for a better day today.

I dozed. The next time I woke, Myrna was fussing, wanting to be nursed. I felt worse than the first time I woke up. She nursed, she fussed, she grunted, and then she had the biggest diaper blow out. No wonder she hadn't felt good the day before. I don't know how she had had that much poop in her little body. I couldn't face clean up. I wasn't up for it. I threw out the entire outfit with the diaper and my T-shirt. I took her into the shower with me. It seemed easier that way.

Once all of that was out of her system, she was back to being a happy baby. Unfortunately, it was my turn to be fussy and unhappy. I was still mad at Ruth, so I called Charlie. Besides, he also lived closer. Had I been clearer-headed I would have arranged for grocery delivery.

"Hey, boss."

"Dani, how is Myrna doing this morning?" I loved how he asked about her before anything else.

"Myrna seems to be doing great. I seem to have picked up what she had. Could I trouble you to swing by the store and grab me some canned soups and ginger ale?"

He never once told me to call someone else.

A few hours later, Linda arrived with bags of groceries.

"Charlie said you needed some backup. I got all kinds of soup and soda for you. Let me look at you."

She deposited her shopping bags on my counter, never saying a word about the mess.

She placed her cool hands on my face.

"Oh Dani, you are warm. When was the last time you took something?" she asked.

"I don't know. When I got up?" My day deteriorated quickly into a bleary mishmash of everything running together. I nursed. Myrna peed. I changed diapers. She giggled and kicked on her play mat. I put Sesame Street on. We did it all over again.

"Go take something, and I'll make you some soup. How's your tummy? You think you can eat some soup?" Linda asked from the kitchen as I went to the bathroom for the medication.

"Soup sounds good," I mumbled.

Linda fed me soup and put me to bed. "I'll watch Myrna, we'll be fine." She closed my bedroom curtain and I finally got some sleep.

~

Liam looked down at me, worry creased his brow. He looked odd. I couldn't figure out why at first.

Oh right, he was here. He was supposed to be in Canada filming, and his hair was longer.

"Why are you here?" My voice sounded like a frog. I pushed myself up and back against some pillows.

Oh, that was a bad idea. Everything tilted sideways and I heaved my lunch onto the sheets.

"Oh gross. I'm sorry. I'll clean that up." I tried to get up but, everything spun like a tilt-a-whirl. I thought I was going to throw up again.

"You aren't going to do a damned thing, Nica. Lay still for a moment."

Where was Myrna? Linda had been here, was she still? And how had Liam gotten here?

"Okay baby, hold tight." I felt him lift me, and then I was laying on the couch. I didn't remember him moving me. A cool cloth was on my head. Not placed, wiped over my face and neck. I could hear Myrna crying.

I heard Linda's voice. I tried to open my eyes but the spinning started up again, so I closed them. Sound bites of the world drifted around and in and out of my awareness.

"Her hair is clean, thank goodness."

"Pediatrician's number is on the fridge."

"Laundry is around back."

"Add the powder first."

"You still need to warm the bottle up."

I was back in bed with clean sheets.

The next time I tried to open my eyes again, I realized it was a mistake immediately and closed them. I found a pillow to hold on to, so I wouldn't fall. I may have been lying down, but the falling sensation was intense.

I patted my arm around on the bed next to me. I could tell someone was in bed with me. I found large firm muscles of an arm and worked my hand up until teeth and lips caught my hand.

"Hey," I cried out indignantly. "I thought you were in Canada?"

"Montana. I came back when I found out you were sick." Liam's voice was soft and gravely.

"You didn't have to do that."

"Yes, I did. You are the mother of my child and you needed help."

My breath hitched. I was going to cry again.

"Where's Linda?" I asked.

"She went home."

"Oh no, she was supposed to only be here long enough for me to take a nap. Where's Myrna?" I panicked. I didn't hear her. My boobs let me know I hadn't fed her for hours.

I tried to sit up. Big mistake. Nausea hit me like a

tsunami. I clamped my teeth together and groaned. I held perfectly still willing the sensation to pass. Liam stroked my arm. It was too much. I grabbed his hand to hold everything still.

"Are you okay?"

I groaned, unwilling to try to speak. I lay still breathing heavily through my nose. Eventually, the sick feeling eased and I could swallow.

"Dizzy. Myrna?"

"She's asleep."

"So what happened with Linda? How are you here?" I think he had just told me, but I wasn't sure.

"When you didn't call or text me, I worried. So I started calling like an idiot. Eventually, Linda got sick of me blowing up your phone so she answered it. Told me you were sick and Myrna was having a hard time adjusting to the bottle, and you were almost out of pumped milk."

I groaned. I hadn't meant to put so much on Linda. If I hadn't been mad at Ruth, I would have called her. Family should have been helping out, not my boss's wife.

"I should call her," I croaked.

"When you're better. We owe her and Charlie a big gift basket or something, like a weekend in Cancun," Liam chuckled.

"Linda is a miracle worker. She stayed and got Myrna to finally take a bottle. And she helped me clean up a bit after you puked all over the bed."

I groaned in shame. I would have tried to hide my head, except moving a little caused the world to spin a lot.

"I haven't pumped. There wasn't enough milk."

"That's covered." Liam sounded overly smug.

I tempted fate and cracked an eye open to look at him. It was a futile effort, everything was dark. I couldn't see.

"We called the pediatrician. I explained who I was and what our situation was, and the doctor recommended we go ahead and try out two different formulas. Myrna really likes the first one we tried. So you don't need to worry about that."

"But I'm breastfeeding!" I cried. I had struggled with getting that to work at the beginning. There were some therapy grade issues I had with lactation consultants about my validity as a mother because I wanted to give up. This felt like some kind of blow. The decision to put Myrna on formula was taken away from me, and I was too sick to get up and fight.

Strong arms wrapped around me and eased me against a warm chest. "And you still can. But you are sick, Nica, and I needed to take care of our daughter."

"How do you know I'll be able to breastfeed again?" My voice stuttered as I cried. "You aren't a doctor."

"No, but I've been reading those baby books. And I look things up like crazy. So far, everything I've read said you should be able to nurse again."

"Nipple confusion." I blathered.

"Our girl is smart enough to figure it out. And thanks to Linda's patience, our girl can."

"Linda got Myrna to take a bottle?" My voice was small.

"She did. She scolded me for giving up so soon when I couldn't do it. Myrna just needed to get hungry enough, and have a squirt of milk on the nipple to let her know what was what."

I relaxed into Liam. Myrna was okay, was going to be okay, and I could learn to adjust.

"Now we just need you to get better." His soft strokes against my arm soothed this time. "I made an appointment with my doctor to come see you tomorrow. This dizzy thing you have worries me."

"Vertigo. It sucks. I get it sometimes when I get the flu. I had the flu right?"

"Probably. Linda said that's what it was. You don't have a fever anymore, so possibly. Try to go back to sleep, maybe you'll feel even better in the morning."

"Right, I'm sorry. Woke you up in the middle of the night?"

"Hmm hmm."

I played with his long hair until I fell asleep.

The next morning, I wasn't able to sit up, but I was able to open my eyes and watch as Liam and his private doctor moved around the small apartment.

I didn't even know that doctors made house calls anymore. I guess the rich had a whole different level of services that us peasants couldn't even imagine.

The doctor, a pleasant-looking middle-aged man gave Myrna a quick once over before visiting with me. The official diagnosis was vertigo. The rapid introduction and departure of the flu left me with excess fluid in my inner ear. I was given a heavy decongestant and diuretic and told to follow up with my OBGYN regarding the breastfeeding situation. While I took the medicines and for a few days after, I should not breastfeed. But for how long?

I had trust issues regarding taking any medication that negated or added something not good into my system. After all, my little surprise Myrna happened because I hadn't understood that antibiotics and the pill did not play well for the entire month.

A few hours later, I felt well enough to sit up without the world spinning. I was finally able to really look at Liam. "How the hell is your hair longer?"

16

I sat up for the first time in a long time. Okay, it had only been a few days but it felt like a very long time. Liam stepped into the bedroom with Myrna in his arms. His hair was weird, but Myrna squealed when she saw me and all of my attention was on her. It was indescribable to have her in my arms again. She smiled and her little headed bobbed and ducked as she worked those baby back and neck muscles gaining control. She gave me a wide-open mouth gummy kiss on the side of my face.

"I missed you so much, Love-bug." I wiggled my face into her tummy and she giggled.

That wasn't the smartest thing to do. I lay her on the bed between my legs and closed my eyes. I breathed slowly in and out through my mouth trying to find my center again.

The bed dipped. "Dizzy spell?"

I clamped my hand down on his arm and willed everything to stop spinning. "Yep."

"Open your eyes and focus on the far wall."

"It's spinning," I complained.

"Nothing is spinning, you'll be fine."

I took a deep breath and focused across the room. The curtain was open so I was able to see all the way to the front wall of the living room.

Liam was right. Nothing moved.

I wanted to rest my head against his shoulder, but I thought anything other than upright might be a bad idea for the moment.

I played with Myrna's feet, getting her to use her strong little legs to push against my hands.

I let my hand rest on his shoulder, and then begin to play with his magically long hair. "I thought it was a wig, but your hair is still really long."

"Extensions. And they did a good job." He flipped his hair to the side so I could see where they had braided, and then stitched the longer lengths into place. He fingered along the connections. "I haven't had time to go get them removed."

"Shouldn't you be on set?" I asked.

"I kind of got fired."

"Can they do that? I thought, contracts and such."

"Well, technically, they hadn't begun filming when I walked off set. So, the studio is calling it a difference of opinion, and I was replaced."

"Difference of opinion?" I asked

"I was of the opinion that I needed to leave. You needed me. The director was of the opinion that I needed to stay. I believe his exact words were, 'if you leave now, don't bother coming back.' So, I contacted my agent on the flight and..." He made a flip with his hand. "We officially parted ways."

"Aren't you going to feel bad if it's a huge success?" I asked.

"No. I've got another Seb Hale coming up. This way, I can help out with Myrna as you transition back to work.

Charlie will be glad to hear you're feeling better. And you should probably call your sister. She hangs up every time I answer your phone."

I sighed. Ruth was going to do her best to make things difficult for us until she settled down.

And that wasn't going to happen anytime soon. After a week off with Liam taking care of everything, it was time to admit I had to go back to work. Charlie was willing to be flexible with my schedule, Ruthie was not.

"You clearly don't need me in your life now that you have that cheating bastard—"

I hung up on her. My reactions to her mouth were not making this any easier. I needed the help she had offered, and Myrna needed her aunt in her life.

About ten minutes later my phone rang. "Hi, Mom."

"I wish you girls could get along."

"I wish Ruthie would stop being a bitch about Liam."

"She says you cut her out of Myrna's life the second he gets back in town."

"Mom!" I was so frustrated with all of this I almost felt like it would be easier if I just went ahead and did what Ruth accused me of.

"You don't have to yell, Danica."

"I do, you aren't listening to me any more than Ruthie is. I did not cut her out. I was sick. My boss's wife had to come over and take care of me because Ruth was pitching a fit. And then my child's father came over and took care of us."

"Why doesn't he just get a nanny? Why is he making you work if he's so involved?"

"Because that's not the relationship we have right now. He's barely known about Myrna and he's stepping up in a big way. But I never once told Ruth she was cut off. She's doing that to herself," I complained.

"I'm going to talk to her."

"Mom..." But she had already disconnected.

Mom was never very hands-on once I hit being a preteen. She figured we were fairly self-sufficient and left us to it unless Ruthie and I argued in front of her. Then she was arbitrator supreme. It was as if we only had one rule she cared about, Ruth and I had to get along. We did for the most part, but at times like this, my limits were tested.

~

"You know I hate to ask this of you." I unloaded an arm full of toys into the sparse and wide-open space Liam called a living room. Stunning didn't adequately describe his house. Inside was all concrete, steel, glass, and hard angles. Outside was all air and sky and view.

Baby proofing would ruin the aesthetic. I guess it was a good thing Myrna wasn't mobile yet. But as soon as she figured out how to move, he was going to have to baby proof this place in a big way.

"Nica, everything will be fine. Myrnoula will help me with the new assistant."

"Oh God, is that today?" I had completely forgotten that he hired yet another assistant.

He smiled a knee-weakening grin at me. They would be fine. Myrna was doing well with the bottle. I pumped this morning so my boobs wouldn't hurt, and the doctor said by the end of the week, we could return to breastfeeding during the times I was home or I could start weening if that was better for us.

I followed him into the kitchen, more concrete, steel, and glass. It was architecturally a gorgeous place, and the bank of windows looked over the other houses and out to the ocean. It was a bachelor movie star's perfect house. A new high chair stood out like a sore thumb amidst the designer setting. Liam swung my Love-bug into the chair, and she rewarded him with a giggle.

"You know I am always happy to spend time with our girl. And your sister will come around. She'll miss this one soon enough." He rubbed his nose into Myrna's tummy.

"She needs to hurry up and get her head out of her ass. You've got Comic-Con coming up."

"I cou—"

I cut him off. "You cannot skip that for anything."

"I'm not going to. I was going to say I could hire a nanny."

"You can't even hire an assistant, what makes you think you could get a nanny?"

"I'll fly my mum in for the week if I have to. If your sister is still not talking to you, don't worry, I will make sure you have the support you need."

I was surprised to find him standing in front of me with his hands on my hips. I wanted to say 'I love you,' instead, I squeaked out a thank you.

"You never have to thank me for taking care of our daughter." He leaned down and gave me the most domestic peck on the mouth. "Go to work."

I almost couldn't move, paralyzed in place by a perfunctory go-to-work kiss.

I don't know how I got to work that morning. All I could think about was that quick, lip closed kiss of familiarity.

I hated the inadequacy I felt every single time I pulled into Liam's neighborhood. And it seemed to be getting worse with each day. It was that cosmic slam of not being able to properly provide for my daughter. The universe reminding me, again, that I lived in a garage, that I would never be able to afford a home like this even though I had a good job that paid well.

It seeped in like an oozy tar around the edges of my consciousness. I didn't even want to live here but the ooze made sure I knew I couldn't. Sure the house was great, but the street view of his wasn't anything much, mostly a garage door, a small entry and a solid wall of grey stucco. Once through the entry, there was a tiny courtyard with a fountain, and then the entry into the house. This really wasn't a neighborhood, it was a street with expensive houses hidden behind walls. No sidewalks and no parking. Liam was lucky because he actually had a small driveway with off-street parking.

I didn't recognize the sleek Mercedes in the drive. Liam's Jeep was typically tucked into the garage, so seeing any car was a bit of a surprise.

I parked and passed through the gate into the courtyard.

An older lady, dressed to match the Mercedes, meaning very high dollar, swept out of the gate. She had Myrna in her arms and turned to laugh at something Liam said as he followed her out.

Myrna had a pudgy grip firmly on one of the gold loop earrings. Sharp gray eyes made contact with mine, and the woman gave me her smile. "You must be the mother."

I was the mother of the baby she held, but who was she?

"Myrna looks just like you. She is so precious. I just love her name, Myrna. It's so deliciously old fashioned, it sounds like a purr." She scrunched up her face and rubbed noses with the baby, repeating her name.

Myrna was delighted with the attention. Another hapless victim lured in to her sweetness and light.

Liam came and stood next to me. "Danica, this is Maggie Fletcher," he introduced us.

I said hi, but didn't shake her hand since her arms were full of Myrna.

She rubbed noses with Myrna again. "Oh, I hate giving them back, but I can't keep them. My grandchildren are in Atlanta, I do miss them. They're older, so it's been a while since I've had a baby to charm me." She hoisted Myrna up and handed her toward Liam.

Myrna kicked and reached for me, so mid handoff Maggie switched directions and handed me the baby.

"You two have a lot to discuss, but I look forward to hearing from you." She shook Liam's hand and patted Myrna on the head. "Such a beautiful girl."

"Thank you," I said as she walked out the gate.

I whirled on Liam. Obviously, Maggie wasn't a nanny interview. Liam had stated if he was going to hire a nanny the person would have to be grandmotherly. He was done with assistants falling in love with him. Apparently, the last batch of interviewees had turned up several flirts and one proposition. But Maggie had been too posh for a nanny. She had a marketing vibe about her. I just didn't know what.

I followed Liam back inside. The hard edges and polished concrete were now rimmed with foam pool noodles. Not that Myrna was mobile, but he had taken special care of making his home safe for her.

I flopped onto the couch while holding her. I was tired and feeling inadequate. Myrna grabbed at my face and put her wide open mouth on my cheek in a happy slobbery baby face-eating kiss. This is what I needed. A stab of jealousy for Liam being able to stay home with her all day prickled in my chest. Then again I knew exactly how exhausting managing Myrna was. He was beat too.

Liam collapsed next to me and handed me a glass of chardonnay. A hidden benefit of not breastfeeding, I could have wine.

"So you gonna tell me who Maggie Fletcher is?"

"Maggie Fletcher is a real estate agent. I'm putting the house on the market."

My stomach plummeted all the way down the side of the cliff. If he was leaving LA, that meant he was returning home to England and I wouldn't see him. Myrna wouldn't have her father helping to raise her.

My hand shook as I placed my wine glass on the foam wrapped coffee table.

"When did you decide to move?" My voice was smooth as silk. There was no way he would be able to hear my internal wails of pain.

"I started thinking about it that first day I had Myrna over. This place is not conducive to children."

I felt my lungs fill with air, apparently, I had stopped breathing.

"Too many stairs. Every room is on a different level. And the way this place is built, there really isn't an easy way to install baby gates. I had a guy come out to give me an estimate, and he did a lot of head shaking. He's the one who suggested the pool noodles." Liam waved his water bottle around indicating all of the padding duct-taped to the corners and ledges.

"Also, I'm more than a little concerned with the balconies. I have nightmares—"

I held up my hand cutting him off. I did not need him to voice that fear, I had it too. Crawling baby, glassed-in balcony, bad combination.

"So you aren't moving, moving? I mean relocating back to England?"

"Why would I do that? You and Myrna are here. I couldn't go back to England without my girl."

I thought for a second he may have said *girls*. I wasn't certain as he had taken a swig of water just then.

"So where are you looking?"

He shook his head. "I haven't started yet. That was one of the things Maggie was here to discuss. What to do with this place, and what kind of house will Myrna need to grow up in."

He took her from me and held her on his knee. He bounced her and she could look at both of us. She deserved the very best. Okay, maybe I wasn't failing as a mother. I had managed to give her a pretty amazing father who loved her. That's what really mattered.

"What's on your dream list for a house?" Liam stood up, one hand scooped under Myrna's booty so he could carry her one-handed.

I followed him into the kitchen. The warm savory smells of roast wrapped around me and invited me in to peek into pots. It turned out Liam's new assistant had a hidden talent for cooking.

I opened the oven and the aroma of dinner made my muscles relax. This was wonderful, coming home to Liam and Myrna and not having to worry about dinner.

"Myrna needs a yard with a swing set," I said as I poked at the food. It looked like it needed another half hour or so.

Liam filled a pan with water and rice. He was quite mobile with the kid in tow.

"Need me to take her?"

He shook his head, not willing to let go of her.

"Then allow me." I hip bumped him gently and took

over, picking up the measuring cup and pouring in rice from the container set aside. The note stuck to the front included all the instructions, including when to start the rice, and for how long to set the timer. Maybe this assistant would work out; meal prep notes, and apparently, Myrna liked him.

"I agree, Myrna needs room to run and play. But I'm asking what do you want?"

"Ooh, can I get my own room? And I'd love a bathtub, one of those super huge ones. This is going to sound nuts but I've always wanted a copper sink in my kitchen. And it has to be a two-part sink. I don't mind dirty dishes hanging out in the sink, but I hate not being able to use it. So one side for use, and one to toss dishes in."

"Sinks are easy enough to replace. But a big bathroom, okay. How many rooms?"

I shrugged. I really had never thought about it. "I guess I always figured I'd get a basic house when I grew up and had kids. You know everybody gets their own bedroom, at least two bathrooms, an eat-in kitchen, and a formal dining room. I'd love an entry so that I'm not walking straight in from the outside to the living room like I have now."

I put the lid on the rice and set the timer. "What do you want?"

Liam slid his eyes from side to side and grimaced, showing me his teeth. "I don't know." He sucked in a breath. "I mean, I bought my famous-actor place. It's pretty, not practical. I've never put much thought into it either."

"We should probably think about school districts. Right?" School was a very big reality in the next five years.

"Districts? You mean locations."

"No, districts. She'll need to be in a district with good schools. I'd be willing to live in a smaller place if I can get her into better schools."

I can't believe we were discussing school already. The girl couldn't even sit up on her own. I guess this made us responsible adults and parents. I sighed.

"I can't afford private schools, Liam. She'll be in the public school system."

"I think I can afford better schools."

Oh, we were talking on two completely different socio-economic levels. "You're thinking private school. Okay."

"I said I would take care of her. That means clothing, food, schools."

"Cars and houses too?" My gut tightened. If he made a play for custody, I would lose. I might be mommy, but daddy wanted her and daddy had money.

I felt wobbly. I must have looked peaked too.

"Nica, are you alright? Sit down before you fall down." With his free hand, Liam guided me to a chair.

He placed his hand on my cheek and I wanted to lean into his touch.

"You don't feel warm. Having a dizzy spell? How long has it been since you had anything to eat?"

"Dinner is almost ready," I pointed out. I swallowed my concern and decided not to bring it up. What Liam didn't think about I didn't need to plant those idea seeds.

Talk of taking care of Myrna turned to immediate needs as she made those noises that indicated she was going to need a serious diaper change in a few moments. While he was off changing and getting her cleaned up I gulped down air and talked myself away from the newest panic ledge I faced. I was already feeling money pangs with juggling taking care of her and having been off work for four months. Driving around grand houses wouldn't help. Hell, even cruising through Ruth's neighborhood of reasonable houses gave me issues.

Liam came back in, pulled a bottle from the fridge and popped it into the bottle warmer. "I think she'll be out by the time our dinner is ready."

He was right. She was heavy-lidded and a little fussy. He managed quite well without me. Myrna no longer needed me now that she was on formula. My heart shattered and tears overflowed my eyes. There was no controlling it.

Liam shifted his glance to me and he closed his eyes. Yeah, I was failing at everything today.

"Come on." He hooked a finger under my arm and led me back into the living room. He sat me in the corner of the couch and placed Myrna in my arms.

I held her while she fed. Her big eyes looked into mine and her lids drooped. She fought it, never fully breaking eye contact with me. Eventually, she drained the bottle and made a shuddering sigh as she finally fell all the way to sleep.

"Why don't you go put her in bed? Dinner is ready." Liam's voice was soft and quiet.

He seemed to understand. She may not need me, but I needed her.

By the time I finished my dinner, my lids were heavy and I was fighting to stay awake.

"You are so done in, Nica. Why don't you stay the night?"

I nodded and took myself off to the guest room where Liam had set up bumpers so Myrna wouldn't fall out of bed. She would wake up from her evening nap soon enough, I needed what rest I could get. I'm not sure how much later it was when I heard her fussing. I woke to see Liam picking her up.

"I've got her, go back to sleep."

Hours later, I woke up again. I was overtired and not sleeping well. I flipped onto my back and stared at the ceiling. I saw a shift in the light out of the corner of my eye. At first, I thought it was light from traffic, and then I realized we were way too high up on the cliff for traffic to reflect off the ceiling, and the blinds were closed. As I closed my eyes again, I saw him.

I stared at him, he didn't seem to see me. Or maybe he did, but he said nothing.

It was weird to see him this way. I wasn't used to actually seeing him with my eyes open, but there he was, shadow and light. Well mostly light, the areas of shadow were see-through. He was a true specter, the ghost of Flint Reese.

I didn't get that odd feeling of static electricity I had gotten used to when he had been around. No goosebumps, no tingles along the back of my neck.

"Flint?"

He floated out the door. I twisted out of bed and followed him.

"Flint!" It was him, and I know he heard me, he had to.

I followed him down the hall and up the few steps. Liam was right, no two rooms in this house were on the same freaking level. So many stairs, and all concrete. Another set of steps and Flint turned into another room. The door was cracked, I pushed it open the rest of the way. Liam's bedroom was huge. I caught my breath as Liam's presence washed over me. The room felt warm and had his distinct scent. He smelled good and comforting.

I watched as the Flint ghost rolled into the sleeping form of Liam.

Stunned, I didn't move for what felt like an eternity. I watched as Liam's back rose and fell as he breathed.

"Flint?" I whispered.

Nothing.

I crossed the room, my toes grabbing onto the shag

carpeting as I crept up to Liam. I reached out to put my hand on his shoulder. What was I doing?

Liam shifted and made small grunts in his sleep.

I froze, hand extended. It was hard to breathe, and I swear my heart made the loudest crashing noise as it banged in my chest, the sound echoing around the concrete cavern. With a loud snore of a sound, Liam rolled over and grabbed my wrist.

I wanted to pull away, I wanted to run. I also wanted to know what was going on.

Liam didn't say anything, his eyes still closed.

"Flint?" I asked again.

"I found you." It was barely a sigh, and possibly not even words. He let go of my wrist and continued to roll over. Liam was in full deep sleep, his breathing even. It was if he hadn't said anything at all.

I wanted to crawl in and curl into him, sleep like we once had. I reached over and moved a lock of hair away from his brow. I saw so much of Myrna in his sleeping face.

I woke up from my dream, Myrna was asleep on one side and Liam was curled around me on the other. Not in his bed, in his room, but here with us. How did I tell him this is what I wanted most in a home for Myrna?

17

"Danica." Ruth's voice was full of sharp edges and disapproval. "Can I help you?"

Maybe this hadn't been the best idea. I swallowed my pride. "How've you been?"

"I've been fine, Danica, can we skip the pleasantries and cut to it?"

I hoped all of this venom wasn't because of me. All I had done was get sick and let the father of my child take care of me. I didn't dare call him boyfriend, or partner. I didn't know what we were just yet. Something beyond co-parents I hoped.

"All right." I took a breath and hoped Mom got through to her. "At one point in time, you offered to help me with childcare for Myrna. I was wondering if you would still consider this, or have you completely changed your mind?"

I couldn't get any straighter forward than that.

She cackled. "So, did he leave you again and now you're stuck?"

I closed my eyes. I would not kill my sister. I would not kill my sister.

"No, Liam did not leave me. But he does need to go back to work. He was never supposed to take care of Myrna for more than a couple of days while I was sick. I haven't been able to find a daycare just yet, and so I thought I would see if your original offer was still available or not."

"Of course, you just needed to ask." The tone in her voice was the complete opposite of how this conversation started.

I let out the breath I held.

"When do you need Myrna to come over?"

"Ruthie you're a lifesaver. Can I start bringing her by next week?" I gushed, and Ruthie hummed. It's what she wanted, to be the hero.

"Of course, do you still need me to just watch her three days?"

"Yeah. I'm still just at twenty hours. Myrna is taking the bottle so much better these days, and she's on formula half-time now. So things should be much easier."

"I am glad to hear that. She's always been such an easy baby."

My sister could spin around on a dime without blinking, and make me be the one to think I was insane because she changed her mind. Myrna had gone from "manipulative" to "so good" in the speed of a blink. At least Ruth now thought the baby was easy.

We finished making arrangements for Myrna to stay again. From what Ruthie said, I expected her to be willing to take Myrna on for more hours as my time with KoS increased, and she said she would start looking at that list of daycares she had found.

That was a huge weight off my shoulders. I needed to call Mom and thank her for talking my sister off that ledge.

Nerves danced through my body as I approached

Ruthie's house. This was stupid. I shouldn't be nervous delivering my child to her aunt, who had taken care of her before.

The door opened and Ruth's attention went straight to the baby. "She's gotten so big!" In seconds she had Myrna out of the car seat and in her arms.

Liam had been right, she would realize she missed Myrna and everything would re-right itself back to the way it needed to be.

With Myrna and Ruth enchanted with each other, I let myself out and sat in the car and cried before heading into work.

"All is good with Ruth." I texted Liam.

"But how are you?" he asked.

Did he know?

"I'll be fine. I'll miss her when I'm at work like I always do."

"She misses you too. I've seen it. I'll miss you both this weekend."

"Yeah." I couldn't bring myself to admit I would miss him, because if I did then the next thing out of my mouth would be I love you, and I just didn't know... *"You too, Liam."*

Comic-Con was the biggest thing going for comic books, and all of geekdom that surrounded them, directly and adjacent. Sci-fi, comics, anime, books, movies, and TV shows. Liam was a double dipper having starred in the cable version of the graphic novel series *Tails from the Urban Jungle* and in the most recent blockbuster from the library of *The Time-traveling Adventures of Sebastian Hale* stories. He'd be lucky if he had time to shoot me and the girl a quick text message between all of the promo appearances, and panels, and schmoozey parties. He would be going non-stop, and he would have a lot of fun.

Charlie was there, in a different capacity. He had his ear

to the ground to catch the rumors of upcoming projects that he might want to hone in on. I'd gone with him in the past to listen in on how our sets were received by the fans. Always an intense few days, always fun, and always worth the time and exhaustion.

Without Liam around the depression seeped in a little more.

I didn't know how to express the feelings I experienced. Hell, they barely felt like feelings. They felt like exhaustion, commitment, obligation. It was slogging and difficult work.

Anything and everything I had done in my life for the past eight years I revisited with tweezer-and-magnifying-glass scrutiny. How could I have changed the outcome? Why didn't I have the outcome I thought I wanted? How could I go back and change everything?

I would wake up because I couldn't breathe.

My apartment felt confining, constricting. I ran outside just to breathe more than once. I had waking nightmares of dropping Myrna. At those times I would look into the side crib, assure myself that everything was all right, and then stay up for hours just watching her breathe. She was here, she was safe.

I hadn't forgotten to feed her or change her diapers. I hadn't left her at Ruth's and then not been able to remember.

I started to look up my foibles on line so many times. Each time, I either couldn't complete filling out the search field, or I would not click on the links.

When I finally clicked on one of the links, I fell down a rabbit hole of patient cure thyself bullshit. Blogs that looked like they had useful articles denied the existence of post-partum depression, others tried to sell me essential oils to get out of my funk. And too many of them assumed I had a partner who could help me with my burden of guilt. I didn't assume anything regarding Liam.

Guilt that I had brought a baby into this world for the most selfish of reasons: I loved her father and I was going to love her. I kept her because she was part of the greatest love of my life, and the embodiment of his afterlife. Only now I couldn't adequately provide for her. We lived in a converted garage. I could barely take care of myself. I collapsed in on myself and cried so many nights it wasn't even funny.

I found an online group of women who all had babies around the same time. I thought if anyone would understand me, it would be them. Vipers. Every last one of them was evil and catty and bitchy. Mostly, first-time mothers, but they would gang up and shame each other over the stupidest things, from diapers to the brand of pacifier they chose. Moms were shamed for breastfeeding, for not breastfeeding. For introducing soft cereals, for following their doctor's advice.

No one had started a thread of discussion regarding postpartum, so I started one. Apparently, I argued with the golden child regarding the unique difficulties that a single mother faced compared to that of one with a live-in partner. I was blocked from the group.

That was probably for the best.

I returned to doing what I knew I could do. I took care of my baby the best I could.

"Dani, I think you might need to watch this."

"What is it?" I swiveled in my chair, pencil still tapping away. I was interrupted mid-contemplation on this design.

The reality was, my numb, over-tired brain was not functioning.

"Feed from Comic-Con."

"Sure." I sighed. Liam was there. I could use the distraction.

Viv slid her laptop onto my drawing table, and not on top of my sketch pad.

"It's one of those YouTube fandom channels, they are having a field day at Comic-Con."

"How did you find it?" I asked.

Viv tilted her head to the side like I was some kind of idiot. She found it because it was her job right now to track any press that involved our big-budget productions where we might be mentioned, and any mentions of King of the Scene. We all kind of did a lot of everything for Charlie: design, build, monitor social media, answer phones.

Right. I hit the arrow starting the video.

I tried not to smile, which meant my cheeks tightened and I bit my lip. Liam looked really good sitting there in his Seb Hale costume, kilt, no shirt. Sigh. There was a moment of awkwardness as he had no place to clip the mic. The film sped up and in a comedic action sequence, someone gave him a zippered hoodie to attach the mic to.

"That's better," he said smoothing down his kilt.

It was possibly more distracting with the hoodie only zipped part of the way up exposing flashes of skin.

"Can you explain your choice of clothing today?" the interviewer asked.

Liam went off on a wild explanation of wanting to have fun, why not cosplay his own character?

The video cut and an image of Liam in a throng of similarly dressed hard bodies flashed across the screen. Seb

Hale was a big hit with the cosplayers this year. And that was a very good thing.

"Are you planning on joining the Johnny Urban contingent?"

Another image of a group of men with tiger tattoos across their chests flashed up. A few furries in full tiger costume also posed in the group. It was an impressive collection.

"I'm no longer blond, besides that tattoo takes a long time," Liam told the interviewer as he rubbed his chest where the large tiger tattoo had been applied when he had that role.

I hit pause. I would happily sit here and watch Liam for hours, but I didn't want to give anyone at work that ammo. I was still very uncertain what exactly our relationship was. I looked up at Viv. "It's a standard interview." I started to hand back the laptop.

She pressed it back down. "Just wait."

She dragged her finger over the scroll bar moving the interview forward.

"...secret family?"

Oh God, is that what Myrna and I were? A secret? Something to be hidden?

Liam shifted in his seat and laughed. "I do have a family, but I wouldn't call them a secret."

"We weren't able to find anything out about them, only there was a rumor that you were let go from the *Mammoth Killers* project because of domestic issues. But since you are still on the slate for that... well, we're curious, and if we are, your fans are."

Liam let out a bit of a sigh. "My family isn't a secret, but I'm learning to keep my personal life personal. And yes, I did walk off set. At the time, I felt my reasons were valid and Whitmore Jaspers did not."

"Those reasons were?"

"My family needed me." That's all he said. My heart doubled in speed.

"He's talking about you, isn't he?" Viv asked. "I mean we all know, even if no one says anything."

"Well, Myrna is his daughter, and he did come home with hair extensions. I guess that was Whitmore's project." I shrugged. He had been fired for walking off set. He had also gotten a call from Whitmore with an apology. After the director's wife found out Liam left because Myrna and I were sick, she strong-armed her husband into asking Liam back. They agreed on delaying filming so that he could make the marketing rounds with Seb Hale a little longer.

"It's cute," Viv said as she took back her computer. "I'm happy for you. You certainly seem happy with him around."

"Thanks, Viv." I didn't really know what else to say. I was thrilled Myrna had her father. I was happy when he was around, I was also worried because I still didn't exactly know what we had together, other than a shared bundle of DNA with big blue eyes.

Liam wouldn't put the baby down. He had his driver bring him straight to my studio before returning to his own home. The smile he gave Myrna had her giggling with delight. The one he gave me made my knees go weak, and made me keenly aware that my body was broken.

"Please tell me you don't have to go to work tomorrow." He held Myrna on his lap as he ate the dinner we ordered in.

"Nope. I don't go in until Wednesday. Why?"

"I want to spend the day with my girls. And I don't want to upset Myrnoula's routine with your sister. It was my fault that got all messed up."

"Liam, it was Ruthie's fault. She's the one who pitched a fit." But damn if I didn't appreciate the fact that he recognized that. I wanted to kiss him for it.

He ran a finger with some rice on it into Myrna's mouth.

"Are you sneaking her solids?"

"Bloody hell!"

"Liam!" I thought he was mad that I busted him on feeding her solid food. Truth is I had been sneaking her little bits of plain rice for the past few weeks too.

"She bit me." He pulled his finger out and looked at it. He swiveled the baby in his arms and looked in her mouth. "Nica, look." He pulled down her jaw and rubbed his finger over her lower gum.

Teeth, my baby girl was getting teeth. Our breastfeeding days were numbered. The first time she bit me, it was game over.

I left my seat to stand next to them to admire her newly emerging pearly whites, to be near them during this milestone of development. I blinked back tears. I was so happy Liam was here for this. I wanted him here for when she crawled, walked, talked.

He lifted his gaze to mine, and I kissed him.

It was nothing like the comfortable familiar peck he had given me. No, this kiss had overtones of our heated past. My lips pressed want and need into his. When he responded and opened his mouth to mine, I plunged into him. I fell in and down and poured longing, and loneliness and all my fear went into that kiss. Liam hooked a hand around my neck and held me to him. He gave as much as I did. I had a year of kissing to catch up on, a year of resentment and worry to atone for. I had words I could not say, that I needed my lips to convey.

"God, I have missed you, Nica." His voice was raspy and thick with emotion when we finally ended the kiss.

I had tears running down my face, and he had a baby with a smelly diaper on his lap. I swiped at my face and laughed. This was us now, passion and family were not separate contained units. He stood to change Myrna. He pulled me hard against him and kissed me again. This time the kiss was a promise of more to come, that we were not done yet.

It seemed forever before Myrna went down for the night. I could tell Liam was exhausted from his days at the con. And I was just tired, my new normal. Liam guided me to bed and wrapped me in his arms. We lay like that for who knows how long.

"I want to kiss you again." His voice felt like thunder in my belly.

I raised my face to him and his eyes did that blue-brown swirling split. It was sexy, intimidating, and thrilling. Somehow, I had both Liam and Flint, and they were one and the same now. I sighed as his lips descended on mine.

Liam rolled me to my back and continued kissing me. I was beyond content to do this, and only this. I loved him, I loved kissing him, but I was keenly aware that the pull in my core this activity should trigger was missing.

He cupped a breast, and I removed his hand. He lifted up on his arm.

"You okay?"

I nodded and gave him a weak smile. "No breasts while I'm still breastfeeding. It doesn't seem right."

He lowered back to me. "I can do that. Just give me a slap if I forget."

His lips were warm and slid over mine in such a wonderfully familiar dance. He filled my senses with his warmth, his smell, his taste. A hand trailed over my ribs and down to my hip. Then he was palming my ass, pulling my hips closer. I could feel his erection pressing against me. I should have been tilting my hips to angle against him, to pulse and rub and grind into him. Nothing.

But I didn't want to stop kissing him, not ever.

When his hand found its way between my thighs, I pushed him back and scooted away from him. "Liam, no."

"Are you all right? Did I hurt you?"

"I'm sorry. I'm sorry. I can't," I mumbled before I burst into tears.

Liam returned to me, wrapping me in his arms, cradling me against his chest. "Sh, sh, whatever's the matter, it will be okay. We don't have to do anything."

I didn't explain anything, and he didn't ask any questions.

18

The sky was a lovely bright cloudless blue, but it felt dark. It was going to be another one of *those days*. Maybe the overwhelming sense of failure wouldn't try to pull me under today. Maybe today it would just heckle me from behind.

Damn. My ass still hadn't recovered. How could it when I didn't have the energy to go out for a walk or make healthier food choices for myself?

I glanced over at Liam. Why was he here with me? It had been two days since he kissed me. Why was he dragging me along to look at a new house? Right, because I came with the baby. He was doing this for the baby. At least he loved her enough to want to help out, and even make sure he had a kid-friendly house for her to grow up in.

I blew air through pursed lips.

"How many houses are on the list today?" I faked interest. Damn it. Black gooey tendrils slipped around my arms. It always started in my arms. They became heavy, difficult to move. Next, my fingers felt swollen, and movement became disjointed like I was some mechanical puppet that didn't quite move naturally.

Liam drummed on the steering wheel. "The Mighty Maggie," he started.

"You gave her a title?" The black coiled around my stomach, squeezing out droplets of jealousy. I wanted a title. Myrna had several nicknames, the fucking real estate agent had a nickname.

"With a name like Maggie Fletcher, she needs one don't you think?"

I shrugged and stared out at the blue sky. "You were saying?"

"Maggie has only two lined up for us today, but I'm sure we could fit in more if I said something. Why?"

I sighed. *Because I'm drowning in tar, because I don't need you to rub it in my face that you are provider mighty man, and I'm fat and broke.* "I didn't sleep well last night."

"Myrnoula kept you up?"

Damn it. I blinked back tears as the ooze hugged my spine and tightened around my rib cage. *No, you not being with us kept me up.* But I couldn't get the words out of my mouth.

"No, she slept really well. Down at nine, fed just past midnight, and didn't wake up until five-thirty."

Liam chuckled. "That's positively sleeping in."

He reached for my knee and gave it a squeeze. "We won't spend too much time with the houses then, and I'll get you home so you can take a nap."

"Thank you." I rested my head against the window and felt the vibrations in my teeth.

Maybe I could shake this oxygen robbing feeling out.

The first house was intense. We never made it past the entry.

Maggie Fletcher introduced us to the listing agent and the property manager. I didn't realize that was a thing. I had only ever been to a few open houses with Ruthie when she and Hugh were looking. That felt like a million years ago. But I do recall only one agent being present, and never a property manager.

"I'm sorry, you manage the property for the current owner. Is this a rental property?" I had to ask.

"This is an investment property. I'm here to ensure the new owners of a smooth transition so that operations continue with the vacation leasing agency. And to provide you with assurance that all units rent out with an eighty percent occupancy rate annually."

Liam groaned low in his throat. He adjusted the car seat carrier in his grip and leveled a stern look at the listing agent, his dark brows low over his eyes.

He lifted one brow and sort of squinted at Maggie.

As if she could read his mind, she perked right up. "This home was listed as a single-family residence. We are not reviewing income properties."

"Oh, it was a single-family home. It's been divided into three rental units. The owner would be able to live in—"

Liam turned around and walked out the front door. I followed him and left The Mighty Maggie to do her thing regarding the misrepresentation of this place.

The acrid smell of a hill fire drifted past on a breeze. The black ooze bled out of my feet a little. I felt better leaving this place behind.

Maggie approached us and Liam finished securing Myrna back in the car. I sat with my seat belt already on.

"I'm tired of all these online bed and breakfast vacation rentals," Maggie complained. "People think they have turned into the Hiltons overnight by letting people rent their spare room. I gave that agent a piece of my mind. I'm going to call the listing agent for the other property in the car to make sure we do not run into this again. It had been a beautiful home, a good school district too."

Liam said something I couldn't quite make out, and then he slid into the driver's seat.

"Ready for the next one?" he asked.

"I almost feel like we should have a camera crew with us. I don't think anyone would believe that if they couldn't see it for themselves."

"Would you really want that? A camera crew following you around as you look at other people's bathrooms?" he chuckled.

I shook my head. "Of course not, but you have to admit that was pretty bizarre. Do you think the property manager came with the house?"

Myrna made a chirping noise from the back.

"She okay?" Liam asked.

I reached back and caught her reflection in the big mirror.

"Hiccups. She's still out." I jostled the end of the car seat I could grab and she squirmed a bit before finding her fist with her mouth. She hiccupped a few more times and chewed on her fingers in her sleep before completely settling back down.

I felt the black ooze slide from my legs. Myrna could be the best balm to my troubles at times.

"She's fine," I said as I sat back in my seat properly.

In a few minutes, Liam followed Maggie's Mercedes through an electric gate. Wow, a gated property.

The driveway climbed a steep hill. As it rounded behind the property I expected to see a lavish mansion. I was a bit disappointed with the smallish mustard yellow stucco façade.

I knew the basic price point Liam was shopping in. If this is what that many zeros could buy I would be stuck in my garage forever. The black tentacles wrapped back up my legs. They bit and grabbed and announced their presence. There was no quiet seduction of depression this time. This time it was taking me down.

I swallowed hard, forcing bile and black ooze back down my throat. The house seemed nice, and only slightly larger than the basic three bed two bath home I grew up in.

There were a living room and a study on the first floor. The lights flickered as we walked in. Myrna woke up fussing.

Liam held the car seat while I lifted our girl out. "Do you mind if I feed her while you take a look around?" I asked.

"You'll be okay?" Liam cupped my arm as I cradled Myrna.

"We'll be fine. The owners won't mind if I sit here will they?" I asked Maggie.

"Not at all. You can join us when you're done." She directed Liam toward the kitchen which apparently was the next room over.

I sat on the couch, a dark gold plush velvet affair. I would describe it as a vintage color on a retro Victorian gothic style with a high back and arms rolled into giant swirls. It was a fun couch to look at, sitting on it, it wasn't the most comfortable thing ever. The furnishings in the room were dark gothic antiques combined with sleek modernistic accessories. I kind of liked it. It was the Addams Family meets Danish Modern. Of course, there were ghosts.

Myrna nursed and I amused myself with thoughts of living in a haunted house for a few moments before I was taken over by a wave of the black depressive ooze that had been threatening me and pulling at me all day.

I would never be in a position to be able to purposefully pick my furniture. No matter how much I liked a piece, there was no buying it new for me. I couldn't even do that before I had Myrna. I was struggling to make student loan payments and rent. I did my very best to sock money away for retirement, but that was so intermittent. I never was able to successfully set aside even the minimum two-thousand annually that the IRS suggested I do for a tax break. There was no way for me to buy a showcase piece regardless of its level of comfort, just because it looked good.

Myrna pulled at me and I was terrified she pulled the black ooze into her body with my milk. I slipped my finger into her mouth breaking the seal she formed. Her mouth was full of milky white. No black ooze. She was not happy with me. I switched breasts, so I could at least claim I had a reason for interrupting her groove.

I felt the weight of the world press down on me. I curled over Myrna, protecting her. I did my best to make sure she was safe as I took the brunt force of the tsunami of depression on my back and shoulders.

The pounding didn't stop, it matched my heartbeat and grew in intensity.

A warm hand slid over my shoulder and the pressure eased back.

"Danica?"

I looked up at Liam. The black ooze whipped around him, repelled by his presence, it retreated.

"Oh, my darling, what's the matter?" He knelt in front of me and caressed the side of my face. He cast his glance quickly over Myrna, running his other hand over her bald head. She still nursed as if there wasn't a storm of guilt and pressure raging around her.

His thumb brushed my cheek and slipped over tears— I didn't realize I was crying. Damn it.

He kissed the top of my head. "I'll be right back." He stood and left me.

I stayed curled into myself, covering Myrna.

She stopped nursing, but I clung to her tightly.

Liam returned. The car seat appeared at my feet, he must have brought it back with him. I felt muzzy headed from the onslaught and beating I took. I didn't want to let go of the baby. But Liam eased her from me and placed her in her car seat.

I wasn't precisely clear on the order of events, but somehow he got us all into the car, and back to his house.

Liam helped me into a bed. I didn't know where Myrna was. He had her, she was safe, so I didn't worry. The black ooze lapped at the edges of my awareness as I fell asleep.

I didn't look at houses the next day.

Sitting on the floor, Myrna and I had a conversation. She chewed on a blanket and moved her lips as if she could talk. Little squeals of giggles and a rousting bout of kicks followed.

I said, "Oh yeah," and, "tell me about it," a lot.

My phone made a God-awful sound. I hated those alert notices, necessary, but annoying. I guess that was the whole point of that sound: to get my attention.

"What's that all about?" I asked Myrna even though she couldn't answer. I reached over and grabbed my phone while bouncing her chair a bit more to settle her after the shocking sound interrupted our afternoon playtime.

Another fire. I swear, I wished it would rain and not stop for a year. We needed moisture badly. I checked the location. We were far enough away from the mountains to technically be safe, but the grass fires had been getting worse year after year and forgetting they were supposed to be limited to grass, and not buildings.

Malibu was taking another hit. I zoomed in the area map and realized it was close to Liam, even though he technically wasn't in Malibu.

I called him, this needed more personal contact than a text.

"Nica." I did love the way he said my name.

"Malibu is burning, you need to get out." A bit more panic seeped into my voice than I intended.

"I like that," he purred. I swear he did. I bet he even had a silly grin on his face like he just figured out that I still had a thing for him.

"Like that you're in danger?"

"That you are worried about me. I'm fine. The fire isn't anywhere near me."

"Liam," I cut him off. "Those things can move fast. They consume houses faster than you realize."

"My house is made of concrete and glass. It will be fine."

He wasn't listening to me. I looked over at our daughter, my daughter who needed her father as much as I needed him. I wasn't a priority. She was.

"Myrna would feel better if you came and stayed with us until the fire is out." I looked at her and nodded. She giggled and kicked. Yeah, she would love to have him here.

"Let me pack."

That was it. That's all it took. I put Myrna's name on the

request and done. And here I had been trying to appeal to his logical, adult, thinking self. Maybe that was my problem, assuming Liam thought.

"Pick up some doughnuts on your way over," I said before I hung up. I wasn't about to give him a chance to say something else.

"Daddy's coming over and he's bringing snacks," I said as I played with her toes.

~

Liam curled in close to spoon. I sighed back against him. He caressed my middle. I still wasn't comfortable in my body. But Liam let me forget all of that for a few moments.

His hand slipped under the hem of my shirt, and his fingers tickled my skin. I squirmed with a giggle and pushed his hand away.

"Stop." I liked his touch, I just could not go down the path this would lead to.

He hummed deep and throaty in my ear. "I don't want to."

"Liam," I whined. I don't know if I whined at him or at myself.

"It's okay, Nica. Can I just touch you a little?" His voice was a caress.

He rolled me onto my back. His gaze captured mine, and I was pulled into the depths of his eyes. Liam lifted my shirt, exposing my belly. I gasped and tried to shove it back down. He held my gaze as he caressed my hip and ran his hand across my middle. He hadn't seen my skin since when we were first together. My belly wasn't pretty post-baby, no shape, and all stretch marks. Myrna left me pastier, all pale squish and goosh. I had never been this self-conscious of my shape, and it wasn't comfortable.

He shifted, pushing up onto his knees above me. His focus shifted to my weakness, the marshmallow fluff of my midsection.

"You have always been so beautiful. As the mother of my daughter, you are even more so." He wrapped his hands around my post-pregnant belly. Warmth spread over me. Nerves tightened in my chest. His lips were soft and gentle as he kissed just below my bellybutton. "I'm sorry I wasn't here for you. I missed so much. This is not the father I ever thought I would be."

He rested his cheek against me.

I threaded my fingers through his hair. My heart ached. I wanted to want him. I loved the feel of his arms and his kisses. But my body had no interest beyond cuddles.

"You're a good father. I..." I felt like I should say something, explain myself.

"You just had a baby. There is no rush."

"But I want to, Liam. I want to want to."

"Is it me or sex in general?" He lifted those infinite depths that were his eyes to mine.

"It's me. It's like something inside of me broke."

Myrna started fussing. We both paused to see if she would settle on her own. Liam was up a second later when she didn't. He scooped her into his arms and cooed as he gave her a clean diaper and bounced gently with a clean baby in his arms before handing her over for feeding. She happily sucked away and gazed at her father as if he was her whole world. He was. He sat behind us and watched her over my shoulder. Her little hand held onto his pinky finger as if she would never let him go.

They were my whole world.

"When is your next doctor's appointment?" He was hypnotized by the beautiful baby in my arms.

"She has a well-baby appointment in three weeks." I stroked my knuckle down her soft arm and tucked the blanket around her a bit more.

"Not the girl, you." He looked at me then.

I shrugged. "Not for another month or so. I'll have to look. I have my six month follow up sometime soon. Why?"

"Would you mind if I tag along? I know I wasn't around for the prenatal appointments, but I'd like to, you know, be supportive now. And this way we can ask about your post-partum issues together if they're still worrying you."

The ooze and my libido, or lack thereof, terrified me.

Myrna made a few loud sucking noises as her mouth lost its attachment to my nipple. She sighed and her little milk drunk body relaxed, her head falling to the side. A little dribble of milk ran down her cheek.

Liam lifted her from my arms and up to his face and kissed her cheek. I could tell by the look on his face he never wanted to put her down. I knew that feeling entirely too well.

"Can I come to the well-baby check-up too? I want to be the father you both deserve."

My heart tightened. I think he already was the father she needed. I knew he wasn't going to be some absentee baby-daddy, and I would never have to fight him over custody or child support. He was going to be in our lives for the better. I didn't know if he would ever be able to see me as anything more than his baby-momma, especially if I didn't start having a sexual interest in him. It wasn't him, it was sex. I had no interest in it at all.

I scooted back down against the pillows and adjusted my boobs when he got up to put Myrna back in her crib. He slid into bed next to me and pulled me against his chest. His heartbeat a soothing steady rhythm. I could lay here with him as the best-damned pillow forever, but I was afraid he would leave. What reason did he have to stay? Were my company and his baby girl really enough to keep him?

I slid my hand over the ripples of his abdomen. I smiled remembering him telling me how when he wasn't in the middle of a shoot, or getting ready for a shoot he didn't have a rock-solid six-pack. Silly man, he did, the cut wasn't as sharp or as deep, but the ridges and valleys were still there. He mindlessly ran his hand back and forth over my arm, and I plotted the actions of my hand over his hips and under the elastic of his shorts.

I ruffled the crisp hairs along the soft skin at the juncture of his leg.

"Hmmm, Nica, what are you doing?"

In answer, I ran my fingers through the curls until I found the base of his shaft. I circled him until I held his cock. It pulsed and grew thicker in my hand.

"I want you to have a reason to stick around," I murmured into his chest.

"Nica, darling, you don't need to do that to keep me hanging around." His voice was thick. I could tell he liked the touch.

"You want me to stop?" I teased.

"God no. But... ahh..." He breathed in deeply, exhaling on a sigh. "I'll shut up and let you do your thing."

He stopped talking, but he didn't stop making noises. I let my fingers pleasure him with strokes and squeezes that I could not get the rest of my body interested in. Liam arched into my fisted grip. His hips assisted with a counterstroke. Right about now, I was used to my body wanting to get in on the action with my hand, but nothing. I was happy to make

Liam feel good. I wanted him to feel this way because of me. I just wish it was all of me and not only my hand.

Liam pulled a pillowcase off and used it to clean up after I brought him to release.

He wrapped his arms around me again, and this time I lay still, no plots of awkward seduction in my head. No, my head was full of worry and black ooze around the edges. I didn't want to lose him because I couldn't make love to him. I finally had him back, and I desperately wanted him to stay with us. Myrna needed her father. And I needed him.

19

L iam sat on the bed, legs crossed, a laptop in front of him. He wrote notes on a pad and typed something into the computer. Myrna did her baby kick and squirm routine next to him.

"You know who Gil Denver is?" he asked, as I cleaned up in the kitchen.

Everything I had felt smaller with him around, closer, cozier. I loved him being here, and I didn't know how to tell him that. He was going to have to go back to his home soon now that the fire was out. As soon as he left, this place would feel empty and inadequate. Much like how I felt a lot of the time.

I needed to make an appointment sooner than later. I couldn't keep on living with the black ooze. I took that post-partum and shoved it into a dark corner. Maybe not the best idea, considering it might fester there.

"Wrote *Tails from the Urban Jungle* right?" I only knew her name because of Liam. I started following her work after I found out I was pregnant after Liam disappeared on me. She created graphic novels. Did the illustrations and the writing. Liam's big breakthrough in action roles came when he was cast to play the burly blond shapeshifter she had created. That series ran for four years.

It was some of my favorite of Liam's work. He was hulking and blond, and shirtless most of the time, but I preferred him a little leaner with his naturally dark hair. The way he was now.

"She's still in town after Comic-Con and wants to go to dinner. Will you come? We can get Linda to babysit."

The smile he gave me made my stomach think about flipping.

"San Diego is a bit of a stretch for getting a baby sitter, don't you think?" I hemmed and then hawed.

"She and her husband are in LA. I'd love for you to meet her. I think you creative types might get along."

I shrugged. "Okay, sure. I'll see if Ruthie can watch Myrna," I said.

Liam groaned.

"What's that all about?" I asked.

"Your sister doesn't like me much. I remember your boss saying his wife, Linda, would sit any time for Myrnoula."

I put the dish towel in my hands down and stared at him. He had remembered that?

"What night? If it's after work, I could leave Myrna with Ruthie. She'll already be there. Maybe she could even spend the night?"

"You'd let Myrna spend the night at Ruth's?" He lifted his brows as he looked at me.

"If we're out late with your friends, that would make more sense than driving out to her house to get Myrna, and driving all the way back. Makes for a really late night."

He continued to just stare at me.

"And we could go get her first thing in the morning. You

can get Maggie to get some properties lined up, and we maximize our time."

"Good." He grinned. This time my nerves positively shifted a little.

Charlie let me shift my schedule around a bit, and that way I didn't have to be at work in the morning and leave Myrna with Ruthie for a full day plus the overnight. I dropped my Love-bug off with my sister right after lunch.

"We're going to have a big day, she won't have a chance to notice you're not here," Ruth reassured me.

I confessed to being nervous being away from her for a full night. She would be asleep most of the time, and I would be there early. It would be okay.

I would be okay.

Tonight, I would not let the dark lurking at the base of my brain seep up. These were Liam's friends. I worked with and for the Hollywood elite, this wasn't a big deal. I had an appropriate sapphire blue dress, and spandex shapewear so I didn't look like I was stuffed into sausage casings.

Liam was toe-curling gorgeous in black on black designer cut suit, shirt, and tie. The bit of scruff around his typically clean shaved jaw made me wish my body would respond to him.

Ruth assured me that Myrna had been good this afternoon, and they were going to watch movies, and play, and everything would be fine. I did not talk or video conference the baby. I did not want to confuse or upset her. Or me. I hoped Myrna would settle for Ruthie tonight.

Liam held my hand as we followed the hostess in a weaving fashion through the restaurant. Had the restaurant purposefully put our party in the back to hide everyone from the general public, or so they could parade the stars through the seating area and show off who their clientele was?

I spotted Liam's friends before I knew that's who we were meeting. A ridiculously large man with a head full of heavy dreads dressed like a rock star, a lithe redhead dressed like a nineteen-sixties mod model, and...

Emi Paul jumped out of her chair and threw her arms around Liam. Liam laughed and returned the hug.

I smiled. It was awkward.

Emi turned to me. She grabbed my forearms in an excited welcome. "I remember you from set. Your team was the best." She flitted her hand over her collar bone. "I was Isis in the Sebastian Hale movie. You made sure my rigging was secure."

I gave her a genuine smile at that point. I always welcomed being remembered for the work, even if it wasn't mine directly. "Miss Paul. I wasn't on that team, but that was our crew. Thank you for remembering us."

"Emi. Hey, I remember and appreciate everyone who keeps me safe. Plus, how could I forget you? We're in the middle of the desert, and you were the palest person I've ever seen after Gil. You know Gil?"

With that, the redhead stood up and extended her hand. "We haven't met yet. Liam was excited to introduce us, looks like Emi stole his thunder. Hi, I'm Gillian, but call me Gil, everybody does."

Emi clamped her mouth shut and her dark eyes went wide. A hint of pink-tinged the tops of her cheeks.

Liam's smile was broad and relaxed. His arm came back around my shoulders and he gave me a squeeze. "It's all good, Emi. This is Danica. You already know Emi from set.

You just met Gil, and this is Brand, who has the double pleasure of being Gil's husband and Emi's brother."

That's when the big guy stood up. And up. And up. Liam is a tall man. He's actually a little too tall for Hollywood standards, which makes him stand out in crowds. Brand dwarfed him.

"Are you joining us?" Liam asked. I could tell he was counting chairs, there were only four chairs and there were five of us standing around.

"No, when Gil said they were meeting you for dinner, I had to crash. I'm actually headed back upstairs to play with the kids. This was a rare moment we were all in town at the same time. I'm literally only in town for three days with this tour, and I happen to have tonight off." She gave Liam another quick hug.

"It was so nice to see you again, and Danica, nice to officially meet you."

Emi, exchanged some quick words with the other two and floated off. I remember her moving like that on set as if gravity hadn't quite discovered her. She moved with grace and fluidity.

I know I had a very puzzled expression on my face when we all finally sat down.

Liam grabbed my hand. "What?"

"So you know Gil and Brand because Gil wrote Johnny Urban right?" I wiggled my finger around trying to make the connections in my head link up.

"Right."

"Emi just happens to be Brand's sister. But you met her on Seb Hale?" I hated it when the interconnections of who knows who and how got my wires crossed.

"I met Emi on Urban Jungle. She was one of the circus performers, and because of Gil," Liam explained.

I shook my head. "Sorry, the connections aren't meshing. I still have baby brain."

"Tell me about it," Gil moaned. "First it's pregnancy brain, then it's baby brain. And they never warn you about toddler brain."

"Does it get better?" I asked.

Brand chuckled. "We're still in the middle of toddler brain."

Gil shot her husband a side-eye. "Oh, like you help."

There was an inside joke there, I was clearly on the outside.

"Paulo, my man." A huge booming voice caught all of our attention.

A virtual mountain of a man approached our table. When I said Brand was big, I clearly had no clue what I was talking about. I don't think Emi, Gil, Liam, and my body masses combined would equal the mass of this guy.

Brand stood and grabbed the other man's hand in a fist, they hugged and beat each other on the shoulders. I contemplated the bruises an embrace like that would leave.

Brand stepped back. "Jameson, you dog, how have you been? Gil, this is Rob Jameson, he's a lineman for the Packers. This is my wife Gillian Denver."

"Ma'am." Jameson shook his head in a slow side to side motion. I could feel the air currents change because of his action. "Boy, don't tell me you aren't paying attention to the game? I haven't been with Green Bay for years. I'm with the Raiders."

Brand tapped his temple. "The memory doesn't work."

"Oh right. They gonna let you back in the game?"

Brand shrugged. "Nope, I'm benched for good. But it's all okay."

Jameson clapped him on the back again. "It was great to

see you. Folks, sorry to interrupt your dinner." He pointed at Liam. "Loved that last movie. Making more?"

"If they let me."

"Night folks." Jameson waved and faded back to his own table and dinner.

"You remembered him?" Gil asked. Her eyes were big, but she looked excited.

It seemed an odd thing to say. After all, Brand had called the other man by name.

Brand sat back and a smile lit up his face. He blinked a few times. Was there a hint of a tear? "I did. I didn't get all of it, but I remembered him. Damn." Brand wiped at his cheek.

Gil turned to me. "Brand had an accident a few years ago that affected his long term memory. He doesn't always remember people without a prompt. It's kind of a big deal."

"Then we should celebrate," I said.

Brand shook his head. "I don't drink. It's bad for the brain."

"Do you chocolate? I think something like this deserves dessert first. We don't need champagne to celebrate."

Gil crossed her arms and gave Liam a serious look. "I like her style." Turning to me, she said, "I think that's a brilliant idea."

I leaned into Liam as his driver headed through traffic toward my home.

"Thank you, that was nice." I sighed.

"It was. You and Gil got along like a house on fire." Liam played with the big coil of curled hair behind my ear

"She's funny. And so is Brand. I mean for someone who was a football player, he has some serious insights into the

Hollywood machine, especially stunt and action stuff. I like your friends." They were his friends and not business acquaintances. That dinner had nothing to do with projects they could work on together or help each other out on. That dinner was so they could be in each other's company. No agenda. Something I missed since being pregnant and having Myrna.

The driver pulled up to the end of my drive and I reluctantly pulled myself from Liam's gravitational pull. I turned to thank him for dinner, and he was on my heels out of the car.

"Am I making an assumption that I'm welcome to stay even if Myrna isn't home?"

My mouth went dry, and I struggled to swallow.

"Not at all. I just thought you'd go home." I held the key to my front door in my hand and looked at him. I knew why he was staying. So why wasn't I saying anything? "Of course." The car pulled away, leaving the two of us staring at each other. I unlocked the door and Liam silently followed me inside.

Before I took enough steps to be properly inside Liam spun me into his embrace. He held me gently, but I could feel his muscles quiver with nervous energy.

"I want to make love to you." His voice was low and thick, a seduction itself.

I started to protest that I was broken.

"As much as you will allow me to. You say when. You can say no at any time."

My brain wanted to, my heart wanted to, my participating body parts showed no sign, no throb, of interest.

"I want you, but I don't know." Nerves rioted through my being. I felt pressure low in my abdomen, not the sexy kind, but the scared, puking kind.

"Can I at least kiss you?" His lips moved so close, he practically already was.

I closed the imperceptible distance so that he was kissing me, and I, him. Our mouths did not fight in a wrestling match of fierce passion, the kiss was smooth and slow and so full of love I'm sure tears fell down my cheeks of their own accord. It was the kind of kiss that turned my brain off.

He took his lips on a sensual exploration of my face, my neck. The kiss he placed on my exposed collar bone reminded me that my body once craved him like oxygen, and maybe I needed to taste that again.

"We go slow." I agreed. "Do you have a condom? I'm not on the pill or anything at the moment."

His expression burned into me. He nodded. His eyes swirled with the distinct brown and blue, never settling, never letting me know who was in charge, Liam or Flint. It didn't matter anymore. This man and who he was, and who he had been, were all one and the same to me. I loved him more than words.

Slowly, he undressed me. Finding the oddly placed side zipper on the vintage dress, he slipped it from my shoulders and folded it over the back of the couch. His jacket, tie, and shirt followed. He worked quietly, reverently. Liam lowered to his knees in front of me, to help me off with my pumps. I rested a hand on his shoulder for balance. Skimming his hands over my legs and up and over the silky spandex undergarment, he hooked the top edge and rolled it down, and off, leaving me in panties and a bra. He made quick work removing the rest of his clothes until he was left in shorts.

I gripped tight around his neck and told my body this is what it wanted as he lifted me in his arms. Liam followed me down onto the bed. His warm capable hands skimmed over my skin. He hooked a finger into my panties and swiped them away. He kicked out of his shorts.

And then he was kissing me again.

I ran my legs over his and hooked one over his hip so I could feel his heat, his hardness. Kisses against my mouth turned to kisses against my skin, and Liam trailed them down between my breasts. His hands cupped my ribs, grazing the sides of that flesh without ever really touching me there.

He shifted. I felt his eyes staring.

"Is this okay?"

He was poised between my thighs, ready to kiss my sex, lick me senseless.

Incapable of speech, I nodded.

His tongue was cool, and I cried out as his lick turned on my switch. Damn, that was the sensation that I was missing. Immediately, no longer a passive participant, I writhed and squirmed under his ministrations of tongue to clit, tongue to soft flesh.

His eyes narrowed and I felt like prey when he eased back and made sure I saw as he sucked a long finger into his mouth. I knew where that finger was going next.

"Yes." I moaned.

I moaned, and my senses flooded with need of him. I still felt tense and nervous, this all felt familiar and new. I wasn't this nervous the first time I made love to him, either of him. That finger slid in and instantly I needed more, and I wasn't shy to say so.

His tongue and his fingers wound me up in the most glorious way possible.

"I want you inside of me," I about cried, the need had been turned on and cranked up.

"I want me inside of you." He moved away with a growl and returned rolling a condom down his length.

He held my gaze, chest lifting with a deep breath. With a slow guided motion, his cock ran around my needy flesh. I closed my eyes as he pressed the head to my entrance.

I sucked in a breath as I felt him slide in. More smooth action, and slow love-making. He stopped moving once we were hip to hip. He shuddered with a deep sigh. My hands ran over his arms and down his chest. I bit my lip as he slid back out before returning, fully sheathed.

"Are you okay?" The expression on his face was full of concern and love and fear.

I nodded, my teeth digging into my lower lip.

He slid out and in again before stopping. "Look at me, Nica."

He thrust with a little more force and I swallowed a whimper.

"Do I need to stop? I'm not hurting you, am I?"

God, he was perfect. In the middle of actually making love, he wasn't going forward with anything unless I said it was all good, and clearly, I wasn't all good.

"Nervous, it's been a long time, and..." I didn't want to kill the mood with baby talk, but there it was. "I don't know if everything still works."

Liam slid back and pulled me to his chest. "It's been a very long time for me too, but I haven't given birth in the middle of it. It certainly feels like everything is working. Did you have a lot of stitches?"

I nodded. "The doctor wouldn't tell me exactly how many, but more than enough. I'm sorry." I tucked my head and tried to roll away. His arms tightened around me, and he wouldn't let me move.

"For what? You gave birth to my daughter. I'm the one

who needs to apologize every day for not being here when you needed me. I've waited over a year to make love to you again. Now that I've got you back in my life, I will wait until you are ready."

I cried myself to sleep wrapped in his loving embrace.

In the middle of the night, I jerked awake. My body was so used to waking up for Myrna, I instinctually did it, even though Myrna was not with me.

Liam sat up and pulled me to his chest. His skin was so hot against mine. My mouth found one of his nipples and I licked and teased it to a hard peak. Nipples were fun that way.

When Liam pressed me back against the mattress my body parts were ready for him, wet and swollen, throbbing with need. This time when he entered me he did not hesitate. His thrusts were masterful and commanding. His body claimed me for his and declared me as the owner of him.

He growled. I cried out. We both moaned, and whimpered, and roared. When he left me to take care of the condom, I had forgotten how physically happy and exhausted my body could be.

20

I had about ten minutes of "life is good" before Ruthie ruined it. Ten minutes where I wasn't worried about the black ooze, I knew Myrna was safe and cared for, and I still floated on cloud nine after Liam's masterful lovemaking. I remembered feeling like this before the hormones triggered the ooze.

I looked over at Liam as I drove us to Ruth's so we could pick up our daughter. All the "us," and "we," and family, and couple vibes reverberated through me and resonated low in my abdomen. I didn't feel broken anymore. I smiled at him, and his eyes sparkled a steady hazel back at me. I think that meant both he and Flint were settled in.

I pulled into Ruth's drive and got out of the car, Liam followed behind. She met us at the front door with a sour look on her face. I thought she was about to complain about Myrna not behaving since she was clearly unhappy and fussing in her car seat.

"What's he doing here? I thought you were just going out to dinner."

"He is here picking up his daughter." I didn't feel like I owed her any kind of explanation.

Her tone and words were clear. She was pissed I had spent the night with him. Little did she know, or care, that we had been sleeping in the same bed for weeks now. All that mattered to her was if I was having sex with him, again. And that was none of her business, either way.

I kept my words and actions pleasant enough. Liam was charming, though its effect bounced off of Ruth's impenetrable armor. The transition visit was short. We got Myrna, and essentially we ran. The original plan had been to stay long enough to breastfeed and make sure she was happy to be back with Mommy and Daddy. Liam locked her car seat into the installed base, and sat in the back with her, while I navigated to a parking lot. I didn't even want to loiter in Ruth's driveway after that encounter.

Once parked, I was in the back, and we had Myrna unbuckled. She was so happy to be out of the car seat. She squirmed her face to my chest, trying to breastfeed. I obligated and adjusted my clothing. She nursed as if she were starving, and not just in need of succor from Mommy.

"It was a long night wasn't it, Love-bug?" I cooed.

Liam sat on the opposite side of her car seat and leaned over so he could watch her. His gaze shifted to my face.

"Did you miss her terribly?"

I gave him a weak smile. The damned black ooze clutched onto Ruthie's attitude and lurked around the edges. "I did." I gazed at my baby before I looked back over at him. "I am so glad you kept me distracted."

"Is that what you call it now? A distraction?" He smirked.

"I don't think I can do that again. At least not for a long time."

"Do you mean me or—"

"Myrna spending the night away. I didn't like it. I missed her too much." I bit my lip and looked up through my lashes at the handsome man next to me in the backseat of the Flex in some random grocery store parking lot while I breastfed our baby. "Now, what you did last night, that I could do again."

～

Maggie had something special for Liam. She sounded so excited about it over the speakerphone, and when we met up in the drive of this property, she definitely was more upbeat than she had been over previous places. We walked into the entry. It wasn't even a foyer, it was its own palace with a movie set quality grand staircase that curved through the entire space.

I adjusted the car seat in the hook of my arm and looked up. Stained glass lined the upper vault of what essentially was the third story of this space. It was huge; it was grand; it was too much. I shifted my gaze back to Liam, he and Maggie exchanged some heated words. The other estate agent had disappeared.

Maggie leaned toward me. "The other agent said the owner wants to show us around. I somehow think they found out who you were."

Liam looked at me. I swear panic washed over his expression before our attention was called, with a cough, to the top of the stairs.

We looked up.

Posed in a bias cut gold-tone designer gown stood Cecilia Saaid. I swear to every god on this planet she was about to declare she was ready for her fucking close up.

She wafted her arms out in a graceful welcome and leaned like a starlet of Hollywood past. She floated down the stairs in what could only be a well-practiced entrance. Her eyes were closed, with the expectation that we were gazing upon her with bated breath until she would open those elaborately made up peepers, with perfect eyebrows, and dare to grace us with the gift of her looking out upon us.

"Oh for Christ's sake. Open your damned eyes before you fall down the stairs, Cici." The words were out of my mouth before I realized I had even thought them.

She stumbled down a step and her eyes flew open.

For such a beautiful woman, she could really get her face to look like some kind of deranged rage monster. The monster visage was quickly replaced with blank nothing, and she no longer saw me but drifted the rest of the way down the stairs and straight to Liam.

"Liam!" she said his name as if she were surprised to see him. She wrapped his arm around hers and started to lead him away. "I had no idea you were looking for a new place. I just love to give visitors the personal tour."

Liam pulled his arm back and didn't budge. Cecilia was forced to let go to continue walking.

"I don't think this fits what we're looking for," Liam said before turning and placing his hand on my back.

I was ready to run out the door, but Cecilia wasn't having any of it. The dress she wore was for red carpet strolls. She had to have sprinted in order to get in front of us. It couldn't have looked good.

"But you haven't been to my place before. How do you know it does suit you?"

"It's not even on the market is it?" I sneered, knowing I wouldn't be heard.

"This isn't going to work, Maggie. Please let the agent know we are sorry for having wasted the owner's time."

"A private listing could—" Cecilia started.

Liam dropped his hand from my back. And turned, slowly. "It's not going to happen, Cecilia. As Danica pointed out, it's not really on the market is it?"

He followed me out the front door.

"Like I said, we need a camera crew with us on this. Maggie?" I turned as the other woman caught up with us outside.

"I am so sorry about that. I was told this was an exclusive listing and they had found out I had a client, and..." she shook her head. "That was a setup. And I can see you are not happy about it. I'll have my assistant do some digging on the next few properties before something like this happens again."

I snarled as I secured Myrna back into the car. I fumed as I put my seat belt on, and I looked out the window in a total huff when Liam got into the car and started the engine.

He drove for a few miles before breaking the silence. "Cici huh?"

"What? She was being overly dramatic. Maggie was right, that was a setup. Cecilia somehow found out that you are on the market for a house, and did some conniving to get you into her lair."

"No argument there. But you called her Cici."

"No, I didn't."

"Yeah, you did. What gives? I get that she is a bitch to people she doesn't think can help her career, but she didn't even act like you were in the room. I didn't catch it last year on set, but looking back... yeah, she goes above and beyond ignoring you. You care to share what that's all about?"

I continued to look out my window, but I could feel his gaze boring into the back of my head.

"Cici Saaid was my best friend in the seventh grade until we hit puberty and she got glamorous, and I got the shaft."

I proceeded to tell him almost everything that happened in the tenth and eleventh grades that changed everything. Almost everything, I left out the parts where Cici's father was surrounded by dead people, and Cici bought the lie that he was some kind of war hero. But, I included how I ended up with creepy Hester who turned out to be a pretty good friend until she followed her boyfriend out of state

"I don't think I've heard you mention a Hester before?"

"She lives out of state. We didn't stay in touch." I turned to watch him as he began driving again. "She met a guy, had a bit of a stylistic and personality change. Said Hester came with too much baggage. Changed her name to Sasha, and I believe is happily living the life of a soccer mom somewhere in middle-America."

"Baggage?" he laughed.

"Yeah, Hester worked it pretty hard. It was a role she played in her life as a coping mechanism. When she realized Hester was a front, she laid her to rest and let Sasha come out."

"Like a split personality?" Liam's brows tried to meet in the middle.

"More like a suit of armor she was finally able to take off. We were the outcasts of the outcasts in high school. I mean, I get that most people think they are, but we really were. I had been ostracized, and Hester had some trauma at her first school, so was a transfer.

"I actually preferred Hester to Sasha. She was different, and not afraid of being unique. In the end, it turns out she was afraid of being too much like everyone else. I guess she got over that."

"And how did she piss you off?" Liam's tone called me out.

"She didn't. She never gave the boy I had a crush on a blow job while pretending to be my friend. Cici deliberately hurt me and pretended to be my friend. Hester never did that. She figured out who she wanted to be, and became that person while never stepping on my feelings. Big difference."

"So who do you consider your best friend now?"

I felt a tingle in my low abdomen and bit my lip. "Charlie is too much my boss, and Ruth is too much like Mom. So I guess, Myrna," I paused, "and you."

Liam cut a glance at me quickly before returning his attention to traffic. He nodded, the biggest grin took over his face.

21

The last time I sat in this chair, in this office, I was pregnant, nervous and worried about how I was going to manage my way through a maternity recovery with no income. Charlie had offered me a permanent position and told me I would have full benefits, including maternity leave starting immediately. The time before that, he tricked me into designing an Egyptian city without telling me it was for a Sebastian Hale movie. I only had positive experiences in this office, but damn if I wasn't still nervous.

I patiently watched as he shifted blueprints, and other project plans from on top of his desk. Sure, industry-standard was moving away from printed records, and everything could be assessed on a tablet. But Charlie was old, old school. He claimed he could get a better feel of the big picture if he could look at a proper schematic, or diagram, or map, or... whatever. He liked big rolls of paper.

He picked up an arm full of the big rolls and dumped them on the floor behind his chair. "I should really move into the twenty-first century, shouldn't I?"

"If you think so, boss."

"I think these old eyes only know how to see in blue lines and scale models."

I snorted. Charlie was far from old. He may have learned at the hands of traditional set designers and builders in the days before computers, but he wasn't old.

"Okay, Dani..."

I gulped. I hated being nervous.

"Sell me on the beauties of a Viking longhouse." He propped his elbows on his desk and rested his chin on his clasped hands.

"Vikings, huh?" I eased back in my chair. See, nothing to be concerned with, I just needed to come up with something great for Vikings. What were we getting in house to work on? My brows tried to meet in the middle as I thought about it.

Unless we were doing something with dragons or a remake of Beowulf, I couldn't think of anything I heard of that was in the pipeline that could be headed our way.

"How fanciful? Space Vikings? Modern Vikings? Comic book Vikings?" We hadn't been involved in any of the wildly popular superhero movies lately, and I couldn't imagine we would be brought in now.

"Your boyfriend hasn't said anything to you?" Charlie smirked at me from across his desk.

I leveled a very even gaze at him. Of course, he knew about me and Liam, by now everyone did. What the hell did Liam James have to do with—

"They're making *Sebastian Hale and the Halls of Valhalla*?" I may have screamed with the enthusiasm of a fangirl at a boyband concert.

Charlie sat back and guffawed at my enthusiasm.

"He didn't tell me it was *Halls of Valhalla*, just there was another one he was shooting as soon as *Mammoth Killers* wrapped."

"I thought he was off that film."

I shook my head. "Temporarily. I think Jaspers's wife has a thing for Liam. She made Whitmore call and apologize and invite Liam back, personally."

Charlie did that thing where he pulls his chin back into his neck, quirks his mouth, and raises his eyebrows. That expression said he had never heard of such a thing coming from Whitmore Jaspers before, so it was a pretty big deal for Liam to be called back like that. I knew a lot of the behind the scenes that went on in this industry, but nothing like Charlie did.

A flutter of happy and nerves twirled in my middle for Liam.

"So when do I start on the new stuff?" I still had a pile of designs that needed to be digitized into functional dimensions for the fabricators. I huffed a sigh. I wasn't starting on the Seb Hale set anytime this week.

"Handoff the 3D rendering to the new intern, she's a whiz at that. I want you and Viv brainstorming on this next time you're in the studio. We have an authentic, yet deceptively advanced Viking stronghold to come up with."

"When you say 'deceptively advanced' are we talking they had running water? Or are we talking..." I paused.

"Viking Atlantis, Steampunk Vikings, Vikings with non-tech modern-tech. Steam power and flight. Unrealistically advanced where the only logical explanation can be aliens."

"Or an unrealistically intelligent man from the future who can engineer machines from flywheels when in his own time he has problems operating a bicycle?"

"Exactly. And that's why you are on the project."

I gave him a stupid cheesy grin. *Ahmentari* was still on

wide release and still making box office sales. Glenn had hit Hollywood gold once again. Liam was along for the ride, and yet, he seemed to be barely affected by it at all. Well, except for the house thing. And he did buy that car without batting an eye. Okay, maybe he was surfing along on a slightly higher plane than I realized. I mean the last house we looked at was pretty spectacular.

"Thanks, Charlie." I bounced to my feet. "Any other project parameters I need to be aware of?"

"Yeah, they really want Seb Hale to look like a giant when he's inside, so we might need to scale everything back."

"I thought Vikings were big guys. You know, burly warriors and all that."

He shrugged. "At least give them small doors. They want Seb to have to stoop down to enter a room so when he stands up, it's clear he's the big guy on campus."

He rested his wrists on the top of his head. "Modern man going up against the old gods. Should be interesting."

Interesting? It was going to be fantastic!

"There's something you're not telling me isn't there?"

Liam looked up at me from preparing a row of bottles with formula. At first, his expression was of confusion with his forehead crinkled up and his brows pulled together, and then resigned guilt.

I did not like that expression. When he put the measuring scoop back in the formula and sealed the lid with quiet precise movements, the nerves in my gut were squirming around uncomfortably.

"So, I guess you found out. I was trying to figure out a good way of telling you."

My eyeballs were about to roll out of their sockets if I opened them any wider. "Tell me what?" What had I uncovered? I sucked in a ragged breath.

He leaned against the counter and closed his eyes. He let out a deep sigh.

I wound up tighter with fear. "Liam, what?"

"Cecilia. She's on *Mammoth Killers*."

That was not what I was expecting. My anxiety crashed into a pile of steaming aggravation. I kicked something on the floor. "Ow, damn it. Seriously? Why her?"

Liam pierced me with clear blue eyes of Flint. "We look good together on film. It's a standard studio practice. Why do you think Flynn and de Havilland made so many movies together?"

"Yeah, but they don't do that so much anymore," I whined.

"That's bollox and you know it." He started counting off on his fingers. "Sandler and Barrymore, Depp and Carter, Wilson and Stiller, it happens all the time.

I stomped around in a tight circle, acting like a toddler having a fit. "The last two are guys, and that's not what I wanted to hear right now," I grumbled.

"You're the one who came at me like you already knew. What are you on about?"

I huffed through my nose at him. "I was talking about the new Seb Hale. You didn't tell me it was *Halls of Valhalla*. Charlie had to," I pouted.

Liam chuckled quietly and shook his head. "You expected to hear all about your favorite time-traveling Victorian dream lover cavorting about with the Norse gods, and instead you got slapped with your arch-nemesis. Poor little Nica." He mock pouted at me.

"I wouldn't call her arch-nemesis. Just pain in the ass. Look, you know what Sebastian Hale means to me." I gestured broadly indicating the collection of framed Seb Hale movie prints I had hanging on the walls in the living room.

He leaned across the counter and narrowed his eyes at me. They swirled with the two colors. Who was in that brain? Who was running the show? Now would be the time to say it, right?

I sat with a thunk and sighed. "If previous lives could incorporate fictional worlds, I would say my obsession for the world of Sebastien Hale would indicate a past life connection." I raised my eyebrows at Liam.

Ball served. He needed to return volley.

"Maybe you were William Powers Stapleton. Or maybe you were one of the early actors? Who were you in your past life?" He picked up a pile of Myrna's folded onesies from a chair—laundry was scattered everywhere— before sitting down.

"Who were you?" I tossed it back at him. He had been one of the early actors. I needed him to give me a better opening.

"I'm not even sure if that's something I believe in. Halen was pretty convinced of it."

"So you weren't in love with your assistant in a previous life?" I laughed, even though on the inside I cringed. I didn't want to mock the situation, but... I also didn't want Liam to run away screaming calling me a weirdo. I had too much of that in my life. Goosebumps broke out over my skin and I realized I was shivering.

"Nica, why are you so nervous? It's me. Come on." He

wiggled his fingers at me. I took it as an invitation to invade his personal space, as well as cough it up. I slid into his lap and rested my head on his chest. I picked up his hand just to be touching him.

"This is important to you isn't it?" He ran a soothing hand down my back.

I sat up and looked him in the eyes. Flint's blue swirled in the same space as Liam's brown. I couldn't do it, not with that gaze locked on me.

"I'm in love with you, Liam. I want you around. Myrna needs you around. You've given me fair warning. You'll be working with Cecilia. I'm just going to have to get over my high school heartache that the best friend I thought I would ever have doesn't like me.

"You're an actor, and even though you will kiss her again, I have to know it's acting. I have to accept that you are going to work with people I don't necessarily like. But can Cecilia acknowledge that you aren't fair game? Can she play nice and hands-off?"

"Are you really worried that much about her?"

I nodded. "Yeah, you saw her completely ignoring that I was even in the room. What if you decided that you were in love with her in a past life?"

Liam pulled me against his chest and laughed. It was a good feeling, it chased any doubts that lurked around the edges away.

"That's never going to happen because, in my past lives, I was always in love with you."

I kissed him then. Maybe I should have used that as an opening for mentioning Flint, but why waste a kissing opportunity when he had basically just told me he loved me?

"NDA," he said against my mouth.

"What?"

"I couldn't tell you the details about the new Seb Hale because of a non-disclosure agreement. NDA."

"Right. Of course. How stupid of me not to think of that." I shook my head.

Liam cupped my face in his large hands. His eyes held mine. "Not stupid, never stupid. Next time, I'll try to remember to let you know I have an NDA on something and then I will tell you anyway. I know how important Sebastian Hale is to you. I wanted to make it a surprise, but I haven't found anything to give you that would make a good hint."

I rested my head against his chest again. I wanted to stay like this, even if we were surrounded by a mess of laundry, and baby bottles of formula on the kitchen counter.

Myrna made fussing noises from her crib.

22

Liam drove calmly through the streets and I gazed out at the ridiculously large houses. The type of house I could only dream of living in. The type of house Liam was shopping for. The ooze wasn't easing out of my system. It had been threatening me for days.

"This is a nice area," he said.

I hummed in agreement.

"Do you like it? Would one of these be good for Myrna?"

"I think any house like these would be great. I mean, they are phenomenal properties. I can only imagine what the back yards look like." I could only imagine what the insides looked like.

Didn't Liam know he was killing me with this house hunt? He would go back to his glamorous house on the side of a cliff, and I would go back to my garage.

I hated this new aspect of my brain. I never cared before. I had been to parties at some pretty posh places. Hell, Charlie had one hell of a swank house, and I never once had a pang of being left out. Maybe it was because I knew there would be the ultimate mom versus dad fight in my future with Myrna. *'Why can't you give me what I want when Daddy gives me everything?'*

She would hate me simply because I didn't have money.

"Liam, I don't want you spoiling Myrna. Don't buy her things just because she asks for them. Say no occasionally," I blurted out.

"What does that even mean, Nica?"

"It means if she wants a pair of Prada heels when she's eleven, say no. Don't go buying her a car in every color just because she's sixteen. I don't want her growing up some spoiled Hollywood princess."

"Can I buy her one car when she turns sixteen?" he asked.

"I don't know. I don't know what I'm even saying." I turned to look at him as he guided the car down the street. I turned and looked over my shoulder so I could see the back of her car seat and Myrna's face in the big baby mirror. She was a sleeping angel, perfect and loved. "You can give her so much more than I can. I'm afraid I'll never be able to compete."

"It's not a competition. We'll discuss big purchases. She won't need heels when she's eleven because she'll be too busy being a kid. But I think I get what you're saying. Don't buy her another pair of boots because this new pair is pink and she only has twelve other colors in her closet?"

"That's exactly what I'm saying." I sighed heavily.

"How about we deal with that when we get there. Let's not rush her into high fashion before she can even walk, okay?"

"Sorry, my brain is stupid these days."

The tires squealed as Liam pulled over to a stop. His belt was off and a second later, so was mine. He scooped me out of my seat and into his arms. It wasn't exactly comfortable, but I didn't care. Any time Liam held me was the most wonderful moment.

His hand caressed the side of my face. "Don't say that. Your brain is amazing, not stupid. You still have hormones in your body making you think some crazy shit. It took your entire pregnancy to move those chemicals in. Your body isn't going to get rid of them all at once. Baby brain is real; tired compounded with postpartum issues. You are amazing for thinking about her future, while I'm struggling with the day-to-day. I think that gives us a good balance. Don't you?"

God those soulful brown eyes did something to my insides. Whoa. I hadn't felt that pull for a very long time, and it was back. My heart quickened.

Liam leaned in and I wanted to cry for very different reasons when he kissed me on the forehead and not the lips. My lips wanted him. They needed him. I closed my eyes and leaned into him.

He wanted to co-parent, and he wanted to provide support, he wanted a house for Myrna, but did that mean he wanted me too?

"Would you like to look at one of the houses with me?" he asked. "I'd love to get your input."

My insides knotted up. He wanted my opinion? It was his house, and he wanted my opinion. I guess I was Myrna's input by proxy.

I gently pushed away from him and re-fastened my belt.

"I think I could handle that. We weren't doing anything else today, were we?" I asked.

"You wanted to run some errands." Liam picked up his phone and gave Maggie a call.

She wasn't available to show us the property, but one of her associates would meet us. I guessed Liam had a specific place in mind when he backtracked through the street of particularly nice houses and pulled up to a gate.

The junior associate was dressed like a wannabe country star, expensive jeans, and an overly relaxed look that at first guess didn't scream money, but at second look said high-end investment. Denim, plaid, cowboy boots, and a slightly spiky yet clean-cut hairstyle made me think country. Had there been more black and long hair, I would have said wannabe rocker.

"You must be the Iakobuses?" he asked as Liam stepped from the car. "I'm Sean. Maggie told you I'd be with you on this walkthrough. I understand you've already seen the property but the missus has not?"

Sean just dropped a handful of mini bombs in that one sentence. Liam was functioning under his given name. Was that a cover or was that still his legal name? I'd have to find out. And Liam was letting the agents think of us as a family unit, not Liam and the mother. Nerves I forgot my body possessed quivered at the thought of actually being his missus.

Sean called me *ma'am* when he shook my hand, and a slight southern accent cemented my appraisal of wannabe country star firmly into place.

The house was something altogether not what I expected. It was better, so much better. And huge. The entry was set back as two wings extended forward. The drive curved in front and around to the side, where I guessed the garage was located.

Sean took us up the few steps and in the front door. I tried not to gasp and look like a kid in a candy shop. This was the kind of house that magazines called *digests* like to feature. Room after room downstairs, but the best part was the large open floor plan for part of it, and still there were separate formal gathering and dining spaces.

"Now this is the kind of sink I want." I ran my hands over the copper. It had better than two sections, it had three. Liam carried the sleeping Myrna while I cavorted and craned my neck looking at everything.

"Can we see outback before we head upstairs?" I asked.

"Sure thing." Sean led the way and we walked through French doors onto a bricked in back patio. Beyond that extended lawn in one direction, and pool and pool house in the other. "The pool house can serve double duty if you decide to have any staff live on the property, such as a nanny, and when you no longer need a full-time nanny, it's back to being a pool house."

I guess people who could afford houses like this could also afford live-in nannies.

Upstairs was just as beautiful and impressively large. The master bath had one of those super deep, super big bathtubs, and a walk-in multi-jet rainfall shower

Sean's phone rang and he excused himself to another room to take the call.

"This is a nice place, Liam. Why are you showing me?"

"I wanted to know what you think of it. Maggie assures me it's in a highly sought after school district if we decide to go with public schools."

As he spoke, I slid in closer to him and Myrna. He placed his free arm around my back.

"See, I am paying attention." His voice dropped low and husky.

I swallowed the rock that formed in my throat and stepped in closer. "It doesn't have a view."

"It doesn't need a view if it has you." His lips were a breath away. I leaned in and—

"Sorry about that." Sean came back into the room.

I jumped back and rubbed my elbow nervously.

"Did you have any questions about the home?" Sean looked anxiously from Liam to me and back again.

Liam handed me Myrna. She felt so snuggly and warm. "Go wander around, see what you think."

I left him to talk to Sean.

I had a strong inkling that if I said yes, Liam would buy this house. How many other houses had he looked at before bringing me to this one in particular? I know there had to be others that I wasn't seeing, not after I had that spectacular meltdown at that one house.

I headed back downstairs. I found the utility room with another back door. This led out to a side yard that looked like it had been their dog's private yard. Okay, this house was set up for pets, and kids, and parties, and staff.

I laughed. Staff.

Liam would have to be able to keep an assistant for more than six months before he should ever consider having staff. I liked Ray but he pitched a fit when Liam told him the house was going on the market.

"But I want to work here." He had sounded like such a brat. I convinced him to not quit on the spot. He was a good assistant and his cooking and meal prep was incredibly helpful. He agreed to stay on until Liam was out of the house.

Apparently, Ray was an architect junky and would only work in beautiful unrealistic places. Would this place be too housey and not enough showcase for him? Probably, but I still wanted to bring him out, maybe he would change his mind.

I pulled up a map on my phone. This place wasn't that far from my studio, or from the KoS Workshop. It wouldn't add extra hours to my commute to bring Myrna over in the mornings, or to pick her up.

My stomach knotted up again. Maybe I would have my own room, maybe I'd be in the pool house. I got the distinct impression that he intended me to be here too. I wanted to moan with my need to be part of his family, with him and Myrna in one place.

"Well?" Liam asked as he approached me.

"Seems big for just one little girl and her father." It was the best way I could think of dropping the *please let me live with you* hint.

"Who said there will only be one little girl?" He lowered his eyes and smoldered at me before heading off toward the drive, his hands shoved into his pockets, his stride casual and confident.

My heart soared. Body parts tingled. My grin tried to split my face. "Your daddy just checked me out," I whispered against her head.

Man, the highs were high today. I hoped there wasn't a nasty crash in my future. I followed after Liam.

The highs stayed high, and maybe I was over the hump on the postpartum. It was hard enough admitting to Liam I had tough days, I didn't know how I would tell my doctor.

Maggie held up her promise of having the properties better assessed before they were shown to us. Sean took us to another home that Liam had not seen before, and there were no crazy property managers and no crazy love-struck owners. This one did have too many ghosts. They tend to congregate in locations, like some kind of after-life house party. It took more than a few minutes before I realized they were all older. And then we walked into the living room, and the mantel was lined with urns.

Maybe these ghosts would move to the new location

with their ashes, maybe not. There were other reasons to not like this house, but the ghost brigade was a hard no for me.

On the way to the car, Liam pressed his palm to the side of his head and clamped his eyes shut. Slowly, he lowered Myrna's car seat to the ground. My arms wrapped around him and I held on tight, anticipating all of his weight to come crashing down.

It was over in ten heartbeats, and Liam stood up. "I'm okay." He smiled at me and picked up Myrna before continuing to the car.

"What's your schedule like tomorrow?" Liam asked as I drove away from the ghost occupied house. He hadn't said anything, just got into the passenger seat.

"Why? How's the headache?" I watched for traffic and pulled out.

"I want to stay with you tonight. I was wondering if you could come to my place or if we needed to be at yours?"

I shot him a glance, worried. "Because of your head?" I was still concerned, even though he seemed to have them less and less frequently.

He chuckled. "I want to stay with you Nica because I want you in my arms. The headache has nothing to do with it. But if you'll stay because I'm having the headaches, then yes, because of the headache."

"So your head is fine?"

"Depends on which head you're asking about," he said as calm as he pleased.

My jaw dropped and I blushed. I was more shocked than appalled. His flirting had gotten dirty. "Mr. Iakobus!"

"Miss Kensington?"

"I do believe you are talking dirty to me." I continued to act affronted.

"I would like to do a bit more than talk dirty to you." I glanced over, his eyes were narrowed and locked on me. The switch in my body that he so cleverly fixed, thrummed to life. I wasn't going to be able to wait until after Myrna went down for the night. I wanted him immediately.

"I would like that too. I think my place is closer." I was breathless from a heavy flirt and a little dirty innuendo.

Cupid and the gods of lust and lovers were clearly on our side that afternoon. Myrna fell asleep at some point on the drive home. And then she stayed asleep.

Liam carried her into the bedroom and placed her car seat into her crib. I looked at the crib, and then at the bed. She didn't have a separate bedroom.

"I can't with her in here." I pulled my shirt off and stood to stare at the crib while standing in my bra. How was I supposed to make love to Liam with the baby in the same room? Sure, she wouldn't know what was happening, but I didn't want to scar my child at such a tender young age with the sight of her parents going at it.

I looked out at the living room. The couch really wasn't big enough for both of us. Well, not for what I wanted. I looked at Liam with wide eyes. He had to have an answer, all possibilities escaped me.

He picked up the car seat, Myrna didn't even notice. Without a second glance at me, he carried her into the living room and set the car seat on the floor.

"She'll be fine there," he said as he returned to me. A warm hand slid around my middle and pulled me against him.

He left soft butterfly kisses across the tops of my breasts. "How soon until you stop breastfeeding?"

He sat on the bed. I followed and climbed onto his lap. "Why?" It was a stupid question.

Liam pulled my bra cup down and lowered his head. I dug my fingers into his hair, unable to do much more than hold on. His tongue laved across the exposed nipple. And he left bites across the rest of the flesh.

I whimpered.

"I miss these." He replaced the fabric, and ran his hands over the underwear, grabbing and kneading.

I covered his hands with my own, stilling the movement. It felt good. It felt like I didn't care anymore and I wanted his mouth on me. I took a deep breath and reached behind me, unfastening the bra.

"Danica." My name was a prayer. He wrapped his hands, so hot around my breasts. His thumbs toyed with the nipples, rubbing in circles. His eyes went wide as they didn't simply peak but grew longer than expected. I stifled a cry when he pulled one into his mouth and began sucking.

I felt the milk pull. But his mouth on me made me not care. "You might want to stop."

He backed away and placed his mouth against mine. He tasted warm and needy. His fingers bit into my hips, and I shifted to straddle his lap. I needed to find and rub against his hardness. He lay back. I shifted above him. Smiling down on the man I loved.

"You have on too many clothes," I said.

"I have on all of my clothes." He lifted his hips and tipped me off balance. I was down and rolled onto my back.

Liam towered above me. I sighed. Watching him undress was a thing of beauty. The muscles in his arms bunched and flexed as he pulled his shirt over his head. I squirmed out of my pants, as Liam shoved his pants down, and he kicked the rest of the way out of them.

He slid in against my body. All that skin and I wanted it

against mine. He palmed a breast again. Milk ran between his fingers.

"Oh damn. Sorry." I started to sit up, I needed to get the bra back on.

Liam held me down, and slowly, like a cat licking his paw, he licked my milk from his fingers.

"Do you have to put them away?" His mouth latched onto the skin of my exposed breast. He ran his tongue around and over the offending nipple. "You taste like life."

I moaned. I arched my back and pushed my breasts up into him. "Liam." I moaned again.

"One last goodbye before you put them away." He ran his tongue around each nipple. He leaned over the side of the bed and scooped my bra off the floor. "Thank you for sharing. I will miss those until later."

He helped me on with the garment. He pulled me into his chest and held me, planting kisses on my face. He rolled putting me on top. I pushed against his chest and wiggled my hips until I was positioned with his hardness cradled against my sex. He tilted his hips. His head caressed between my folds and hit my clit. I shifted and he thrust into me.

I ground down against his hips. He pushed back into me again, and again. I wanted to cry out with every thrust.

We locked eyes, and I panicked. I jumped off and rolled next to him in bed.

"What's the matter are you okay?" Liam pushed up into a sitting position and cast his gaze around. "Did Myrna wake up?"

"Condom," I growled out. I flopped onto my back and let my knees fall open.

Liam scrambled from the bed with a stream of curse words. Only moments passed before he lowered himself between my legs. His head dropped to my middle and he peppered my belly with kisses. He lifted his face and smiled into my eyes. He mouthed "I love you," as he slid home.

I threw my head back and wanted to cry out and scream. Every thrust brought a small noise of need from my throat. Liam lowered to me and bit and kissed along my neck. He bit and sucked and shoved. I could feel the pressure building. I counter thrust against him, crashing our hips together.

Liam shuddered and pressed into me, holding me against the mattress. We crashed together. I grabbed a pillow intending to burry my screams into it. Instead, I simply clutched it and cried out. Liam laughed when he could move again. He held me to his chest. "That was the best use of nap time."

"I agree. You still want to spend the night? We can do that again when she goes down for the night."

"Yes please, and thank you."

We both stopped moving and listened. She was still asleep.

23

I flipped through a history book, looking at pictures of what Viking life was like. Apparently, Vikings were originally simply referred to as Danes, and they were always invading warriors in longboats. Sebastian Hale fans would be disappointed, not a horned helmet in sight. And not a single big bosomed blonde in a steel bra on the back of a white horse.

I was going to need to know about the history before I could artfully break it, and do it properly. I wanted Valhalla to be the most epic place ever. And I wanted to be on set when they filmed it. Of course, that probably wasn't going to happen a second time.

A flicker of blue light caught my eye. I blinked and wondered what the guys on the other side of the workshop were working on. King of the Scene was a giant studio warehouse. The only walls in the place blocked off Charlie's office, the conference room, and the bathrooms. The rest of us were out in the open. Okay not quite wide open, but it was essentially a single continuous space.

The blue flicker was probably the flash of an arc welder getting fired up.

Except it wasn't. It was too close, and it was moving toward me.

I looked up. I blinked hard. Reaching out toward me, and expression of pain on his face, wavered Flint. Flint, whose eyes I've been seeing blended with Liam's. Flint, who hadn't come to me in this form in years. Ever since Liam had that car accident.

Viv ran through the ghost and stopped in front of me. "Oh God, you heard?"

The sound of my own blood rushing through my veins crowded out any other sound from my ears. "Viv, what's going on?"

Flint continued to flicker, and look beseechingly at me. My stomach lurched with the familiar sensation of needing to puke. I felt cold.

"You're pale as a sheet, Dani. I thought you heard."

"Heard what?" I was yelling in the growing panic.

"Liam's been in an accident. Charlie told me to send you out front. He went to get his car. I don't think it's good."

The details were blurry. Viv somehow got me outside and into Charlie's car. He didn't say a word but got me to the hospital. He was by my side and did the talking when we encountered scrub-uniformed hospital employees. They said words, I heard the rush-rush, rush-rush of blood in my veins.

I didn't breathe again until I stood next to an emergency room bed with Liam laying in it. Flint flickered in and out of focus next to him. Liam was covered in leads and IVs. Monitors blinked and jumping lines followed his heart, his breathing, and things I had no clue about. A bandage on his forehead covered a few stitches.

Charlie rested his hand on my shoulder. "You take all the time you need. Talk to him."

I turned to Charlie. I didn't understand. I blinked back tears that finally started to form in my eyes. I was confused. Liam looked asleep. He was hooked up to all the monitors, and there was a tube up his nose. He was breathing on his own.

"What's wrong with him?" I asked.

Charlie shook his head. "They don't know. He's not coming out of it. Didn't you hear the doctor when he told you everything?"

I shook my head. "I... I didn't hear a thing. I couldn't."

Charlie pulled me into a bear hug. It felt like my dad wrapping me in a bubble wrap hug from when I was little. "You talk to him, he can hear you. Brain activity goes up. Do you need me to call your daycare? I can have Linda pick up Myrna."

I swallowed hard. Myrna. I should have brought her, she would have been good for Liam to see, to touch. I took in a shaky breath. "She's with my sister. She's taken care of. I guess I should call Ruthie to let her know."

Charlie eased me into a chair, and I focused on my phone and called my sister.

"Leave a message..." I waited for the beep.

"Ruthie, can Myrna stay with you tonight? There's been an accident. Liam's in the hospital, and I need to be here. I'll give you a call later."

I scooted the chair in as close as I could to the unconscious man. Everyone had left us alone. I gazed at his face. He was breathing on his own, that had to be a good sign right? I shifted my attention to the ghost. He stood on the other side of the bed.

"You bastard," I hissed at the ghost. "Couldn't you have somehow told me? Did you have to just up and disappear?"

Flint looked from me down at the body he had so recently occupied.

"I get it. I think. His accident right? You're the headaches and the swirling eyes. What are you doing out in the world? I mean if you could come and go, why has it taken you so long to come see me on your own?"

Flint shook his head at me. His hair was a mess over his eyes, and he wore modern clothes. He wore the clothes I'm pretty sure Liam had on when he had the accident.

"Why aren't you talking to me? Say something."

He continued to shake his head and cast his worried gaze between me and Liam's form.

"No," I whined. I collapsed over Liam's arm and cried. If Flint could not talk to me, did that mean his connection was no longer strong? He looked so worried for Liam, did he know if Liam was in danger?

I couldn't stand the thought of losing Flint again. The thought of losing Liam had me out of my chair and throwing up in the biohazard trash can.

I heard a whir in the back of my head. I was too busy puking to worry about it until a loud beeping came from one of the monitors Liam was hooked up to. I turned and stared in wide-eyed panic. What did it mean? I caught my breath and realized I needed to go get a nurse when one pushed through the swinging doors and into the room.

She went straight to the monitor and hit a button. The sound continued. She wiggled a wire, checked the connection by Liam's arm, and then gave the monitor a solid thump. The noise stopped.

I wiped my mouth with the back of my hand. "What was that?" I asked.

"Blood pressure cuff acting up. You okay there? Let me get you some water." She exited the room, and I returned to my chair and my worry.

I stared at the shimmering form of Flint. The nurse returned with a cup of cold water, and Flint blinked out of my peripheral vision.

"Let me know if you need anything, or if he decides it's time to wake up." She left again.

I nodded and returned my gaze to Liam. He had a scrape on his chin, and dust across the bridge of his nose. Airbag powder I guessed. He was going to have an interesting set of black eyes when the bruises that were forming finally set in. I looked up at Flint.

"I need you to try, Flint. What happened? Why isn't he coming out of it?"

Flint shrugged. He seemed so helpless.

"You've seen Myrna right?"

He nodded. Good, he could hear me.

"I'm not crazy thinking you've been inside this guy's brain. Or am I?"

He shook his head no. It was going to be a long conversation without Flint being able to do more than nod or shake his head.

"You brought him to me, didn't you? I don't know if you're why he fell in love with me. I don't know if that's why I fell for him, but I love him, and I cannot lose him again. If it weren't for Myrna I don't know how I would have survived last year. I didn't have you, I didn't have him. And then by some miracle, I got you both. I haven't had enough time with him. It's really only been a couple of months, weeks really, and I know I want him forever." I clamped my hand around Liam's arm that wasn't covered in tubes or wires.

"Did you hear me? I can't lose you. I need you. Your daughter needs you."

The lights flickered and suddenly Flint was as solid as he could ever get. I felt the familiar shiver when he touched me. It had been a very long time since I experienced intentional ghostly contact. I looked into his eyes. They were still blue while the rest of him was almost in color.

My lips buzzed with the brush of energy as Flint kissed me. I wanted to be able to kiss him again. I really needed to be able to kiss Liam again.

"I love you too. She's your daughter, have you seen her eyes? Those are your eyes. I don't know how that happened. But it did."

I sat and babbled at Liam. I told him what the doctors said. He had hit his head, and it should have only been a concussion. There was no reason for him to be out cold like this for this long. They would be back for him later for a CAT scan. I tested Liam to see if he was faking it. I lifted an arm over his face and let go. His hand smacked him right in the nose on the way down. He didn't flinch. How bad had the accident been? He hit his head, the airbags deployed, but did they before or after he was knocked out?

"Liam, you need to wake up and tell me what happened."

Charlie came in and brought me some food, and then told me he needed to go home. I told him to leave and I would stay here as long as I was needed.

Nurses came in and checked on Liam, they gave him more bags of fluids when others ran out. They called me Mrs. Iakobus. Apparently, my picture was next to "ICE Wife" in his phone, and so in their minds, I was his wife. I hated that I found out I meant that much to him this way.

I wanted to be his real wife. "I love you, wake up and

marry me. Flint, can't you jump back in and make him wake up."

Liam made a thrumming sound deep in his throat.

"Liam?" I squeezed his hand harder. Had he heard me? My heart raced and my breath quickened.

He groaned, and his lids flickered, but his eyes stayed closed.

"Did you call me Flint?" The words were barely a slurred mumble.

"I was talking to Flint."

"Not Flint anymore."

I stared at him. He knew. I cut my gaze to the flickering collection of light that was Flint, before returning to Liam's face. I was too scared to say anything to a conscious Liam, but he clearly knew. Unless he really wasn't quite all the way awake. Mostly asleep Liam had said stuff like that before. Mostly asleep meant he was waking up. He was waking up!

His eyes blinked open.

He looked at me for a split second, just Liam, no Flint. His eyes were dark velvety brown, and full of panic.

My hands, already resting on his for arm tightened. I stood up. He flinched.

"It's okay, Liam. It's okay. You were in an accident. Do you remember what happened?"

"Danica?" His voice was raspy, unused as if he hadn't even been mumbling moments before.

I smiled. He was going to be all right.

His face contorted and clenched in pain. He curled up into himself. His hands crashed to the sides of his head. Buzzers and beeping alarms abounded on the monitoring equipment. He groaned in pain.

"What's happening?" he asked through clenched teeth. His skin was red with strain, and sweat dotted his brow. His eyes locked with mine once more before rolling up into the back of his head. He slumped back against the bed, unconscious again.

My own panic froze my voice. I didn't know what to do. I looked frantically from Liam to the specter of Flint who hovered by his other elbow.

"Do something!" I cried to Flint just as a nurse rushed in. I'm certain she thought I was talking to her.

I had to step away from Liam so she could help, but I didn't want to. I needed the contact, the connection. I wrapped my arms around my middle and hovered against the wall. The nurse moved with speed and efficiency. She was joined by another nurse.

Liam was completely blocked from my view, but Flint was not. His focus was all on the man they checked. Liam was still breathing, and that was good. No indication of a cardiac event, though they took blood to check for the related enzymes. I thought they would leave us alone for a bit, but that never seemed to happen.

As soon as everyone left an orderly came in to take him for his CAT scan.

I sat and waited. I was too nervous to be able to focus on anything. I called Ruth.

"What's going on, Dani?"

"I'm not sure yet. He was conscious for a second, but now he's not. They just took him back for a test. Are you okay with Myrna for tonight?"

"I don't like you springing this on me at the last minute like this. But Hugh is fine with it. Of course, Myrna can stay overnight. I have enough formula. She'll be fine." Ruth's speech was dotted with many heavy sighs. This was such a burden I was putting on her.

I wanted to rant at her. I was pretty sure no one wanted

something like this sprung on them. It was a big inconvenience for everyone. But, I was good. I behaved and I promised I would be there first thing in the morning after getting my car from the KoS Workshop. I needed to stay with Liam right now.

Eventually, they brought him back. He was followed in by a doctor. Dr. Cohan introduced himself and shook my hand.

"Brain activity looks fine. We can't see any reason why he's decided to check out for as long as he has. We'll get him into a room and see if he doesn't come out of it on his own. If not, we will have to get a plan into place for long term care."

Another orderly pushed into the room. "We have a room for you. Ready to take a ride?"

He pulled out a scanner, scanned the band on Liam's wrist. "Mr. Eye-ah—"

"Yah-koh-bus," I corrected.

"Sorry. You know he looks like that actor?"

"He gets that a lot," I answered.

I followed them down one hall, up an elevator, around a corner to another bank of elevators, and eventually into a room. The orderly scanned something on the wall, and Liam's bands again.

Once in the room, new nurses came in and introduced themselves. Their names went in one ear and out the other. New monitoring equipment was plugged in and attached. A different nurse came in with a heart monitor and wired Liam's chest. That was followed by someone else attaching stickers and leads all the way from his head to his ankles.

It felt like a flurry of activity, but it was almost an hour before we were alone again.

I stared at him. He was a little pale, he still had dust

across his nose, and the bruises around his eyes bloomed into a more lurid color scheme.

In the morning Liam's assistant Ray burst into the room. My initial reaction was to shush him since Liam was asleep. But he needed to wake up. Maybe the noise was what he needed. Ray's much older boyfriend, Jerry, followed behind.

Ray made a pitiful gasp and covered his mouth before collapsing against his boyfriend's shoulder. I loved this guy but was caught off guard by his melodramatic display. Jerry held Ray with one arm and held out his other hand to me.

"How are you holding up?" He gave my hand a squeeze.

"The fold-out chair is horribly uncomfortable. I've spent all night staring at him, afraid that if I go to sleep that's when he'll wake up, and I'll miss it."

"Do you need anything?"

I shook my head. For now, I needed to be here with Liam.

Nurses came in and left. Liam's monitors made a soft constant hum, no jarring alerts, no alarms.

Ray and I sat close together, leaning on each other, staring at Liam. Jerry sat somewhere behind us, quietly running to the Coke machine, or down to the cafeteria. He watched over us while we watched over Liam. Flint hovered close to Liam. Occasionally, he would look at me, and give me a sad expression. He never slipped into my head. He never attempted to speak with me in any way.

Flint was too much like other spirits I'd encountered in the hospital. People whose bodies died, but they didn't know what to do or where to go. He flickered like a silent movie cast against a sheet from an old reel-to-reel projector. A bright phantom ready to vanish when the film stopped rolling. It scared me. Did this mean that Liam's body wasn't going to survive? Did it mean Flint was in a place where he would fade, and move on to where ever it was that spirits moved on to?

I held a little tighter to Ray, needing comfort when Flint didn't offer any, and Liam could not.

At some point, Charlie and Linda showed up.

"You need to go home and get some rest Dani," Charlie told me.

I gazed at Liam. "But he might wake up."

"And if he does, we will call you. Hell, I'll send a car to pick you up. Hell, I'll drive you myself." Jerry joined forces against me.

I tried to complain and wiggle out of their comforting hands on my shoulders. I was wobbly from exhaustion.

"Myrna is going to need you to be strong so you can take care of her. And you are going to need to be strong to take care of Liam when he does wake up," Linda began saying.

"Myrna!" How tired did I have to be to forget my own child?

"She's fine. I called Ruth this morning. She has everything she needs at her house, and she's going to keep the baby for another few days." Linda said.

I turned my sad and tired gaze at Linda. I melted at that point and cried onto her shoulder. Here she was being a better mom than my own had been, taking care of me and my baby when I couldn't take care of myself.

Charlie and Linda drove me home. Linda even tucked me into bed to make sure I went to sleep. They were right. I wasn't going to be any good to anyone if I didn't get some rest, or take care of myself. Note to self: when the plane is going down, put the air mask on yourself first. It barely made any sense, the crash and the burn were going to take us all out in the end right?

When I woke up, I foraged for some food. I felt better. I

checked in on Myrna. Ruth assured me one more night would not be a problem. I arranged for a car to take me to KoS so I could get my own car, before heading back to the hospital.

Liam's room was quiet and dark. The monitors hummed. It was as if he were asleep. I even moved as if I thought he was asleep, and then I realized that was stupid. I turned around, flipped on the light switch and announced my presence.

"Wakey wakey eggs and bakey."

Nothing. Flint still flickered in the space near his shoulder, behind the bed.

"Can't you do anything? You know, jump back in?"

The apparition looked at me with those soulful eyes.

I spend the afternoon telling Liam, and Flint about all my fears. He was a better listener than a therapist could ever be. In the end, he couldn't provide insight to my woes. I did talk myself into calling my doctor and scheduling an appointment to specifically discuss the postpartum tendrils of despair that liked to grab at me.

I called Ruthie to see how my baby girl was doing. Everything was fine and she could keep her for another night. I agreed to pick her up in the morning.

"You know how much I hate that right?" I asked the comatose man in front of me. "So you better wake your ass up soon."

His ass didn't wake up. They ran more tests. There were no identifiable reasons they could point to. I called Liam's mom.

24

"He's being selfish, you know that right?"

My jaw hit the ground. "He's unconscious, Ruth. You could show a little empathy, maybe?"

I didn't want to be here any longer. I thought a visit with my sister would be a good thing, especially since I had left Myrna with her for two nights in a row. I didn't want Ruth to think that all she was to me was glorified free babysitting. But I didn't need her to be so rude about Liam. Especially right now.

I grit my teeth together and adverted my gaze so I didn't glower directly at her. Myrna squealed a happy baby noise and my whole attitude changed. I felt the tension and anger literally melt from my shoulders. I clapped for her and smiled. She was my joy, my reason for breathing. I knew Liam felt the same.

"We have to go," I said abruptly.

"I thought you were staying for lunch?"

"I just remembered something I have got to get done for Charlie," I lied. "I haven't been able to do anything these past two days, so I should take care of it before the place closes." The lie was so blatantly obvious, maybe Ruth didn't notice all the hemming and um-ing in the middle of everything.

"I need a day off, you have to take Myrna." Ruth sounded as tired I had been every day since she was born.

"Of course. No, you have been so great taking care of her during this situation—" I can't believe I had to call it a situation and not the emergency it was. Liam was unconscious in the hospital, and if he didn't wake up soon it was coma time and his mom was probably already on an airplane on her way over from England "—I'll take her with me, it's just a simple errand really, but I need to talk to this fabricator in person." Lie, lie, lie, lie, lie.

If Myrna was my light and life, maybe she could coax Liam back to active status. I bundled her up, said goodbye to my sister, and left. Ruth had been right, the plan was to stay for lunch. So I hit a drive-through on my way back to the hospital.

Nothing had changed.

Liam lay as if he were asleep. Flint hovered and gazed down on him with more longing than I think I even looked at the man, and I was in love with him. Maybe the body-life connection was one I wouldn't be able to understand until I was a spirit. I could wait.

Myrna slept in her car seat. I gently eased her out and tucked her into the crook of her father's elbow. Flint reached out and stroked the soft hair that was finally growing in. Dark and wispy. I hoped for curly Greek hair for her, and not the boring hair-is-hair, not-quite-a-color, not-exactly-body but definitely-not-straight hair that I had.

"I wish you could tell me what happened," I whispered as if I needed to be quiet since Flint was so thin and near invisible.

He rested his hand on my wrist. It felt like someone blew on me instead of the electrical, fuzzy zap-tingle I was used to. Images flashed into my brain. None of the images were strong, mostly flashes of light and shape. There had been a bang and then a jolt. Confusion. And Liam's head hit the steering wheel. The next images were all looking back at Liam. He slumped against the steering wheel, and then with an explosion, the airbag went off, effectively punching him in the jaw, and throwing his head back.

I blinked as the images left me as quickly as they had invaded my brain. Flint no longer touched my arm. I looked at his flickering presence. Hitting his head explained the cut. I reached up to run my finger just over the bandages, not touching, but caressing the space above his skin. But neither of those hits should have been enough to knock him out for very long. Liam should have a concussion, not a coma.

"I know he knows all about you. He has to. You've been inside his head. He knows, right?"

Flint shrugged, never taking his attention off the baby that was his, but also Liam's.

"I'm telling him. Liam, I'm telling you all about ghosts and all about Flint."

And I did.

"I see ghosts." It was easy to talk to sleeping Liam, no judgmental squinting of eyes, or throat clearing noises that sounded remarkably like "bullshit."

"I couldn't tell you before because it's not exactly something I go around telling people. They don't react well. I told my parents once before their divorce."

We all sat around the dinner table. We did that before the divorce, did things as a family, the way families were supposed to behave. The table was a long rectangle. I sat next to Ruth on one

side of the table, and Mom and Dad sat across from us. I was five
or six.

"I saw Mrs. Phillips again today."

Mom always served at the table. She made grand presenta-
tions of food that we would admire as a group before we could dig
in. She plopped a scoop of potatoes or rice on to my plate and just
stared at me.

"Honey, Mrs. Phillips died last year, are you talking about
Ms. Reiner who lives there now?" Dad asked.

Mom didn't move. She stayed frozen in time and space, that
big spoon twisted to the side.

"No, I mean Mrs. Phillips. I don't think she knows she's dead."

That's when Mom dropped the spoon. And the yelling began.
The yelling at me, the yelling over my head. I wasn't allowed to
eat dinner that night. Dad wasn't upset, but Mom was fit to be
tied. I never said another thing about it to either of my parents
again.

"It was years before I said anything to Ruthie. I sort of
told her about Flint. No names, just that there was this old
movie star that seemed to be around. She harassed me
something fierce. I never told another person after that. But
now I'm telling you, even though I don't think you need to
hear this, because Flint has somehow been with you since
that car accident you had three years ago."

I told Liam how I first met Flint sitting on top of Cecile
B. DeMille's tomb. I gave Liam details of our sex life and the
details of my sex life without him.

"I consider Flint my first. Always will. But at some point,
I figured I actually needed to have real sex, or it would be
weird. And it was, because Flint was there the whole time,
like some kind of pervy mat coach. And no matter how
many times I did it with somebody else— I even had a
steady boyfriend for a few years— we never hit a sexual

groove the way Flint and I did. The way you and I did. I cheated on every single one of them with Flint. Or would that be the other way around? I cheated on Flint with all those living boys, all three of them."

"Liam, you need to wake up." I tried to not cry, but it was fruitless. I swiped at the tears running down my face.

"You and Flint have control issues inside that head, I can tell. Sometimes your eyes are brown. And every now and then Flint's blue ones are looking at me. And then when you are in harmony your eyes swirl together to make a half blue half brown hazel mix. It's sexy as hell."

Myrna began making a fuss. I reached for her. Did what I see just happen? The baby shifted and resettled, and I swear Liam sighed. My eyes quickly ran over all of the monitors. I could not identify any change in any of the information being recorded.

He shifted. He definitely shifted.

"Liam? Liam?"

I buzzed the nurse.

Her voice was cracking up over the intercom. "Can I help you?"

"He just moved! And he sighed."

"Coming."

A few moments later a nurse came into the room.

"I went to pick up the baby and he shifted. And then she settled and he sighed."

Her stethoscope was out and she listened to his chest. She peeked under his eyelids. Shaking her head she said, "I'll go see if there was anything recorded. How long ago?"

"Not even five minutes."

She nodded and left. I eagerly watched her go, and turned to Liam, and then to Flint. "It's good right?"

I stared hard at Liam pushing my will into him.

Myrna finally did wake up. I let her play with her toes and do her kicking and tummy time while on the bed with Liam. Somehow, down deep in my bones, I knew she was good for him.

"I don't know what kind of opening you got when he died, but you need to find a way back in there, Flint."

I changed diapers and fed the baby. We watched cartoons and sang songs, all on Liam's hospital bed. Hours passed before the nurse came back.

"I didn't forget you. I had to chase the doctor down and have him look at the tape. There was a burst of brain activity."

I surged forward, ready to jump for joy. She put a hand out to keep me in check.

"Apparently that can happen. Unless we get continual activity, it's nothing to write home about."

I deflated. I was so sure Liam was aware that Myrna was snuggled up to him, and that she would be his magical cure.

It was hard to maintain a smile for the baby when the nurse left us alone. I got angry. Angry at Flint who was the heart of this. Angry at Liam for tearing my heart out. I reached out and pinched him hard on the soft skin at the back of his upper arm. I pinched hard enough to leave a mark that would bruise.

"Fu—" Damn no cursing in front of the baby. Didn't want her first words to be 'fuck you.'

"Come on, Liam. Wake up."

Eventually, I took Myrna home. I needed to sleep and take a shower. I was going to be meeting Liam's mom at some point the next day.

~

There was a flurry of activity when I approached Liam's room. Ray and Jerry stood in the hallway outside his door, with a middle-aged woman who I guessed was Liam's mother.

"What's going on?" I asked Ray.

He gestured to the room, "They kicked us out so they could clean him up."

"I kicked us out," the older lady said. "My son deserves some privacy and dignity."

I lowered the car seat to the floor. "You must be Liam's mother. I'm Danica. And this is—"

She turned all of her attention to me before dropping her gaze to the baby strapped into the car seat. "Myrna?" She lowered down and began cooing at her granddaughter.

She looked back up at me with sparkling gold eyes. "She looks just like him. May I hold her?"

I nodded and unfastened Myrna. She was sleepy and ready for her morning nap. She snuggled into her grandmother without a fuss. "Hi baby, I'm your Nan."

Nan's name was Rose, and she cooed and bounced Myrna up and down the hall until we were let back in Liam's room.

He had fresh linens, and his face looked damp from being wiped down. What we couldn't see, is that he probably had a fresh catheter also.

I think Myrna was a balm for Rose. That child was never put down, and happy all day long. Even Ray and Jerry spent time holding and cooing over her. When she got fussy and it was time for a nap, I tried to convince Rose to let her snuggle in with Liam. But Rose refused to put her down until she was well and truly asleep.

Snuggled up to her unconscious father I was convinced Liam moved a little. I glanced up at Flint, who kept his vigilant position near Liam's head. I had no way of talking to him today, not with everyone around. "I love you," I said the words looking into Flint's eyes, and then I kissed Liam on the temple. "Get better. We need you."

At some point in the middle of the night, Liam had a crisis, and I wasn't there.

In the morning, Ray called and told me. He didn't give me details, only Liam woke up, but he wasn't in good shape. It would be a few more days before he'd be released. I wasn't allowed to see him. Too many tests. It would be better if I just waited until he went home and I was called.

"Doesn't he want to see Myrna?"

"There's what he wants, and there's what the doctors are allowing." Ray's manner was subdued.

"Will you call me?"

That day the creeping black ooze was bad. It brought with it every stupid embarrassing thing I had ever done or said. It dangled Cici and Hester and the failures of every female platonic relationship I'd ever had in front of me. It taunted with why I wasn't a better sister and pointed out all of my failures as a mother, and that was why Liam had obviously told Ray to not let me come back to the hospital.

25

"I heard he's recovered. Thank you for not bringing that man here again." Ruth sounded smug like she knew something. Like she knew why I hadn't heard from Liam for a few days.

I squinted at her and shook my head. "He's out of the hospital and doing better." I didn't know much more than anything she could have known, seeing how my Hollywood gossip news was probably the same one she got her information from. "I know you don't like him. I wish you would try to be nice. He is Myrna's father and he is sticking around." *I hope.*

"I don't think I can. It's better with him not around. I'm happy to not see him at my house, thank you very much."

I gave Myrna a kiss on her forehead and headed out for work.

Ruth's choice of words did not sit well with me. I let the car idle and I sent Ray a quick text. *"Is everything all right? Haven't heard from you for a day or two. Please check-in."*

I then sent Liam a text. *"I heard you are doing better. I'd like to see you."*

I started worrying days earlier. He hadn't gone more than a day or two without seeing his daughter since he found out about her if he was home. I hoped I fretted over nothing. He was probably out of town and I missed the text. Scrolling through my back messages I found nothing.

I sent him pictures of Myrna. *"Love-bug says hi."*

I texted him the little bits of our day that I discovered I really liked being able to share with him.

"My doctor recommended a therapist for the postpartum. I'll keep you posted."

"OMG, how does such a little girl poop that much?"

"Any luck on the house front?"

"Myrna really likes this rice cereal. I know we should wait, but she is going through so much formula. The nurse said it would be okay."

"My appointment is this afternoon. I'm nervous. What if she tells me I need to give up Myrna? You'll take good care of her right?"

"I really like this therapist. She said I'm not a horrible mother and gave me a prescription. I should start feeling better soon. Apparently, it takes a while for the meds to kick in."

"Are you mad at me? Did I do something wrong?"

"Did I piss your mother off somehow?"

"You've been crying." Ruth pointed out my pink rimmed eyes.

Of course, I had. I couldn't help it. I hadn't heard from Liam in almost a week. I was sad; I was nervous; I was so very scared.

"What did that man do?" she sneered.

"What makes you so certain it was something Liam did?"

"Because you didn't immediately correct me and say it was work." She was right. I hated it when she was right.

I sniffed and stood up a bit straighter. "I'm worried. Haven't heard from him for a few days. That's not normal."

"Have you seen that therapist yet?" She pulled together the few things I needed to take Myrna home with. Ruth convinced me to leave a few things permanently with her, it would be easier that way since Myrna was spending more of her days with Ruth as my hours increased. I noticed she purchased a few things on her own. It was great to see her enjoying Myrna so much. I didn't have to worry that Myrna wouldn't be well cared for in my sister's company.

"Yeah. The meds haven't really kicked in yet. She said to give them a few days to build up."

"I'm glad you finally went." She buckled Myrna into her car seat.

I lifted it with two hands. My kid was getting heavy. That was good.

"Me too. I didn't want it to get any worse. The therapist said it takes a while for the hormones to really settle, so I might not have to be on the medicine for very long. But she also warned me the pregnancy could have flipped a switch and I might need maintenance meds for the rest of my life." I shrugged. I would take the medicine for the rest of my life if it kept the ooze at bay.

After about a week, maybe a bit longer I realized Ray and Liam weren't texting me back on purpose.

I had the TV on while I folded laundry, Myrna kicked at one of her padded arch toys. She had mastered the roll, and now rolled over and did a little push up before rolling back and kicking at the toy. She wanted to do things like sit up, but she wasn't quite strong enough.

Hollywood Entertainment News flashed by and I dropped the clothes in my hands.

The footage was grainy as if it were taken from a

distance with a cell phone camera. But there he was. He looked a little thin around the neck. And very tan. Must be getting ready for *Mammoth Killers.*

I had to stop and rewind. Thank God for streaming TV with instant replay. Yep, that's what I thought I saw. My stomach bottomed out. Maybe he was going to buy her house after all, and that's all this was. Why was his hand on her back like that?

"Liam James and Cecilia Saaid are seen here together strolling through shops on Rodeo Drive..." pretty much all sound stopped reaching my ears at that point, all I heard was the loud rushing of my own blood.

"...amid rumors of a secret family hoax so that James could keep his role in the upcoming Whitmore Jaspers big-budget *Mammoth Killers*, which begins filming next month. The actor and director had a disagreement on set they have since resolved."

I wanted to puke. We had become a hoax so he could keep a part in a stupid movie about stupid cavemen?

But the worse part of it all was how he smiled at Cecilia, how she gave small furtive, almost shy glances back. How he touched her, and— "No!"

Myrna jumped at my yell and began crying.

I stared at the television in utter shock. Myrna continued to cry by my feet, and I couldn't move. I was completely frozen in place. The commercial for fried chicken disrupted my shock, and I scooped my poor frightened baby up.

"I'm sorry, Love-bug. I'm so sorry." I cooed, trying to soothe her.

I hit replay and watched it again, and again. No matter how many times I replayed it, it didn't change. Watching Liam lean over and give Cecilia a familiar kiss on the lips destroyed my world.

My phone rang. I grabbed it as fast as I could without unsettling Myrna, praying it was Liam with an explanation.

"Dani, oh honey, you need to sit down. I've got something horrible to tell you," Ruth said through the phone.

"I saw it. I saw it." I had a hard time speaking.

I didn't stop texting him. And I started crying.

"Can you please tell me what's going on?"

"Did it have to be Cecilia?"

"Please, Liam will you please talk to me. Or text me. Please."

I barely stopped crying long enough to function at work.

My stomach hurt from swallowing so much snot. I could not stop crying. Through bleary eyes, I texted Liam again, and again, and again.

"Please tell me what I did wrong. Just tell me."

"You never have to see me again, but will you please come see Myrna. She knows you're not here."

"Please."

I begged in a way I never begged before.

The last time he completely disappeared on me I was so focused on eating healthy and staying positive for the pregnancy, and so busy with work that I didn't have time to break down. This year, all I had was time. Time and the tentacles of black ooze wrapping me in their sticky grip pulling me under its bubbling surface of despair.

On the days I didn't go to work, I barely functioned. I had a hard time remembering to buy food for me. Fortunately, Myrna still breastfed part-time. Through all the crying and all the bleakness, I made sure to smile for my little girl.

"Has your doctor adjusted your new meds?" Ruth asked.

I shook my head. The antidepressants were working some, but only some. There was a level of heartache that they couldn't touch. A level of crushing pain that made the black ooze look like a child's plaything squished under the treads of a tank.

"They need to build up. It's only been a week." I flashed a limp smile at her as I unpacked the bottles into the fridge. "Hey, did you get new bottles, or am I completely forgetting how many there are?"

Ruthie danced around the kitchen with Myrna on her hip. "Oh I ended up grabbing some more a week or so ago. It just seems easier if I have a set here, instead of you having to lug them back and forth. I mentioned it to you, but..." She waved her hand around dismissively. "You were going through some shit. I'm sure you just missed it."

She was right, I was missing so much.

My eyes were perpetually rimmed in dark pink from my daily crying jags.

"Liam I am sorry."

"Myrna misses you."

"My doctor put me on a good anti-depressant."

I texted him every day. I called, but I never was given a chance to leave a message. My number had been blocked.

The routine kept me going for another week. Take care of Myrna, go to work. Work was the only reason I showered on a regular basis. Even Seb Hale's set couldn't really pull me up from the gloom. After all, Liam was Seb; Flint was Seb, and I had no way of knowing what was going on with either of them.

I collapsed on one of Ruth's kitchen chairs. My arms were too heavy to lift. I barely slept the night before.

"Dani, why don't you let Myrna spend the night tonight? You can take a sleeping pill and get some rest." Ruth rubbed my back. I blinked my bloodshot eyes at her. It was the best idea I had ever heard.

After work, I went to Liam's house. He wasn't home.

I left a note. It looked like some kind of kidnapper's note, written in eyeliner on a napkin, but there was a note.

I wasn't going to take any sleeping pills. In my state, that was a tragic accident waiting to happen. I was, however, going to drink myself into a stupor. One large bottle of red wine, a shit-ton of Mexican drive-thru, and I had my entire evening ahead of me. Alone. All alone.

My phone rang. I hurried to put the shopping bags down and fumbled for my phone.

"Hello?"

"Danica." It was Liam's assistant.

"Ray? Why isn't he calling me back? What did I do?" I didn't give the man a second to say anything as I bombarded him with needy pleas for assistance in getting Liam to at least text me back.

"Look, Danica," he finally was able to cut me off. "He's going to fire my ass if he finds out I called you. But you cannot, absolutely cannot, drive over here and leave notes again."

"Ray, please. Can you at least tell me if he is okay? He's recovering okay?"

"Physically he's fine, but I've never met anyone so pissed off at the world. I'm not supposed to be talking to you. Look, his lawyer should be calling you this week."

"Does he get my texts?"

"Honey, your number is so blocked." He let out an evil chuckle.

"Tell him I'm sorry. Tell him Myrna needs her father."

"I ain't tellin' him shit. I shouldn't have called. You never should have done that, that's all I'm saying."

He may have hung up on me at that point, but I kept asking, "Done what? Ray, what did I do?"

One bottle of red wine was not enough. I did not sleep. I

spent the night curled up on the floor in the corner behind the couch. The TV flickered blue light across my living room. I was so alone. I didn't even have a ghost to keep me company.

There was a knock on my door. Expecting it to be a package delivery, I tossed the dishrag over one shoulder and hefted Myrna a little more comfortably on my hip. She was getting so big. Maybe spending the nights with Ruth was good for her.

Stupid me did not look through the peephole and pulled the door open.

I stepped back, surprised to see a bike messenger.

"Miss Kensington?" He handed a large envelope out to me.

"Yeah? Can I help you?" I took the envelope and looked for an address or some kind of marking on it.

It was plain, no identifying information at all.

The messenger flipped his bike around and clipped his toe to the pedal. "You've been served." He slid away from my door.

I watched him coast down the drive and start pedaling once he hit the street. I turned my attention to Myrna. "What do you think this is?" *What the hell did he mean I've been served?*

I put Myrna in her bouncy chair and plopped onto the couch. I slid my finger in under the tab.

"Ow, fuck." I sucked on the paper cut before looking at the damage to my finger. Great, that was going to sting for the rest of the day. I slid the papers from the envelope and apparently forgot how to read.

276 | LULU M SYLVIAN

The words were English, but the combination of them made no sense.

Liam Iakobus wanted full custody of the minor named Myrna Love Kensington.

That made no sense what so ever. Why would Liam sue for custody? He could see her whenever he wanted.

I scrambled around for my phone. "Mom, I think I need you to come for a visit. Do you think Hugh knows any lawyers? Liam's suing me for paternity."

26

I hated lawyers' offices. Okay, so this was really the first one I had ever been in and I hated it. I hated what it represented. I hated everything about what today represented.

Ruth squeezed my hand.

I gave her a weak smile. She had been right all along. My big sister looking out for me, having my back. Mom had Myrna, I had my family, the one that I needed.

Liam and his lawyer walked past the office. Neither of them looked at us. Liam didn't look in through the glass wall of the office. He didn't look at me.

Apparently, the laser daggers I was shooting from my eyes did not cut or burn.

Connor Frank, Hugh's lawyer friend, stood up. "Ladies." He adjusted his impeccable tie and gestured for Ruth and me to follow him out of his office.

I took a deep breath and let the anger crease my face. I'd rather Liam see my scowl than the red-rimmed eyes from all the crying I had been doing the past few weeks.

Liam and his lawyer were already seated on the far side

of the table. No one stood as we entered. Some assistant or note-taker followed us in. I didn't pay much attention, just that the young man sat in the corner behind a laptop and typed as the legal guys did their chest-pounding and dick sizing bullshit maneuvers.

Liam looked like shit. His hair hung limp and greasy; he hid his eyes behind dark glasses; his forehead was going to take on permanent grooves from the intense furrowing he was doing. The cut on his forehead had healed into an angry red line.

I rested my fingertips against my own brow to remind myself to relax the muscles there. I didn't need a headache on top of everything else today.

A large document was passed between lawyers. A copy was handed to me. I knew what it said. I didn't want to read it. I didn't understand why any of this was happening.

"Why?" I couldn't hide the pain in my voice.

"Ms. Kensington." Frank chastised me. I wasn't supposed to speak to Liam.

Liam just stared at me. His face pinched in more like he squinted at me like he was trying to understand a foreign language.

"Mr. Iakobus requires a paternity test, and upon confirmation of paternity—"

"I'm not talking to you," I slapped my hand in the air in a hard stop action at the other lawyer. Oh my God, I hated that man.

"A paternity test is necessary to establish—"

I closed my eyes and breathed in heavily. "Will all of you just shut up for a minute? I'm not dumb. Legal paternity needs to be established before Liam can proceed with suing me for custody. That's not what I'm asking." I ground out the words through clenched teeth.

This was the first time I had seen him since he had been in the hospital unconscious. Maybe he had heard me? Maybe he was fully aware of everything I had said? I hadn't seen Flint since that last night either. Was he inside there with Liam?

"This isn't about Flint is it?" I bit my lip and looked at Liam, letting him see my pain.

Ruthie groaned. I knew that sound well. That was the sound of the imbecile little sister saying the most inappropriate ignorant things ever. "I cannot believe this. You're actually bringing your obsession of Flint Reese into this? It's not about some dead actor, Dani. It's never about that dead actor. I can't believe this."

My gaze tried to lock with Liam's through those stupid dark glasses.

Liam didn't move. No nod, no shake of the head.

"If that's not it then why are you doing this? Cecilia?" This hurt so bad. Breathing felt like a million bees stinging my lungs. I had been a complete mess for the past few weeks. I was more confused than ever. I honestly thought I would see him again and be so angry that the pain would dissolve into hatred or at least indifference. But that's not what was happening. The anger went away and I was left hollow and scared.

Liam didn't speak for so long. His nostrils flared, but he gave no other indication of movement, no nod or shake of the head. How he must hate me.

My eyes burned. I was going to cry again. And now everyone in the room was staring at me. I no longer felt like I had the support of my own lawyer, or of Ruthie, simply because I asked a simple question: why?

"Why don't you tell me why you're doing this first?"

Liam's voice sounded raw like his vocal cords were sandpaper.

I took a deep breath. "Because you're suing me for custody of our daughter, and I hadn't asked for anything."

"Bullshit!" He exploded from his seat. The chair flipped onto its back. The sunglasses went flying.

"Mr. Iakobus, please." his lawyer tried to calm him down.

Liam leveled a glower on the other man and growled low in his throat.

"Didn't ask me for anything!" Liam yelled.

I flinched. He was a big man, and I had only ever seen him be this intense on-screen. In-person he had never been aggressive. Flint had never raised his voice. And I was staring into their eyes, both of them, in that beautiful blue-brown hazel blend. The last time I saw it the colors moved and swirled. Now it appeared as if the colors were locked in, a perfect balance of pale blue and dark brown. The colors that told me both men were in that brain. His eyes were rimmed like mine, in the tell-tale pink of tears.

"I would have given you anything you wanted or needed but you had to go and try to keep Myrna away from me." He drove his finger hard into the table. "That's what this is about."

"What? No." It was my turn to have the expression of not understanding the words being said. I leaned forward, I needed to understand him.

"All you needed to do Danica was ask and I would have bought you and Myrna anything. I was in the middle of buying you a fucking house and you have..." he turned to his lawyer. "Where is that summons?"

The lawyer handed over a document that had been folded and severely handled. Liam scanned the top page, nodded, and then threw it at me. The pages flapped open. The staple in the top corner prevented them from scattering from his action.

"You had me served while I was in the hospital!"

I forced myself to breathe. It wasn't easy with my world falling apart like this. I looked at the papers. Shaking my head I showed them to my lawyer, hoping he could provide some clarification.

"This is the Summons and Complaint you filed against Liam Iakobus, but it says James here." He pointed at Liam's name. "You should have told me you initiated a custody suit."

I knew my mouth was hanging open, but there was nothing I could do about it. Words did not work. Breathing became even more difficult.

I worked my jaw, forcing sound to come out. "I... I... wha... what?"

"It's a demand for him to relinquish custody of Myrna, sweetie," Ruthie explained.

My head swiveled from Connor Frank to her. I leaned in. Things were not making any sense at all.

"You sued me first, Danica. What's so hard to understand?" Revulsion dripped from his lips as he spoke to me.

"I didn't do this." I have no idea if I managed to get the words out, or if I spoke with any volume. "Why would I do that? I'm in love with you." Sobs and then hiccups racked my body. I couldn't see through the tsunami of tears that overwhelmed me. Oh God what was happening? I reached out needing to grab hold of anything, anyone. I found my lawyer's suited arm and the table. There was comfort in neither. I felt everyone staring at me, yet no one did anything. Liam didn't do anything. I closed my eyes, and held on to the little support I had found.

My chair swiveled and I felt my hands clasped into familiar large ones. They were warm and strong and held mine in my lap.

"What did you say, Nica?"

Liam was blurry and out of focus when I opened my eyes again. But he was right there.

I tried to smile. He had come to me when I needed him.

"Why would I sue you? You're Myrna's father. She needs you. I need you."

He blotted the corners of my eyes with a hankie.

"You don't want to cut me out of her life?"

God no, I wanted him in her life. I shook my head.

"Then who does?"

I blinked and my vision came back into focus. His eyes held my gaze. Together we looked at his lawyer, and then at mine.

Conner Frank flipped through the summons. "Your name is on this." He shook his head and returned my gaze.

"But I didn't do that. There has never been a reason for me to do that." I reached up and cupped the side of Liam's face. "How many times did I say I wasn't interested in asking you for child support?"

"Am I the only one who sees that as a problem?" Ruth snapped.

I turned so I could look at her. Everyone else did too.

Ruth gestured at Liam. "You weren't looking out for your or Myrna's needs. I filed that because you wouldn't."

There is no sound in an absolute vacuum. Nothing for the sound waves to surf across. That's the reason in space no one can hear you scream. There was even less sound in the conference room at that moment than in deep space. Not even the sound of breathing could be heard. The stenographer had stopped typing. Silence, as we all stared at Ruth.

Why were words so damned hard today? Yet again I was stuck with my jaw hanging open trying to get words to form and come out of my mouth.

My hands reacted first as if the gesturing could trigger my vocal cords.

"I know you don't like me, but I don't understand why you would do that?" Liam was calmer than I ever could be.

My sister, whom I thought loved me, who I loved unconditionally, no matter if she was being a bitch or a control freak initiated a custody suit. She was still my big sister, my built-in best friend for life. "What the fuck, Ruthie? You had no right!"

She had judgment all over her face as she sneered at me. "He wasn't paying child support that you clearly needed. He wasn't getting you a nanny. You were still in that studio that is a million times too small to raise a child in. Why did I do it? Because you needed to see that you didn't really have his support, Dani. You can't raise that baby on your own."

"So you wanted to cut her father out of the picture?" My own sister was trying to ruin my life.

"You needed to see he was no good. And he proved it by demanding a paternity test and suing you for custody instead of just letting it go." Ruth crossed her arms and glowered at me.

I shoved my fingers into my hair and squeezed my head together before it exploded. Liam stayed crouched in front of me, his hands gripping the arms of my chair as if they were the only thing keeping him from lunging at her. I could feel the heat roll off him in waves.

I closed my eyes and breathed slowly, blowing the air out between pursed lips. I couldn't deal with Ruth right this second. I couldn't. I blinked up at Liam and put a hand in the center of his chest. "I love you, and I never want to take

Myrna away from you. We are so much better with you in our lives."

He smiled at me. From the strain in his jaw, it looked like it was the first time he had smiled in weeks.

I turned my attention to my lawyer. "How do we stop the suit? How do I cancel all of this?"

"You want to settle the custody?" he asked.

I shook my head. "No, I don't want to do any of it. If Liam wants full custody, then he can have her."

"You are just going to give Myrna up like that?" Ruth shrieked.

"That's not what you want, Nica. What do you really want?" Liam's voice, even rough with emotion, soothed my soul.

"What I want?" I swallowed hard. "I want us to be a family. I want you to officially adopt her so she has a father. And I want to be with you both. Together. That's what I want. But if I can't have that, Ruth is right. I don't think I can raise Myrna alone. I don't have money. There is so much I can't give her that you can. You can give her a better life."

"Shut up, Danica," Liam spit out the words, wanting me to stop talking.

"For once, I agree with the man," Ruth scoffed. "If you're going to sign over custody, at least let me take her. Hugh and I can provide a stable environment better than an actor can."

Oh. Realization.

That was it. Everything became amazingly clear. How many times had Ruth dropped hints about me giving her custody? How bitter was she that I had a baby when I had no husband, and I lived in a converted garage while she lived in a nice house, in a nice neighborhood, with absolutely no film industry connections? Proper, boring, stability with income.

I managed to find the words just fine this time. "Wow, Ruth. I mean, damn, I always thought you weren't exactly serious every time you made some comment about raising Myrna as yours. I never thought you would actually do something like this."

"Where is Myrna now?" Liam asked.

"My mother flew in from Santa Fe. She has Myrna." I cut my gaze from Liam to Ruth and back.

I pulled out my phone and dialed. "Mom, what are you doing?"

"I'm putting Myrna down for a nap. Why?"

I looked at Liam, my eyes wide with panic. I swallowed hard, my throat dry. My heart thudded in my throat.

"We need to go."

Liam was on his feet and leading me out of the conference room. He barked orders at his lawyer, "Have my car pull up front now!"

"Liam. What is going on?" His lawyer was on his feet.

"Cancel everything. I'll call you from the car."

And then we were running. I followed as Liam crashed thru the stairwell doors and he flew down the stairs jumping three, four steps at a time. I was too shaky to even try that, but my feet blurred as I ran.

His car sat idling. The driver stood by, with the back door open, waiting. We slid in. "Go!" Liam barked. The car swerved into downtown traffic. I yelled the address to Ruth's house I was so scared.

"Mom?" I hadn't ended the call.

"Dani, what is going on?" she asked.

"Put Myrna in the car seat, and I want you to start packing everything of hers up. Put it in garbage bags, I don't care. I just need to get her and everything of hers out of that house."

"How am I supposed to do that with the crib and dresser?"

"Oh my God, Ruth bought a crib?"

I glanced over at Liam. His phone was to his ear. He mouthed "I love you," and laced his fingers with mine. I was too panicked to celebrate those words coming from Liam's lips.

"Myrna has a whole bedroom here, you know that," Mom said.

No, Myrna had a pack and play she could take naps in that doubled as a playpen. I hadn't been upstairs in Ruth's house for so long I never noticed, never saw that she had set up a baby room.

"On second thought, Mom, just get Myrna, the bottles, and her pack and play ready for me," I spoke in a rush.

"What's going on? Myrna needs a nap," Mom said.

I didn't want to tell her. What if she was in on Ruth's attempt to steal my baby? I hated this, I couldn't trust my own mother right now. I could never trust my sister again. I doubted I would ever speak to her after this.

"I'll tell you when we get there." I ended the call.

Liam was still on his call with his lawyer. He nodded. Grunted. "I want a restraining order against that woman, keep her away from Myrna." He paused and listened some more. "Right. Yes."

I knew what they were discussing. My heart ached at Ruth's betrayal, and my stomach clenched. I needed Myrna in my arms before I felt that I could breathe again.

"Yes, start the adoption process. No. I don't need a paternity test. I never did. And I want a simple prenup drawn up."

I looked at him with wide eyes. His were closed and he

shook his head. "No. No. She is stubborn enough to refuse any support. I want it to make sure she and all children are taken care of. That's right. Good."

He ended his call. I collapsed against his chest and he wrapped an arm around me and stroked my hair. I must have been a sight: no makeup, puffy and blotchy skin, pink eyes, and messy hair.

"I'm so sorry, my Nica." Liam's voice rumbled against my head. "We'll get Myrna, and everything will be all right. I almost ruined everything."

I shook my head against his chest. "No, that would be my sister. I never expected that. Ever."

"I don't think anyone in that room expected that." His fingers played with my hair.

I pushed against his chest and sat up so I could look at him. "You're gonna marry me?"

"Is that a proposal?" He smiled.

"I heard you say prenup."

He nodded. "I want to make sure you and the kids are taken care of if something happens."

My eyebrows shot up. "Kids?"

"You want Myrna to be an only child?"

I smiled at him. The thought of having more kids with him did quivery things to my insides, in a good way.

"I love you." I leaned in and for the first time in weeks, I kissed him.

"Hmm, I remember kissing you. It's one of my most favorite things from before the accident that I can remember."

I pulled back and stared hard at him. His eyes were mostly blue in the middle and rimmed with brown. The color transition between the two blended for a light hazel. The colors hadn't shifted since he first took the sunglasses off. They were beautiful eyes, the perfect blend of Flint and Liam.

Yet again words failed me.

The car pulled to a stop in front of Ruth's house.

"Come, let's get our girl."

"What's he doing here?" Mom's voice was dry and full of thorns as she opened the front door. Mom had Myrna all wrapped up and asleep in her car seat.

Liam picked up the car seat and gazed at her. He loved her so much, how did I ever believe Ruth when she spewed such malevolence toward him?

I picked up the padded insulated bag with bottles and the diaper bag.

"He's her father." I watched him carry her to the car. When I saw the driver lean in to assist with strapping her car seat in I turned back to Mom. "Did you know what Ruth was up to?"

Mom cocked her head to the side. "Your custody arrangement? You were getting papers signed. That man was going to sign over his rights, and then you were granting custody to Ruth and Hugh. I think it's a great idea. We were all going to go out to dinner to celebrate. There's a cake in the fridge for later."

I didn't even bother trying to speak. I turned and walked away. I left the pack and play and walked out of the front door.

The driver held the car door for me and I slid into the back next to the car seat. Liam sat on the opposite side and gazed down at Myrna.

She was so beautiful, so was he. And he wanted to marry me and make more babies. Be a family.

"What did your mother say?" he asked.

I shook my head. I was done with that part of my family,

and right now, I wasn't interested in talking about them. "Myrna James sounds nice." I sighed.

"Myrna Iakobus sounds better," Liam said. "You know, Nica Iakobus sounds positively Greek."

"It's a good name. I'm going to like it." I was crying again, this time happy tears.

My face hurt from smiling, or maybe it hurt because it hadn't had a reason to smile in weeks, and now, I was out of practice.

He instructed the driver to take us home.

I didn't pay any attention until I realized we were nowhere near Malibu.

I shot Liam a quick glance. "I thought we were going home?"

Liam just hummed.

"You aren't telling me where we're going are you?"

"I'm taking you home with me, Nica, where you belong."

I decided not to argue; maybe the driver had a shortcut that involved heading in the opposite direction of the coast. If I didn't know better we were headed towards my studio.

27

The driver pulled in front of that beautiful house Liam had shown me, the house with the perfect kitchen sink, and all the bedrooms.

"Liam?"

He looked at me with eyebrows raised. "We're home," he announced.

I followed as he carried Myrna inside. Boxes were piled in the hallway. A couch and table sat in the middle of the living room.

"I moved in this week. Ray hasn't had time to coordinate the unpacking in the rest of the house. There are more rooms than I have furniture for right now. But our room and Myrna's nursery are done."

"Our room? Myrna has a nursery? Ray decided to stay with you?"

Liam chuckled, "Yeah, he changed his mind when he saw the place. Plus, I think he missed Myrna."

The nursery was perfect. All the furniture I wanted and could never afford in polished dark cherry, combined with sunshine yellows and happy floral designs.

"Mum picked it all out. She was heartbroken when the papers arrived. She's the one who said I needed to get custody, and then set up the nursery."

Liam placed the car seat into the crib, clicked on a monitor, and we left Myrna to sleep.

"You too, rest." Liam pulled me into his bedroom. The furniture was the same, though organized slightly differently than his other house.

He sat me on the edge of the bed and pulled my shoes off. Kicking his own off, he pulled me into the middle with him. He sighed and I felt him relax. I nestled into his warmth. I had missed this so much.

"Better?" he asked.

I was exhausted. I needed to collapse and not think, not cry, not worry about the grief others brought to my doorstep.

"Almost." With everything coming to a head today, I couldn't let this go any longer. I needed to know. "Why did you kiss Cecilia? Why was that on TV?"

Liam let out a sigh and rolled his eyes. "I wasn't called back to *Mammoth Killers* because Jaspers's wife liked me. That sounds so much better than the truth."

"Which is?"

"Cecilia refused to do the movie without me, and I'm betting he's banging her on the side."

I scoffed, "That's not a bet I'd take. The kiss?"

"Jaspers kind of pimped us out to do a Japanese beer commercial. I wasn't up to travel, so they filmed it here. It was acting."

"A commercial?"

He nodded. "I think I figured out why you don't get along with Cecilia."

"She's a bitch?"

"So, you can see ghosts? Let me guess, you told Cecilia you could see her ghosts?"

"Oh, God." I closed my eyes. "You heard me? I thought you were unconscious."

"While we were filming the commercial, Cecilia told me I needed to get far, far away from you. Said you were insane and told everyone you saw ghosts. And she doubted the baby was mine. She said I should run," he paused. "What do you mean you thought I was unconscious?"

Crap. "I talked to you the entire time you were in the hospital. I told you everything. Everything and that includes that I see ghosts, and sometimes they talk to me."

"And you told her all about it?"

"Of course I told her. She was my best friend, and going to be forever." I picked up his hand and focused on playing with his fingers. It was easier than looking him in the eyes.

"Let me guess, she didn't take it well?"

"No, she took it really, really well. At least, I thought she had." I didn't want the memories of that pain to come back. Cici's betrayal hurt worse than anything I had ever experienced at the time. She crushed me.

"In front of my high school crush Jaleb Morrow, of all people, Cici had some sort of split personality attack and became the person she is today."

I didn't want that memory back, but there it was...

"Sorry, you can't come with me to my Dad's anymore. Amanda is insisting it's family only time." I rolled my eyes. My step-mother was ruining my life.

"But he said he would tell me all about camera angles and..." Cici huffed and threw her arms up in the air dramatically.

"I'm sorry she's being a total bitch."

I watched Cici storm down the hall to third period. I

couldn't help it if my step-mom all of a sudden didn't want me to bring Cici over. I wasn't about to tell her that, it would hurt her feelings. I didn't know how to even tell her Amanda thought Cici was being inappropriate with Dad. And my dad was just too clueless to see that. He thought she wanted to learn about movie cameras.

So now Amanda was mad at me, fine, whatever, I dealt with that often enough. No big. But Cici being mad at me was big.

I ran after her. I could be late for math. I didn't want Cici upset. I turned onto the English Hall and stopped. I backed up and tucked back around the corner. Cici was flipping her hair around and smiling up at Jaleb. God, he was so hot.

What I saw next could not have been happening. Jaleb leaned down and kissed Cici. I should have let her be mad, she could have stewed in those damned juices all day for all I cared. She was kissing Jaleb. She knew I had a crush on him. Had since the end of the eighth grade. I whimpered.

Cici spun around and saw me.

"Really Dani? Geez." She sounded so disappointed in me.

"I didn't want you to be mad, because Amanda's being a bitch. But you're kissing Jaleb. I thought..."

"You thought what?" Jaleb asked.

"She thought she should be kissing you. Dani's had a crush on you since forever," Cici told him.

My cheeks burned with a blush of rage and embarrassment. "Cici!"

"Please, it's not like he hasn't figured it out."

"Oh, she's the weird one who sees ghosts? Her dad was going to get you a screen test right?"

I stood there with my jaw hanging open. Kids buffeted

into me as they rushed into their classes before the bell rang.

"Well, that's not going to happen anytime soon. I'll have to audition the old fashioned way. Go to class, Dani." She bugged her eyes out at me and shook her head and made a face that told me everything. Her expression said how much she thought I was stupid, how she only stayed my friend after she found out Dad knew people in the business.

I found out how good of an actress she was that day.

"Whatever happened to respecting your friend's feelings?" I sniffed and gestured at Jaleb. "Hos before bros?"

"You'd have to be my friend first." She turned to Jaleb and pointed back at me. "She has fantasies about giving you blow jobs."

"No thanks, yours are just fine." He laughed and kissed her again. "Sees ghosts." He chuckled as he brushed passed me into the closest classroom.

I stared at Cici. She stared back, hand on hip, head cocked to the side. I was wasting her time. She turned with a toss of her perfect hair and sashayed toward her class.

"Your mom's not wrong, your dad keeps his demons with him," I called after her.

She faltered before continuing.

"He wasn't some war hero." I kept talking.

She stopped.

"And I can see ghosts. Your dad is surrounded by the people he killed."

I told Liam the story.

"It probably wasn't the nicest thing to say to her, but she had pretty much just ripped my heart out and stomped on it right there in the English Hall. It was rather satisfying though. I may have gotten a broken heart, but after the black eye she gave me, she got in-school-suspension for a week." I continued to stare at Liam's hand. When he didn't say anything I looked up into his eyes. That beautiful hazel blend that quickened my heart.

"Do you see my demons, Nica?" he asked.

"Okay, I've got to do this. Please don't think I'm crazy."

I took a deep breath and squirmed out of Liam's comforting hold and sat up. I didn't look at him. This was hard, so hard. There were two outcomes, and the wrong one could be worse than bad.

I took another deep breath. "Flint?"

"Yes, my Nica?"

I wanted to melt back into him. But I didn't. I sat ramrod straight and held onto my knees. His warm hand caressed the small of my back.

"I'm not crazy, am I? It is you?"

He pulled me back into his arms. "My love, it's always been me. I just didn't know it."

"Huh?" I reached up to caress his face. I loved this man. This one. Not the one I thought he had been, and not the one I never knew before the accident, but this version of Liam.

"I've been trying to give you openings. Letting you take the lead. After all, maybe I had just been dreaming? How could I say something when I wasn't fully sure of what was happening to me? Those headaches had something to do with it." His voice was soft and quiet. "I've had dreams of a life with you, but not with you. I remember not being able to touch you but I could take you to a place that wasn't exactly real where we could touch, and make love. I died, and when I came back, I wasn't the same. It took me a while to remember things, and when I did I was remembering two different lives."

He took my hand and held it to his lips, kissing my knuckles softly.

"Two different sets of incomplete memories; I've lost parts of who I was, but I didn't lose you. And I gained Myrna. I fought to get the part of Sebastian Hale so hard because I knew it was vitally important, and not for my career. I had this feeling deep in my gut that said I was Sebastian Hale but I couldn't say why. When I met you, memories solidified. Snippets of black-and-white dreams I had when under sedation roared to life in blazing color. And you were touching me. Every time my body remembered your fingers from someplace, some time. That night when you fell asleep on my hotel bed, there you were with your pink burned and pale skin, and that full moon of your ass."

"Geez." I blushed and squirmed, realizing there was nowhere to hide now. "But you remembered your parents, your sister."

"I also remembered growing up without a father in a different country, because he left my mother during the Great Depression. It was very confusing, and my doctor told me that the unconscious brain can do amazing things to help protect itself and to heal. He said I had scenarios that would explain pains and scars so I didn't have to remember the truth behind them. And they thought the headaches had something to do with that repressed memory. The only problem with that is I remember with vivid clarity watching that fucking Corvette flip over and over and disintegrate around me. Only I was outside looking in. I watched, I didn't experience."

He pulled me closer and nuzzled into my hair.

"I remembered you and how much I loved you, and it scared me. I decided that was just my recovering brain saying it liked you. But when I walked into that garage, the colors were all wrong. I was right, your walls had been purple."

"Are you Liam or are you Flint? How do I know?" I let my fingers toy with a button on his shirt.

"I am both. I was Flint, but I was also Liam. This past accident finally melded us together. You saw what it did to my eyes. The doctors have no explanation for it. There is only one of me inside my head, and I remember both if that makes any sense."

"It makes perfect sense. I'm not crazy, and you're not crazy."

"I'm completely crazy, for you." He flipped me and pinned me beneath his weight.

"I love you," I laughed breathlessly. All the zing and anticipation and desire swept back. My toes curled just being pressed against him.

"Those are the magic words that brought all the memories back to me." The expression on his face as he gazed into my eyes stole my breath and my reason.

"When did that happen? You knew you were Flint long before I said I loved you."

And I remembered thinking after the words came out of my mouth in the lawyer's office that no one cared, and it didn't matter when after all, it's the only thing that did matter.

"Nonsense, you talk in your sleep. You also call me Flint sometimes when you're really tired."

He kissed me then, and nothing else mattered.

EPILOGUE

Liam and Gil lounged in relaxed conversation next to the pool. I waddled up behind him and slid my arm across his chest. He reached up pushing the sleeve of my UV jacket out of the way to kiss and then bite my arm.

"Practicing for a zombie role?" I asked as I snatched back my body part from his mauling jaws.

"Hungry," he grunted.

"Go make a sandwich." I plopped down across from them under the gazebo and watched Ray, who had taken on part-time nanny duty, alternated pushing Myrna and then Ember, Gil and Brand's son, on toddler-safe swings.

Devon, their older son, ran around chasing bubbles Brand made from a giant bubble wand. All of the kids squealed with giggles. Even the older ones in the pool.

I ran my hands over my huge belly. "Make me a sandwich too. We're hungry."

Liam fought gravity with a groan and sat up. "One of us should probably start the grill if we're going to actually cook dinner on it today."

"One of us should be you. You're the host, and I'm too pregnant." I laughed.

"I could just order delivery," Liam suggested.

"Don't be so Hollywood." Emi's voice from just below the lip of the pool called out. She hiked herself up on her elbows so we could see her face. "You invited us over for a backyard barbecue. I'm here for charred meat."

"You're a vegetarian," her friend, another performing artist from the traveling equestrian cirque experience, pointed out, before splashing her.

"If I was 'So Hollywood,'" he mocked Emi, "I would have hired a caterer."

"Do not let that time-traveling Brit use the grill," Charlie announced his arrival.

Linda kissed me on the cheek and sat on the edge of my lounge. "I brought cake. I left it in the kitchen. How are the babies?" she asked.

"So much drama with you people." Jerry laughed as he walked past us with all the grill accouterments. It turned out that he was the one who taught Ray how to help Liam, and now me, with meal prep, and that included organizing this semi-pot-luck cookout.

I pulled Linda's hand to my very pregnant baby bump. "They've been kicking like crazy. Feel."

She smiled and laughed when one of the twins landed a roundhouse kick right under her hand.

Our backyard was full of the people I now considered my family. I couldn't be happier.

Liam leaned in close. "Do the boys need a little snack?"

"Yes, please. Flint wants something spicy and Reese would like something with cheese." At least, that's what I wanted. I'm pretty sure the twins were perfectly happy floating in their amniotic goo.

He kissed me. "I'll make something with an extra side of love."

"Oh God, no. I think it's that extra side of love that put these two in here."

~

When tragedy strikes Emi Paul, she starts seeing ghosts and hearing voices.
*Read more in the next Second Ending book **Fallen Star**.*
Keep reading for a sneak preview.

It's not too late to get the box set of the complete series.

EXCERPT FROM FALLEN STAR

I patted my face dry and stared at myself for a good long time in the mirror. I hadn't worn make up since the accident, and I didn't feel like putting any on now. But this was a meeting with Hank Parsons, and who knew who else he was bringing.

I fluffed my hair, and decided to braid it back. Maybe after I was done with that I would decide to put on some makeup.

"Hey Mom?" I called out as I left the bathroom.

"In here," she answered me from the dining room. I followed the sound of her voice and found her with her lap top in the middle of the table, glasses perched on her nose, and the vacuum cleaner half gutted and up ended on a towel.

I paused taking in the scene. "Whatcha doin?"

"I'm fixing this stupid vacuum cleaner. Your father keeps putting it off, and now with his shoulder," she sighed heavily. "I'm tackling it. What's up? You look nice. Where are you meeting Hank?"

"Some touristy fish place out by the house his group has rented."

"What no luxury hotel?" she asked.

I sat in one of the chairs. And poked at a part on the towel. "Probably can't get a sense of local if you're staying at the Hilton. You know room service isn't the same as wearing slippers down to the shops for musubi."

She gave me that look. That mom look that judged me

for loving musubi. Guess Spam was one thing she just never acclimatized to.

"Do you think you could braid my hair?"

She glanced over at me from watching her how-to video on the laptop. "Let me wash my hands."

I settled into the chair and closed my eyes when I felt her hands run over my hair.

"How tight?"

"Not tight. I was thinking two French braids and then down the back."

She began working. I could have sat on my bed and taken care of this, but I didn't want to wear myself out. I didn't want to risk triggering an episode, especially since all the documentation, and we just didn't know.

"How are you getting there? Did you ask Dad to drive? Is Hank sending a car?"

"No, I thought I would call one. It's not that far. And what would Dad do while I had my meeting?"

"Find trouble,"

We both said, "Mess his shoulder up," at the same time.

The door bell rang. Mom stopped, and handed me the tail of my braid to finish. I hadn't called for a car yet, and it seemed kind of late for a delivery. I played with the ends of my hair, contemplating my split ends, and that I should probably get a trim when I heard her foot steps return. "Who was that?"

"Jeremy."

I startled at the sound of his voice. I turned to see him give my mom a charming grin. I had yet to be on the receiving end of a smile like that. His hair was combed back so it curled just above his collar, and he wore designer slacks, with a tight silk T-shirt that showed off the muscles in his chest, and strained at his arms—it was almost as if he bought it a size too small just show off his physique. I've been around enough actors to know the good clothes when I saw them, and Jeremy wore his outfit tonight like a Hollywood A-lister.

"Emi, Jeremy said he's come over to volunteer to drive you around this evening."

I closed my eyes, and tried to wrap my brain around those words. "What?" Comprehension clearly wasn't working.

"I figured you could use some help. Someone who knows what to look out for in case you had a seizure. I figured your producer friend probably doesn't have all the details yet, and some stranger driving you around wouldn't know what to do."

My jaw slowly dropped open. There about a million things I could say to this. Anything ranging from righteous indignation, to flattered modesty, to reading way more into it that a simple kind gesture from my neighbor.

"What about your mom, and Hami? Will they be alright on their own?" Marj was still not moving around very well, even though she had stepped back on the pain meds.

"I can go over and check on them," Mom chimed in. "You know what, I'll pop over there right now, and see what I can bring over for dinner."

I stood up nervously. "Okay, let me finish getting ready. It won't take very long."

Jeremy lifted the corner of his mouth into a half smile, and I could have melted.

"No rush. I just wanted to get over here before you called for a car, or wrestled your dad out of his lawn chair."

I indicated he should sit, and I scuttled back to my room. I closed the door and eased down on to my bed. I closed my eyes, and then gathering my wits about me, I kicked and punched the air like a toddler having a joyous fit. What I didn't do was squeal, or giggle, or shout. I don't know why I was so excited to be stuck in a car with Jeremy for half an hour, plus whatever it took for parking, but I was.

Maybe I would get to see the charming man I knew he could be. Hell maybe he would smolder the entire time.

He looked gorgeous. I had to accept that there was a very strong chance that was not for me, but that was just how he dressed up. I mean so far I had only ever seen him in shorts or jeans. Definitely not dressed up.

My stomach clenched. Damn, that was probably his one nice outfit that he had packed to take Leonie out in. Assuming he had planned on doing that this trip before she left him.

I sighed, trying to get my head back on straight. I needed to finish getting ready. Mom had given me two loose braids that wrapped around my head, instead of two tight braids running straight front to back. With my volume and curl, this worked just fine. I tucked the braid tails in, and voila I had a fancy up-do. My hair was the fanciest thing about me tonight. My dress was a flowy handkerchief boho style with an uneven pointed hem line. The thin straps of the dress showed off the extra glow of tan I picked up at the beach the other day, and showed off that I wasn't wearing a bra. I found my fancy sandals, the shiny Birkenstocks, and slid my feet in. I crossed the hall to the bathroom, and stared at myself again. I needed to calm down. This was not a date, not with Jeremy, and not with Hank. No date meant no makeup.

I calmed myself before heading back to the dining room. I stopped before turning into the room. I leaned against the wall and watched Jeremy. He was bent over the vacuum cleaner, humming, and tinkering. From the way expressions crossed his face, he was problem solving at a rapid speed. Concern knitted his brow one second replaced with a grin, and a lifted eye brow the next.

"Having fun?" I asked.

"Yeah, I've almost fixed your mom's problem." His focus stayed on the machine. "She went to go check on my mom and Hami."

We had time, so I stayed where I was and watched his long fingers, twist, clip, rip hair—that was my fault—and move parts around.

"Can you plug this in for me?" He handed the end of the cord out without even looking at me.

I took it and plugged the cleaner in. He flipped the power and it roared to life. As far as I could tell, it sounded just fine. He cupped his hand over the hose and it made a hard stop sound as it suctioned to his hand. While it continued to run, he plugged the hose it to another piece and ran his hand around inside the machine. The noise it made changed to more of a whining sound.

His face scrunched up with concentration, and he looked into the guts of the vacuum. He took a screw driver and started to poke it into the depths.

"Shouldn't you maybe turn the vacuum off?"

"Nope." With a grunt he got the screw driver to move, the machine noise changed to a more throaty sound. He reached his hand back in and smiled to himself. "That should do it." He clicked the machine off and wiping his hands together he turned to me.

Time slowed down. I was very much aware this was not a seizure. Our eyes met, and I swear lightning crackled through the dining room. Everything seemed to flow and have an extra sparkle for the charge that lingered. Jeremy gave me one of his dazzling smiles. The one I had seen him give to other people, but not me. But there was something different about this one, like he couldn't breathe around it, and that made him even happier.

"You look beautiful." His voice was soft, and there was none of the typical disapproval in his eyes.

I smiled back. "Thanks."

The back door banged open, and whatever had just happened in the room between us vanished.

"Did you fix it? That was fast. You didn't have to," Mom gushed the second she saw the reassembled vacuum.

"Yeah, let me just wash up, and we can go." Jeremy looked confused suddenly. He gestured as if he were going to run his hands through his hair, but then realized his hands had vacuum cleaner grease and grime on them. I pointed him to the bathroom.

Mom played with the vacuum cleaner for a minute. "This is fantastic. He was able to figure it out in less time than it took me to watch that video."

When he returned, he looked composed. His hands were clean, and his clothes had stayed immaculate through the entire process.

"Shall we?" He swept his hand out indicating we should head out the front door, like this was some kind of date, instead of just the neighbor kid taking me places because I couldn't drive.

Damn, his car was parked in our driveway, out front, as if this were some kind of date.

Get Fallen Star Now!

Sign up for Lulu's newsletter to keep up to date with new releases and happenings. And get a free sexy short story.

https://lulumsylvian.com/newsletter/

ALSO BY LULU M SYLVIAN

Check out these other series

Legatum

Paranormal romantic suspense

The World of Wet Waterfalls

Paranormal reverse harem romance

Rockers

Contemporary Rockstar romance

Holiday Strippers

Contemporary, ridiculous, romance

ABOUT THE AUTHOR

Bio-engineered to be the only redhead in a generation of blonds, Lulu feels that "aliens" may actually be the best answer for a life-time of being asked, "Where did you get that red hair from?"

She did not come into writing from years of scribbling words on paper. Her background is rooted in visual arts and making pictures. Encouraged to make those pictures out of words Lulu began writing just to see what would happen. What happened was two full-length manuscripts in three months.

Lulu cannot ride a horse, a motorcycle, spin a hula hoop, or play roller derby. Yes, she has attempted all of those, even if it has been decades since she's been on a horse or a motor-cycle. She embraces the crazy that comes with that one little genetic mutation, and attempts to live up to the reputation that proceeds her. Lulu would like to apologize for her contribution to the hole on the ozone layer from her use of hairspray in the 1980s.

For more information, visit:
www.LuluMSylvian.com

facebook.com/lmsylvian
instagram.com/lmsylvian

* 9 7 8 1 9 4 8 0 5 9 6 6 4 *